FOREVER
COMES IN THREES

Praise for D. Jackson Leigh

Blades of Bluegrass

"Both lead characters, Britt and Teddy, were well developed and likeable. I also really enjoyed the supporting characters, like E.B., and the warm, familiar atmosphere the author managed to create at Story Hill Farm."—*Melina Bickard, Librarian, Waterloo Library (UK)*

Ordinary Is Perfect

"There's something incredibly charming about this small town romance, which features a vet with PTSD and a workaholic marketing guru as a fish out of water in the quiet town. But it's the details of this novel that make it shine."—*Pink Heart Society*

Take a Chance

"I really enjoyed the character dynamic with this book of two very strong independent women who aren't looking for love but fall for the one they already love...The chemistry and dynamic between these two is fantastic and becomes even more intense when their sexual desires take over."—*Les Rêveur*

Dragon Horse War

"Leigh writes with an emotion that she in turn gives to the characters, allowing us insight into their personalities and their very souls. Filled with fantastic imagery and the down-to-earth flaws that are sometimes the characters' greatest strengths, this first *Dragon Horse War* is a story not to be missed. The writing is flawless, the story, breath-taking—and this is only the beginning."—*Lambda Literary Review*

"The premise is original, the fantasy element is gripping but relevant to our times, the characters come to life, and the writing is phenomenal. It's the author's best work to date and I could not put it down."—*Melina Bickard, Librarian, Waterloo Library (UK)*

"Already an accomplished author of many romances, Leigh takes on fantasy and comes up aces...So, even if fantasy isn't quite your thing, you should give this a try. Leigh's backdrop is a world you already recognize with some slight differences, and the characters are marvelous. There's a villain, a love story, and…ah yes, 'thar be dragons.'"—*Out in Print: Queer Book Reviews*

Swelter

"I don't think there is a single book D. Jackson Leigh has written that I don't like…I recommend this book if you want a nice romance mixed with a little suspense."—*Kris Johnson, Texas Library Association*

"This book is a great mix of romance, action, angst, and emotional drama…The first half of the book focuses on the budding relationship between the two women, and the gradual revealing of secrets. The second half ramps up the action side of things…There were some good sexy scenes, and also an appropriate amount of angst and introspection by both women as feelings more than just the physical started to surface."—*Rainbow Book Reviews*

Call Me Softly

"*Call Me Softly* is a thrilling and enthralling novel of love, lies, intrigue, and Southern charm."—*Bibliophilic Book Blog*

Touch Me Gently

"D. Jackson Leigh understands the value of branding, and delivers more of the familiar and welcome story elements that set her novels apart from other authors in the romance genre."—*Rainbow Reader*

Every Second Counts

"Her prose is clean, lean, and mean—elegantly descriptive."—*Out in Print: Queer Book Reviews*

Riding Passion

"The sex was always hot and the relationships were realistic, each with their difficulties. The technical writing style was impeccable, ranging from poetic to more straightforward and simple. The entire anthology was a demonstration of Leigh's considerable abilities."—*2015 Rainbow Awards*

By the Author

Romance

Call Me Softly

Touch Me Gently

Hold Me Forever

Swelter

Take a Chance

Ordinary Is Perfect

Blades of Bluegrass

Unbridled

Forever Comes in Threes

Cherokee Falls Series

Bareback

Long Shot

Every Second Counts

Dragon Horse War Trilogy

The Calling

Tracker and the Spy

Seer and the Shield

Short Story Collection

Riding Passion

Visit us at www.boldstrokesbooks.com

FOREVER
COMES IN THREES

by

D. Jackson Leigh

2022

This Trade Paperback Original Is Published By
Bold Strokes Books, Inc.
P.O. Box 249
Valley Falls, NY 12185

First Edition: June 2022

CREDITS
Editor: Shelley Thrasher
Production Design: Stacia Seaman
Cover Design by Tammy Seidick

Acknowledgments

I'm most grateful to the inspiration for this story—my rescue pups Tucker, Molly, and JT. Their antics and affection have enriched my life more than I can express. Their distinct personalities and dynamics as a pack have taught me so many life lessons and provided endless hours of entertainment. The Terrors (https://www.facebook.com/djlterrors) were my first experience adopting rescues, which I'd encourage all dog-lovers to consider. So many incredible pets need forever homes.

Ironically, the publication of this book is both a celebration of my little pack and knife to my heart because it has unexpectedly become a tribute to my very special little guy, Tucker. A few weeks after I sent this manuscript to Shelley, I held him in my arms, our hearts beating together until the vet's needle slowed, then stopped his. He had suffered a catastrophic, completely out of the blue, attack of pancreatitis that damaged his kidneys beyond repair.

I was Tucker's third try at adoption, the first two having failed because of his shyness and strong bond with his foster mom. I came to see those failures as destiny because he and I were meant for each other. He rescued me from mourning over my first Jack Russell terrier, and he was the reason I later adopted Molly, his mother, because he needed company while I was at work, then JT because Tucker needed a playmate who liked to run and wrestle as much as he did. I love them all, but Tucker was the one who stayed up with me during long nights of writing. He was the one who would sleep next to me with his chin on my shoulder after I returned from an out-of-town trip. His loyalty and unconditional adoration lightened many sad or lonely moments, and my love for him grew to be as fierce as his for me.

Rest easy, my little man.

In loving memory of Tucker
2010–2021
Your brave little heart will always hold a place in mine.

CHAPTER ONE

Perry opened her eyes, instantly alert, nearly a full second before her alarm chimed and her smart house assistant, or SHA, greeted her.

"Good morning, Perry. It is oh five thirty Eastern Daylight Time. Today is Friday, July 15th, 2022."

Perry rolled up to sit on the side of the bed, stretched her arms above her head, then stood to perform several more stretching exercises during the next ninety seconds. "Good morning, SHA. Four minutes, please. On my mark." She dropped to the floor and began counting out twenty-five push-ups. "...twenty-three, twenty-four, mark," she said, cuing SHA to start timing her four-minute plank, arms straight, after completing the twenty-fifth push-up.

"SHA, weather?"

"It is currently fifty-three degrees and clear," SHA's disembodied female voice recited. "Today is forecast to remain clear with a high of seventy-four. Air quality is moderate."

"Well, that's unusually nice weather to start off the weekend," Perry muttered to herself.

"The air-quality improvement is unusual before the weekend respite from commuter traffic," SHA noted.

Perry slipped in her earbuds, keyed her favorite exercise music, and ignored the computer's unsolicited response. Her mind was already on next week's podcasts—organizing your personal life so you're more productive at home and better rested for the next workweek. She smiled to herself. This idea could generate another best-selling book for her.

"Four minutes."

Perry was so engrossed in her thoughts, SHA's announcement was like yanking off headphones that had been blocking the scream of her abdominal muscles. She dropped to the floor, sweating and panting for breath. No pain, no gain. She'd be sore, but she would stretch her abdominal muscles out later while she prepped for today's podcast that would set the stage for next week.

"Shower at optimum temperature in ninety seconds," SHA reported.

Perry rolled to her feet and dashed to the kitchen to grab a pre-prepared breakfast from the freezer and pop it into the microwave. "Start microwave in six minutes. Cook three minutes on high temp," she said as she headed back to the master suite.

"Confirmed," SHA responded.

Nine minutes until her breakfast would be ready. On Mondays and Fridays, she doubled her three-minute shower time to allow for shaving armpits, legs, and, um, private areas that might need shaping up. That left three minutes to dress, semi-dry her short hairstyle, and return to the kitchen as the microwave buzzer sounded the end of its cooking time.

She multitasked—mentally cataloging the studies she'd bookmarked on the most efficient work schedules—while she completed her morning grooming ritual.

Some podcasters trying to gain subscribers would pay "boosters" to call in with prepared questions if real-time stats showed listeners were getting bored and dropping off to click onto something else. Perry never needed to do that.

Today's *Timed for Success* podcast would give her steadfast followers something to think about over the weekend so their questions could stimulate Monday's discussion.

Before her framed master's degree in business needed its first dusting, she'd already built a solid reputation in the business and manufacturing industry as an efficiency expert. While still in graduate school at Columbia, she began building teams that traveled to factories and business complexes to evaluate and advise them on how to streamline their workflow.

She also was in high demand as a speaker at business conventions. In fact, requests for her expertise were so frequent, she hired a production company to video a series of her training workshops that she sold from her website to small businesses that couldn't afford her team's consulting services.

Questions generated by samples of those videos on her company's website were the catalyst for her two very successful books and, eventually, *Timed for Success.*

The timing of the new podcast—just before the pandemic locked down travel and office buildings worldwide—couldn't have been more perfect. While her teams became busier than ever helping businesses transition their operations online so their employees could work from home as much as possible, the reduction in travel and speaking engagements mostly freed her to handle the twice-weekly podcast and begin research for a third book.

Even when the pandemic lockdown basically ended, businesses were still rethinking their workflow. Having employees operate from home had saved the companies and the workers valuable time and dollars. Organizations would still need smaller main corporate offices and have occasions when a project team would need to come in so they could physically work together, but the no-longer-commuting employees were happier, sick days were significantly fewer, and overhead expenses were shrinking. So many firms were taking the next step and exploring flexible working hours and more work-from-home positions, making next week's podcasts a hot topic.

She shook the last of the shaving cream from her razor and rinsed before shutting off the shower.

"Initiating microwave," SHA recited.

She took precisely three minutes to dry and dress herself in the clothes she'd laid out the night before, mousse and dry her hair, then brush her teeth, and returned to the kitchen just as the microwave beeped to signal her breakfast was ready.

She carried her breakfast tray to her office, where an industrial hot-beverage prototype machine was pouring the last drops of a steaming hot chia latte. The amazing machine could produce up to thirty different hot or cold coffee or tea specialty drinks, in addition to regular coffee. She'd already decided to invest in the start-up company that was about to go public to gear up for production and market it as equipment that could replace 90 percent of a business's human baristas. It would never call in sick, demand health insurance, ask for paid vacations or holidays off, or require payroll taxes or unemployment insurance. Plus, a rent-to-own agreement could be a huge boost for a small business.

In short, it was another win-win. She was rolling, with no obstacles in sight.

She shoveled her scrambled eggs onto half of her English muffin to take a big bite. While her multiple computers booted up, ideas for more podcast topics sprang up like the dandelions in her neighbor's lawn.

She yawned before she stuffed the last of her eggs and muffin into her mouth. What was up with that? Her day had barely begun, and she was bursting with ideas. Perry stretched her arms left, right, then overhead to loosen her shoulders. She was about to pass the mid-thirty mark. Maybe she should add some quick yoga poses to her morning or before-bed routines. Yeah. Before she made any changes, she'd research which time would be more productive.

Her breakfast consumed, she returned to the kitchen, quickly washed and dried her plate and fork, and then stowed them in the cupboard. She glanced at her Apple watch. She was actually thirty seconds ahead of schedule, so she gulped the last of her latte and jogged the few steps back to her office to shove her mug onto the coffee/tea altar.

"SHA, dispense twelve ounces of Earl Grey and three teaspoons of sugar." The caffeine should bring her up to regular speed and alertness levels.

She tapped preprogramed keys on one computer to initiate a rotation of top stories from news sites she trusted. She listened as the computer-generated voice read a headline, then followed with a summary of the story before going to the next. While she listened, she scanned her email, which automatically triaged into folders identified as podcast, seminars and events, personal, and "other."

Weeks could go by without new personal email, which consisted primarily of a rare note from an old college buddy. Her current friends would text to get in touch. The still-empty folder did trigger a reminder, though, and she quickly texted a time-and-place confirmation to the woman she'd arranged a first date with for tonight. She was pleased to get an immediate "looking forward to it" reply.

Perry hunched her shoulders and rubbed her palms together before settling her fingers on the keys to peruse the email from her last podcast. Some days, it was hard to focus on the foundation of Chandler INC because the desire was so strong to check the response from a vigorous podcast discussion. It was like having Christmas every day.

Because the podcast had millions of followers in every time zone around the world, she had three assistants who worked in shifts to read each email and create a spreadsheet that would summarize the subject or question and rank it according to the number of similar emails.

She eagerly scanned today's spreadsheets, then dove into the thirty or forty individual emails they considered worthy and unique enough to forward in full. She took notes as she read, her pen slowing after the first dozen.

Who the hell is Dr. Lee? And what does her woo-woo podcast about Finding Natural Balance have to do with efficiency?

❖

Perry checked her watch again. Her date was six minutes late, but she spotted the tall blonde standing at the hostess station and scanning the restaurant for her. She stood to catch Diane's attention, then waited as she glided to their table like the runway model she could have been.

They'd met when Perry attended a men's soccer match with business colleagues, and she had been instantly intrigued. The daughter of the soccer franchise's owner, she secured sponsors for the team. If men handed out those sponsorships, Perry imagined Diane was very successful at her work.

"So nice to see you again," Diane said as she settled in the chair Perry held out for her.

"Thank you. I've been looking forward to seeing you again, too." It was an overstatement, because Perry hated first dates. She'd had a lot of them, and very few second or third dates, in the past couple of years. "Did you have trouble finding a place to park?"

"No. And traffic was light for a Friday."

"I see." Perry hated people who were late for no real reason. They demonstrated a lack of consideration for the other person's time.

"How's your day been so far? Mine has been total crap, so I'm looking for tonight to make it better." Elbow on the table, Diane propped her chin in her hand and gave Perry a once-over like she was on the menu. Hmm. Although she hadn't scheduled time for sex after dinner—it was only their first date—schedules could always be revised. But dinner first.

"Let's hope so. But we should order, then talk while the food is being prepared," Perry said. That was a more efficient approach and could make up the six minutes of lost time.

"I haven't eaten here before, but I love Greek food."

"Excellent. Their service is very prompt." She handed Diane a menu. "I can recommend several small plates."

"I love gyros."

Perry cringed when Diane mispronounced the word. "Yee-row," she said, carefully rolling the *r*, before she could censure herself.

"What?"

"The *g* is silent. Greeks pronounce it yee-row."

"Whatever."

Okay. Perry wasn't a social idiot. It was rude to correct her date, and she wouldn't even blink at the lack of a rolled *r*, but she expected someone with Diane's family money and assumed education to be more knowledgeable. And she cringed at Diane's "whatever." Maybe she'd overestimated her age, or possibly just her maturity. Still…that body, naked under Perry's. She could make some allowances.

"No matter. We're not in Greece, are we? A lot of Americans pronounce it that way."

Diane waved off her pseudo-apology. "The caterer for the skybox buffet makes little mini ones that are about two or three bites. I think it's the cucumber sauce I like so much. I forget what it's called."

"Tzatziki."

"And that soft bread. So good."

"They do have gyros, but I find so much more to try on the menu." Hoping to impress, Perry had chosen this restaurant because of the extensive, authentic menu.

"I'll stick with what I know. The chicken gyro sounds good."

Perry nearly groaned. Not even the lamb. She could have taken this woman to a food-truck roundup instead. She ordered a grape-leaves appetizer, hoping to at least get Diane to try something else, and the Lebanese-fried-trout entrée.

As soon as the waiter brought their drinks and took their order, Diane launched into a recounting of her terrible day.

"Is it my fault that I'm so good I sold the sponsor spot on front of the guys' jersey to two different companies? I told Daddy to put the one that bid the highest on the jerseys and give the other one the shoe contract. He said the lower bidder didn't make soccer shoes. I said, well, there you go. It's a perfect opportunity for them to expand."

Diane's story of her terrible day was growing past movie length to that of a ten-day miniseries. Luckily, Perry was practiced at multitasking and was making mental notes for her next podcast while Diane prattled on in the background.

"Daddy didn't like that idea either, so I told him to break the contract with the lower bidder if they didn't want their name on something else, like the warm-ups or equipment bags. His lawyers always write contracts so they can get out of them if they want."

Perry tuned back in to Diane's story at the mention of this disreputable business practice. "I'm not saying lawyers don't routinely try to slip in termination clauses and other lawyers always try to catch them before they sign, but your father will damage his business reputation if he breaks contracts often."

Diane gave her the same bored stare as when Perry had corrected her earlier. Time to get this date back on track. Diane had ignored the appetizer, and Perry had nearly finished her trout while Diane talked and didn't eat her dinner. She didn't want to think about how much time they'd wasted on Diane's bad-day diatribe.

"How about we get to know each other better?"

Diane's glare transformed to a near leer. "I'm all for that."

"I'll go first to give you a chance to eat. You know that my company is built on helping businesses be more efficient."

Diane broke off a small piece of the gyro wrap and nodded as she slipped it into her mouth.

"Well, you can't make a business more efficient without studying the humans involved—the owners who started the company, the employees, and the customers. So, I've read a lot of studies on human nature."

Diane's attention span appeared short because she had turned her attention to eviscerating the gyro so she could pick out pieces of tzatziki-covered chicken to eat. Perry preferred to think she was simply multitasking.

"Anyway, studies have shown that when people are on a first date, they want to know five basic things about the other person. Can you guess what they are?"

Diane looked up. "Five things?" Though she spoke while she was still chewing, she had the good manners to cover her mouth.

"Yes." Maybe they could salvage this date.

"I know what I'd ask." Diane swallowed her food and raised a finger as she cited each answer. "One. Do you live with your parents? Two. Do you currently have a job or some kind of steady income? I'm okay with trust-fund girls. Three. Which social media are you on? Four. Do you like to shop online or at the mall? Five. Have you ever been in prison? I don't mean overnight for drunk driving, but sentenced and dressed in an orange jumpsuit. Daddy makes me ask that one."

Perry sat back in her chair. *Wow.* She cleared her throat. "Uh, those weren't exactly the questions noted in the studies."

Diane tore off another small piece of gyro wrap. "Can you answer them for me?"

Perry held up her hand to mimic Diane. "I haven't lived with my parents since I was seventeen and left for college. I'm the chief executive officer of my own company, among other things, and have a seven-figure annual income. I started and host a very successful twice-a-week podcast, but my marketing manager pretty much handles the rest of my company's social media. I don't have any personal social-media accounts. I shop almost exclusively online and hate going to the mall, even though I can be lured into almost any sporting-goods store. And I've never even had a traffic ticket, much less spent time in prison."

Diane shoved her plate and mostly uneaten food aside. "Wow. What do you do when you're not working?"

"I enjoy my work and spend a lot of time researching the things I need to keep it relevant and successful."

"No. I mean, what do you do for fun? Please don't say you organize your closet."

"I go out with friends. You and I met at a soccer game."

"Don't forget that I work in business, too. Those weren't friends. You were schmoozing business contacts."

Fun? She had fun. "I run most Saturdays with a friend and go to dinners and parties at friends' houses. I follow professional women's soccer, the WNBA, and several NCAA sports."

"Do you hit the clubs much—dancing and stuff?"

"The nightclub scene became too boring and juvenile by the time I hit my mid-twenties." Perry discreetly checked her watch.

Diane gave her a long look, then folded her napkin to place it on her plate to signify she was done with the meal and shouldered her purse.

"Wait. You're leaving? I haven't asked my questions."

Diane's smile was a mixture of disappointment and condescension. "No need. The lesbian world is pretty small. I called around and checked you out before tonight because I couldn't believe someone so attractive was actually available. What I learned turns out to be true."

Perry stiffened. People discussed her? "I don't know what you're talking about."

"You were nearly red in the face when I was deliberately six minutes late without offering an explanation. You've checked your watch at least five times during our meal because I wrecked your schedule of order, eat, answer your scripted questions, then plan a second date that is scheduled to allow for possible sex afterward. You're too gallant to schedule sex for the first one."

Was she so predictable the entire Fresno lesbian community joked about her routine? No. She wasn't.

"That's not true. I had already considered changing my plans for later tonight in the hope that you wanted to follow through with the seductive looks you've been giving me all night."

Diane laughed. "I'm flattered. And I am tempted. But I know I'll take offense if I want a second orgasm only to have you announce time is up and show me the door." She stood, then stepped forward and took Perry in a sizzling kiss.

Stepping back, Diane touched her fingers to her lips as if to hold the kiss there. "I might regret this, but the reality is, even though I work for Daddy's organization, I hate sports, love shopping at the mall, live on social media, and enjoy club-hopping. We'd never be compatible."

Hot body or not, Perry had to agree. Scratch off another first, and only first, date.

CHAPTER TWO

"Just find them a good home, Perry," Janice Chandler said. "Together if at all possible."

"Mother, no. What am I supposed to do with three dogs? I don't know anything about dogs."

They'd never had a pet when she was growing up because Perry Chandler's parents didn't have time for their only child, much less the responsibility of a pet. Not to mention that their research work often landed them in other countries, sometimes for a few months or, occasionally, for several years.

So, she was now shocked speechless when her mother showed up on her doorstep and handed her the leashes of three mutts, whose fate had fallen to Janice when a colleague died suddenly of some jungle disease while researching native medicine among Amazon indigenous tribes. Now, Janice, with whom Perry's only contact in the past year had been a one-night visit initiated by Perry at Christmas, was headed out to replace her associate on that same research team and dumping the dogs on Perry.

Perry tried a different angle. "I don't even know if my homeowners' association allows three pets in a townhouse."

"Hopefully, you won't have them long enough for your HOA to know they're here."

"No, Mother. No."

But Janice wasn't listening as she walked back to the Uber ride that waited in the driveway.

Perry looked down at the three canines at her feet. All appeared freshly bathed and groomed. The bluish haze of cataracts was a clue to the advanced age of the plump white-and-black lap-dog mix but didn't detract from the calculating gaze that met hers. The haircut of the slim, white-and-brown dog indicated schnauzer genes, his unusual golden eyes seeming to plead as he sat hip to hip with his chubby companion. Was he clinging to or protecting his elderly friend? The third dog—a male tricolored, wire-haired terrier—paced in a tight circle behind the other two. His dark eyes darted between Janice, Perry, the Uber, and the new neighborhood, while he made small, nervous noises deep in his throat. He paused at intervals to prod the other dogs with his nose, as if imploring them to make a run for it. Perry mentally shook herself. They were just dogs, not abandoned children.

Janice returned from the waiting vehicle with two overfilled cloth totes. The Uber driver followed with two large bags of dog food.

"All the instructions are in the bags, along with food, toys, and various other things. You have two doctorate degrees, Perry. I'm sure you can figure it out."

"Mother, no."

The Uber driver returned from the car a second time and deposited two wire contraptions next to the dog food, then piled three fluffy pet beds on top.

Perry stared at the wire panels. "What's that?"

"Those wire things unfold into cages. The beds go inside them, I would think."

"Mother, no."

She held out the leashes for her mother to take the dogs back from her, startled when her mother stepped forward to place an awkward kiss on her cheek and squeeze her shoulder. It wasn't exactly a hug but as close to one as they got in her family.

"It was Amanda's dying wish that I make sure they don't end up in a pound where they kill them if they aren't adopted in ten days. I owe her that after all the papers we co-authored. Sorry to blindside you like this, but I didn't have anyone else to turn to."

"Did you check with Dad to see if he would take them?"

"Last I heard, your father was in England."

Well, that was more than Perry knew. After her parents had divorced while she was in college, her father popped in on her only every few years, usually unannounced.

Janice handed over a folded note. "Amanda left this local contact for assistance if you need it."

"Mother…"

"Got to run or I'll miss my plane," Janice said, waving as she got into the back seat of the Uber. "I'll email from the Amazon."

❖

Perry walked her three charges directly through the townhouse and out into the miniscule twenty-by-forty-feet backyard. Enclosed by a six-foot privacy fence, they'd be safe here while she called this phone number her mother had left to get those people to take them off her hands.

She grimaced when the schnauzer mix immediately lifted his hind leg and urinated on the base of her birdbath. She doubted he could harm the concrete, but the expensive never-needs-mowing synthetic turf she'd installed would probably start to smell like a men's urinal if the dogs were here very long. The terrier followed his pal, lifting his leg to pee everywhere the first dog did. When the older female dog squatted to relieve herself, she made a show afterward of scratching the ground next to it like a bear claws a tree to leave his mark. Both boy dogs dutifully hiked their legs to add their contribution to her chosen toilet spot, and Perry began calculating the cost of replacing the turf as she dialed the phone number her mother had left.

A rich, melodic voice answered on the third ring. "Hello?"

"Hi. It seems I've gotten stuck with three homeless dogs because their owner died, and I have no idea what to do with them. I was given this number to call for someone to take them."

"Where are you located?"

"The Fresno area." Perry rattled off the address. "When do you think someone can come get them?"

"As it happens, I'm at the dog park a few blocks from your address, helping with a puppy obedience class. It will be a little bit, but I can swing by when I leave here."

"Wonderful." Perry breathed a sigh of relief. "I'll see you then."

Ten minutes later, SHA announced, "You have a visitor at your door," and the dogs whirled toward it when the chime sounded.

"Awesome. Your ride is here," Perry told the dogs. She quickly slipped inside and slid the glass patio door closed as they charged, barking like a pack of wolves.

"You stay put," Perry said, pointing her finger at them. "And be quiet."

To her surprise, they stopped barking. She paused to look back before answering the front door. The townhouse's open concept allowed a clear line of sight from the patio door to the front entry, and they sat in a row, watching her intently.

Perry shook her head and said a quick prayer to the universe that her mother had had second thoughts and was returning to retrieve the dogs. She swung the door open, and karma bared its teeth.

"So, you're not dead or in the hospital or in jail." Julie, Perry's longtime friend as well as right hand at work, stood among the dog paraphernalia still strewn about on her steps. "After the time-management lecture I got last week for being five minutes late, I was sure you must be incapacitated or imprisoned when you were a no-show ten minutes past our meet-up time. But you don't appear incapacitated, and you certainly aren't in jail, since you answered the door so fast one would think you were expecting a hot blonde on your doorstep."

Perry hung her head. "I was hoping it was my mother."

"Oh my God. You are sick." Julie frowned and lifted Perry's chin with her hand to look into her eyes. "You're not just sick. You're delirious. When did you begin feeling ill? I thought you were vaccinated." She laid her other hand on Perry's forehead. "Crap. Now I'm contaminated." She swept her hand out to indicate the pile of supplies left by Janice. "Is that what all this stuff is? You've been having everything delivered rather than going out to shop. Oh, hon. You should have told me. I would have packed a bag and come to quarantine with you. Now I'm stuck here without my essentials."

"No. Wait, wait." Perry clamped her hand over Julie's mouth to stop the verbal onslaught. "I'm not sick."

Julie eyed the pile of items after Perry released her. "Is Chandler INC collecting donations for a local animal shelter? You should have let your marketing-slash-public relations manager," Julie pointed to herself, "know so I could post it on our social-media accounts earlier."

"That's not exactly the situation."

"The company gets a lot of points for that kind of stuff, you know." Julie continued as if she hadn't heard Perry's weak clarification. "Especially after a year of pandemic lockdown when everyone sat home watching feel-good videos about rescued dogs being nursed back to health and finding their forever homes."

Among other things, Julie had been her roommate most of her years in college and was now Perry's public relations/social media/marketing guru. They had both worked from home since the beginning of the pandemic and kept in touch virtually each workday, but they met in person most Saturday mornings for a four-mile run, followed by a strategy session—the standing appointment Perry had forgotten because of her mother's startling visit.

Perry temporarily forgot Julie again when a sleek, white

Mercedes convertible parked next to Julie's car. A woman with midnight-dark hair resting on her shoulders like spun silk gave them a long look before exiting the car. Large sunglasses hid her eyes but not the finely arched brows.

Turning to see what had captured Perry's attention, Julie joined her in watching this perfect female specimen in skinny jeans stroll toward them.

"You called about some dogs that need to be rehomed?"

"Yes. Yes, I did," Perry said, finally finding her voice. "Inside." She held her arm out, indicating the door to her condo. Women didn't normally cause her to trip over her own tongue, but she couldn't seem to get words to form correctly. "I mean, please come inside. The dogs are in the backyard."

The stranger lifted her sunglasses to rest on top of her head, revealing velvet-brown, slightly almond-shaped eyes. Perry had seen—even dated—many beautiful women, but something about this woman mesmerized her. She almost felt…familiar.

The woman held her hand out. "I'm Ming."

Perry's neck and ears heated with an embarrassed flush. Taking Ming's hand in hers, she smiled. "Hi. I'm Perry. The one who called you." An elbow to her ribs reminded her that she wasn't alone. "And this is my friend and colleague, Julie."

"Nice to meet you," Ming replied, gently withdrawing her hand from Perry's grasp to shake hands with Julie.

"Should we put this stuff in your car?" Julie asked.

Ming shook her head. "No. Sorry. My apartment is in a high-rise building, which is not conducive to keeping dogs. I just help the local rescue groups by evaluating possible intakes to point them toward the right new home or foster home, if no adoption prospects are immediately available."

Ming spotted the dogs watching them through the back sliding-glass door when Perry opened the front door. "Our three subjects, I assume?"

"That's them. Darling little dogs," Perry said, hoping her enthusiasm would influence Ming to act quickly. "They belonged to my mother's colleague, who died suddenly. I'm sure you can find homes for them right away."

Ming hesitated, then bent to heft one of the twenty-pound bags of dog food. "You should bring everything inside. You wouldn't want anyone to mistake it for free stuff."

"Right." Perry awkwardly wrestled the collapsed wire crates and three large, fluffy dog beds into her arms. "But don't you worry about it. Julie and I can get it. Why don't you go meet the dogs?"

Ming nodded and headed inside. Julie and Perry watched her drop the bag of dog food in the kitchen before walking into the backyard. The dogs greeted her like an old friend.

"They didn't even bark at her," Perry said.

"When did I become your pack mule?" Julie's tone was teasing. "I'd say it was time for me to go home, but I think I'd rather stay and watch you drool. Besides, I haven't heard the story of how your mother got away with dumping these dogs on you."

"Can you cut me some slack, please? I'll explain to both of you together." She gave Julie her pleading puppy-dog-eyes face—no pun on the current situation intended.

An eye roll, then a shrug of acquiescence rewarded this blatant attempt at persuasion. Deceptively strong given her feminine appearance, Julie easily tucked the other twenty-pound bag of dog food under one arm while grabbing the handles of the two overstuffed totes with her other hand, then using it to also open and hold back the storm door.

"Shit." Perry dropped the dog beds onto the polished hardwood floor, realizing that her navy running suit now looked like she'd used it as a lint roller. She'd also scraped the skin off the knuckles of her left hand as she squeezed through the doorway because she was too stubborn to make more than one trip to bring the cages and beds inside. It was actually bleeding. Bright, red...uh-oh. The room was starting to look a little fuzzy, and her knees felt suddenly weak.

"Oh, no, you don't." Julie dropped her packages, then

grabbed Perry's arm and half-carried, half-dragged her toward the L-shaped island that separated the kitchen from the rest of the downstairs living area.

The dogs abandoned Ming and went crazy, barking and jumping against the patio's glass door. Ming looked up and slid the door open.

"What happened?" she asked.

Perry was afraid she'd puke if she spoke, so she let Julie answer for her.

"It's okay," Julie said. "She scraped her hand on the door frame coming in, and the big baby faints at the sight of her own blood."

"Do not." Perry's faint protest was lost among the howling that had replaced the chorus of barks.

"Sit," Ming said, as Julie guided Perry to one of the tall chairs next to the island.

Perry wasn't sure if Ming's command was meant for her or the dogs, but it didn't really matter. She immediately sat, closed her eyes, and bent to rest her cheek against the cool granite countertop.

"I'll round up something to bandage her hand." Julie opened the laundry nook and retrieved a first-aid kit.

Perry's nausea began to fade, and after a few seconds, she realized the canine ruckus had gone silent. She opened her eyes and lifted her head. The howlers were sitting quietly, watching as Ming examined Perry's bloody knuckles—the bloody knuckles Perry could no longer see because Ming had turned her back as she stood next to Perry's outstretched arm, blocking Perry's view of the wound. Ming's dark hair hung within inches of Perry's face, and she closed her eyes to inhale Ming's spicy scent. If they were better acquainted and the circumstances different, Perry would have wrapped her legs around Ming to pull her closer, buried her nose in Ming's silky hair, and kissed her slender neck. Julie's return interrupted her momentary fantasy.

"You look like you know what you're doing," Julie said.

"I hope so, or else the state of California might want to take back my medical license."

"You're a doctor?" Perry's mouth was near, so near Ming's delicate ear, she could almost...

"Yes. Family medicine and naturopathy." An infinitesimal tightening of Ming's neck muscles was her only reaction to Perry's breath brushing her cheek.

"Very cool. I dated a physical therapist once." Julie sidled closer. "She had great hands."

Perry scowled at Julie's flirtation and obvious ploy to let Ming know she romanced ladies. "Please. You're being modest, Julie. I'm pretty sure you've dated enough medical people to staff an entire hospital."

Julie stuck out her tongue at Perry's sarcastic remark. "I'm going to write off that remark as you being stressed about the dogs and your hand."

Ming interrupted their bickering. "Could you find a couple of bottles of water and two bowls, please, Julie?"

Perry eyed the array of medical supplies Ming extracted from the first-aid kit. The thing that worried her most was the large syringe lying next to the bandages. "What are you going to do?"

"Squirt some saline over your hand to wash out any dirt, paint particles, or fur that might have adhered to your wound rather than your clothes." Ming mixed a saline packet with water in one bowl and drew the solution into the ginormous syringe.

"Saline is salt water."

"Damn, you're smart," Julie said. "And your point is?"

Perry scowled. "That's raw flesh. Salt water is going to hurt...a lot."

"It's a very weak solution, not table salt," Ming said as she gripped Perry's wrist to hold her hand over the second bowl. "It won't sting much." Ming's fine-boned, five-five body was small compared to Perry's five-foot, eight-inch athletic frame, but her grip on Perry's wrist was iron.

Julie grinned. "Buck up, buttercup."

Ming released the saline in a gentle flow, increasing the pressure of the spray only when a stubborn dog hair clung to the wound. Still, Perry flinched, and Ming apologized as she carefully patted the knuckles dry with a sterile gauze pad. "You've mostly just lost a few layers of skin, which will make it pretty sore for a while, but I see only one cut, and it's not deep enough for stitches," Ming said.

"Thank God." Perry couldn't hope that Ming carried a suture kit in her car, and she sure didn't want to spend hours at a doc-in-the-box on a Saturday. She glared at the dogs. "You've been here less than an hour and are already causing trouble."

The wire-haired dog ducked his head and slinked away a few steps, while the schnauzer mix waved his tail tentatively. The female snorted, her stare challenging Perry's accusation.

Ming's melodious chuckle instantly softened Perry's irritation. A good dousing with an antibiotic/lidocaine spray and a nonstick bandage and flex-wrap covering finished the job, and Ming turned to face her. "Molly questions whether you would have scraped your hand if you hadn't tried to carry so much at once through the doorway."

"Who's Molly?" Julie asked.

Ming pointed to the female dog, the apparent pack leader, and the blue tag engraved with MOLLY that hung from her collar.

Perry examined her newly bandaged hand. The dog discussion could wait. "Thanks. I'm lucky you were in the area when I called."

Julie laughed. "Luckier than you know. My usual treatment for a boo-boo is a kiss to make it better, but I wasn't about to kiss that bloody mess."

When Ming rounded the island to empty the bowls of saline into the sink, the dogs followed, focused on the bowls.

"They act like they know you already," Julie said.

"They do," Ming said, washing out one of the bowls and filling it with cold water before setting it on the floor. Two of the dogs crowded around to lap up the water, but the wire-haired boy hung back while Ming washed and filled the second bowl. "How long have they been in your backyard with no water or shade?"

"Huh?" Perry was contemplating a kiss treatment, but from Ming rather than Julie. Apparently, she'd missed the subject change, and Julie was charging ahead in their competition for Ming's attention.

"They were out there when I arrived, but that was only minutes before you got here," Julie said. She turned an accusing stare on Perry, blatantly aligning herself with Ming. "How long have those poor pups been left in the yard?"

Perry glared back. "I'd just taken them out back to relieve themselves when you showed up. So, minutes. Not hours. If they were thirsty, it's because Mom hadn't watered them before she dumped them here."

Julie shook her head. "They're not plants or horses, Perry. You don't water them." She turned to Ming, dramatically overplaying her hand, in Perry's estimation. "She's never had a pet and doesn't know anything about caring for dogs."

Her hand forgotten, Perry mentally reviewed their conversation. "Wait. You know these dogs? Did you know…you knew Amanda?"

"We collaborated on a research project concerning naturopathic medicines used by indigenous people. I've been to her home several times while working on the paper we published on the project. We worked together only a few months but became friends because of our mutual interest in dog rescues. I was shocked to hear about her death and wondered what happened to her pets." Ming sat on the floor, and the two dogs, water still dripping from their beards, jostled to claim her lap. The nervous wire-haired terrier danced around them but didn't pile on with the others. "She was torn about an opportunity because she had to spend several months among Amazon River tribes in Brazil, cataloging the plants they use for medical purposes. She didn't want to leave these little guys, and the last time I talked with her, she was looking for a student to live at her house with them while she was gone."

Julie frowned at Perry. "So, how did your mother end up with them? I know she didn't offer to pet-sit, because she's never had time for her daughter, much less three mutts."

Perry cleared her throat and shot Julie a warning glare. She didn't need to share Perry's failed childhood with this beautiful stranger. "Well…Amanda, who is a long-time colleague of my mother's, did go to the Amazon. Unfortunately, she caught a virus and died before she could be airlifted to a hospital. Her dying wish was for my mother to find homes for them, rather than let them be taken to a shelter."

"So, Janice dumped them on you," Julie said. "This is over the top, even for your mother." Her voice rose with each angry word. "She treated you like you're one of her lab assistants she can just order to take care of anything she doesn't want to."

"Kind of." Perry couldn't help thinking about her mother kissing her cheek and squeezing her shoulder.

"What does that mean?" Julie threw her hands up in exasperation, and the terrier scrambled for the patio door and huddled there when he found it closed. "Oh, honey. I'm sorry. Did I scare you?" He looked from his companions cuddled with Ming to the water bowl to Julie and finally to Perry.

"Mom was asked to finish Amanda's research in the Amazon, so she left the dogs here to catch a plane to Brazil." Perry offered Ming a shrug. "And she left your phone number in case I needed help."

Ming stroked the schnauzer mix, who closed his eyes and snuggled against her chest. "Julie, would you place that second bowl at the end of the counter, then bring those two bags of their things over here?"

The nervous terrier eyed the bowl of fresh water but skittered away when Julie walked near him to retrieve the bags.

"Don't look at Tucker," Ming said, indicating the skittish

dog. "Pretend you don't see him." She patted the floor beside her. "Both of you sit next to me so I can introduce you to them."

"This floor might not be clean," Perry said. "The cleaning service came Thursday, but the dogs have been walking all over."

Julie and all three dogs, their fur pristine and neatly trimmed, stared at her. "Look at them," Julie said. "Now, look at you." She indicated Perry's hair-covered, blood-stained jogging suit. "Who do you think should be worried about the floor being dirty?"

The female dog sniffed at Perry's leg and sneezed as if to point out her untidy state.

"No comments from the canine chorus," Perry muttered as she sat.

Ming kissed the top of the female dog's head. "This is Molly, as you've probably deduced. She's an old girl, estimated to be about thirteen. She was an adult when Amanda adopted her, so her age is a veterinarian's educated guess." She stroked the dog in her lap. "This love sponge is JT."

As they talked, Tucker edged over to the water and began drinking.

"Tucker is the dog we're ignoring, and Molly is Tucker's mother. The litter was only a few days old when Molly and her pups were rescued from a bad home. Obviously, his father must have been a Jack Russell terrier, or something close, because other than identical black spots on their backs, he looks nothing like Molly."

Tucker stopped drinking, pricking his ears forward, apparently at the sound of his name.

"Amanda told me that she adopted JT because Tucker needed a younger dog to run and play with. Molly just wasn't interested or up to the job. If you forget who's who, their names are on their collar tags."

Tucker began to move closer.

Ming didn't hold her hand out to him but pointed to the bags

Julie had brought over. "I'll bet we'll find treats in one of those bags."

All three dogs perked up at the word they recognized, and JT abandoned Ming's lap to stick his nose in the bags Julie was searching. She came up empty-handed.

"Do you have cheese in your refrigerator, Perry?" Ming asked.

Perry stood to open it. "Let's see...string, goat, feta, or American slices?"

"Let's stick with string cheese. It's mild and easy to break into bits."

The dogs seemed to agree with the choice. Molly and JT instantly plopped their butts on the floor and watched Perry expectantly.

Ming waved her away when Perry tried to hand over the cheese. "Your house, so you are the alpha. They'll recognize that fact and listen to your commands if you are their source of food and control their access to the outdoors."

"I already have one injury. What if they nip my fingers?"

"They won't. They're very well-mannered."

Uncertain, Perry eyed the dogs, then puffed out her chest, more to convince herself than her audience. "I am the alpha."

"If you pee on the fridge, I'm leaving, Ms. Alpha Dog," Julie said.

Perry was warming to her new role. She was an alpha—during her student days and now as head of her own successful company. She looked at the dogs and pointed to her chest. "I'm the alpha in this house, and you guys better listen to what I say."

Molly tilted her head—clearly thinking this statement over—while JT wagged his tail. He seemed okay with that arrangement. Tucker shrank back a few feet. They all came to attention again when Perry sat and peeled the plastic from the first stick of cheese. She broke off a piece and held it out, but the dogs didn't take it. "What am I doing wrong?" Perry asked.

❖

Ming studied the tall, handsome woman. Perry was a puzzle. She didn't appear to fear or dislike the dogs, but she displayed no natural instincts for handling them. No, the instincts were there in her body language toward the animals. She was just so… controlled. Why did Perry keep such a tight leash on herself?

"Molly is senior but still strong enough to bully JT, who is the second most dominant," she said. "Tucker's nervousness indicates he is the lowest in their hierarchy, but don't mistake that to mean he won't defend and protect."

"Defend and protect?" Julie sidled closer to watch.

"Bite someone if they move to harm his pack or alpha." Ming hesitated to share much about Tucker, but Perry needed to understand the dogs if she was going to have them for a while. The chance of finding a foster home that could take all three was slim, and she hated to break up the bonded trio so soon after losing their owner. "Tucker is a great dog but displays strong Jack Russell traits. The breed is intense about everything—like fetching a ball, protecting their territory, or catching vermin, which is what they were bred to do. They also are intensely loyal and normally attach to one person, unlike JT, who likes anybody who'll pet him." JT wagged his tail in confirmation. "Amanda was Tucker's third try at adoption because he'd attached to his foster mom and needed someone with a lot of patience to persuade him to transfer his loyalty. Losing Amanda, too, must be very lonely for him, even though he still has Molly and JT."

Something flashed in Perry's eyes but was gone before Ming could read it. Did Tucker's loneliness touch something in her? Perhaps Perry needed company as much as the dogs needed a home. Ming made a silent decision.

"The dogs didn't take the treat because you held it between them. The alpha keeps order in the pack, so they expect you to reinforce that system by giving the first treat to your second, then on down the line."

Perry's entire demeanor changed from reluctance toward the dogs to curiosity. She offered the first bite of cheese to Molly, who took it carefully from her hand. Tucker inched closer when she broke off another piece for JT, who also was careful when taking the cheese from Perry's fingers. Without prompting, Perry spoke to Tucker in soft tones.

"That's right, Tucker. We're sharing treats. Would you like one?"

He took a tentative step toward her but stopped and turned his head as if he wanted to flee again.

"Talk to him," Ming said.

"Hi, Tucker. I'm Perry. Looks like you're stuck with me until I can find you guys a home."

"Compliment him, Perry," Julie suggested.

"Oh, for Christ's sake. It's not like he can understand what I'm saying."

Tucker took a step back.

"He can understand your tone," Ming said.

"So, I could say his shit stinks in a sweet voice, and he'd think it was a compliment?"

Patience, Ming reminded herself. "No. Studies have indicated that most dogs can detect deception—whether it's by reading our expressions, or our scent, or simply because they're empathic. So, don't try it."

Tucker's dark round eyes were filled with distrust, but the treat was a powerful lure. His ears pricked forward when Perry held out the tasty morsel on the very tips of her fingers. The tricolor markings on his face were perfectly symmetrical, and his attractively set ears made a handsome picture when curiosity overrode his fear.

"Hi, handsome. I'm Perry. I'm not going to hurt you, buddy. I just want to give you this treat before I start looking for a good home for you guys. I'm really sorry about your mom, Amanda. She got sick and, uh…"

"Crossed over the rainbow bridge." Julie filled in what Perry was struggling to say.

Perry nodded but gave Julie a sidelong look for injecting the euphemism. "She crossed over the rainbow bridge. So, you guys are going to stay," she glanced at Julie and smirked, "stay with Aunt Julie for a few days while we find you a new mom or dad, or both."

Julie chuckled as she shook her head. "Good try, but no can do. My housemate, Jeff, is allergic."

Tucker took another tentative step, then another until he got close enough to stretch his neck and pluck the offering from her fingers. Perry's broad smile lit her face and ignited her blue eyes as she turned to Ming. "He took it."

Julie added brief, very quiet applause, and Ming nodded for her to continue.

After a few more rounds, Tucker was no longer scuttling away after accepting each treat. But once all the cheese was gone, he resumed his post by the door. Molly sniffed Perry's hands to confirm all had been consumed, then ambled over to the stacked beds and scratched at them until she pulled the top one down and flopped into it.

"You poor baby," Julie crooned. "I know you must be tired. Don't judge my friend. She's just not a very good hostess."

"Not my fault they drew the short straw and got me." Perry sounded bitter.

JT went to Perry and settled himself in her lap, pressing his head against her chest like he'd done with Ming. She stared down at him for a long minute, then began to stroke his head and back. Her stiff posture began to relax as she stroked, confirming Ming's earlier decision that these pups had found their new home. She only needed to convince Perry.

"JT seems to think they won the long straw."

Perry looked up quickly. "No, no, no. I don't have time for pets. I travel a lot for work."

"Not since the pandemic," Julie said. Her expression turned wistful. "I don't know if we'll ever get back to the way things were."

Ming heard the "too busy" excuse frequently, but she didn't want to press Perry too soon. "You can find plenty of professional pet sitters or boarding kennels if you need to travel for business while you're fostering them."

"Whoa. I never said I would foster them. I called you to find a home or a foster for them."

"JT would be easy to rehome, but not many people are willing to adopt an older dog like Molly because she might die soon after they became attached to her. Any foster would have to consider they might have her for several years if she's not adopted. Tucker will be even more difficult. I couldn't recommend him for a home with young children or even a teen who plays loud music. He needs a quiet home and a pack to feel safe. He's been with Molly since he was born."

JT left Perry's lap and went to Tucker, as if he understood their conversation. He nudged his packmate, then flopped down beside him and closed his eyes.

"Aw, that's so sweet," Julie said.

Tucker finally stretched out next to JT and rested his head on his paws, but his gaze stayed on Perry.

Ming gestured toward the dogs. "You can see how bonded they are. I'm really reluctant to separate them so soon after losing their owner. Studies have shown that dogs have long memories and mourn the same as humans."

"Come on, Perry," Julie pleaded. "You can't break up the band. The poor things are already traumatized. I can't take them to my house, but I'll help you with them."

Perry's face visibly softened as she stared back at Tucker, and Ming wanted to cheer. This might be a match. She could almost see the first tendrils of a bond between them. What a pair they will make—a handsome, anxious little dog and this beautiful, uptight woman. For a moment, Ming wondered what Perry would be like if she ever let loose of that control.

"Okay. But just until you find a foster home or new permanent home for the three together. And you might get texts at odd hours because I have zero experience caring for dogs."

"You can call me anytime." Ming felt unreasonably happy that Perry had accepted. "Let's get you organized."

For the next hour, they vacuumed dog beds, then Perry, so she no longer looked like a walking lint brush. They sorted dog toys, bowls, and food, and then Ming interpreted for Perry the written instructions that had been included. She even demonstrated how to prepare their dinner, then explained JT's allergy prescription and Molly's arthritis supplements.

Perry frowned and rubbed her chin as she stared at the two wire crates Ming helped her assemble. "There's only two cages."

"We call them crates, not cages," Ming said. She scanned the instructions. "The two boys like to sleep in the crates, but with the doors open. A lot of dogs trained to crate as puppies prefer to keep sleeping in them as adults. It's their safe place."

"But there are three dogs. Where will Molly sleep?" Still ensconced in her plush dog bed, Molly let out a long snore as if answering the question.

They all laughed.

"I'm guessing she'll be comfortable if you place her bed near the boys, with their beds in their crates."

"Okay. The landing at the top of the stairs is a pretty large space. Maybe I'll put their beds there so I won't be tripping over them down here."

"Sounds like a good idea." Ming decided Perry didn't need to know the dogs were used to sleeping in Amanda's bedroom, and that Molly slept on the bed with her. She'd let Perry and the dogs reach their own agreement on the sleeping arrangements.

"Food, beds, meds." Perry ticked the list off with her fingers. "What else?"

"They'll need a bathroom break pretty much when you do—first thing when you wake up, a couple of times during the day, and last thing at night before bed. They're all housebroken, so they'll probably bark at the door when they want out during the day." Ming checked her watch. "Sorry, but I need to go."

"Do you see patients on Saturdays?" Using the pretense of reading the dogs' instructions along with Ming, Julie had pressed closer than Ming found comfortable.

"Uh, no." Ming tried to inconspicuously move away from Julie. "I have a standing date to play cards with my grandmother, then take her out to dinner."

"Oh, there's a new Thai place in The Plaza. Have you tried it?" Julie obviously wasn't giving up easily and edged closer again.

Ming resisted taking another step back. "No. Grandmother loves a small Mexican restaurant near her house and refuses to try other places." She turned to Perry and smiled. "But I love Thai. Maybe I could pick some up and drop by next Saturday to see how the dogs are doing. We could walk them down to the dog park a few blocks away."

Perry smiled and walked with Ming to the front door. "Any time Saturday sounds good. I have your number, and now you have mine since I called you earlier."

Ming lingered in the doorway, turning to face Perry. Now *she* was intentionally pressing into someone's personal space, but Perry didn't step back or seem to mind. "If you have questions before then, just text or call me."

"Thanks. I will," Perry said. She stayed in the doorway, watching until Ming started her car and waved another good-bye.

❖

"Well, I hope you gave her a towel to wipe your drool off her before she left." Julie's remark held no jealousy.

They had started out as lovers for a short time years ago as college undergrads, but had evolved into best friends by mutual consent after only a few months. Julie was bisexual, while Perry was firmly lesbian. Also, Julie mostly preferred women who were as feminine as herself over even a soft butch like Perry. Neither had kept a lover for more than a few months, so they were occasionally still intimate with each other. But those encounters were moments of comfort, fun after a night out drinking and dancing with friends, or sometimes a frustrated need for release. Sex between them was a convenience and never figured into their separate dating prospects.

"I'd have to wipe your drool off her first," Perry said.

They laughed together.

"She was really cute, but I think you must be more her type," Julie said.

"Maybe she doesn't date women."

"Please. She's blowing off Grandma next Saturday for Thai and the dog park with you. That's a date, hot stuff."

"My stuff is hot, isn't it?" Perry strutted back to the kitchen with Julie trailing her.

"It might be if you didn't have enough hair on the back of your pants to make a small dog. We must have missed that side when we vacuumed you. Why don't you take that suit off and throw it in the washing machine now?"

"Right. You just want to see me naked." Perry opened the laundry nook and stripped down to her sports bra and boy-short underwear.

"You're not naked, and even if you were, I've seen everything you've got before, darlin'. I certainly wouldn't mind seeing it again since we didn't get to run, but we've got work to do before we even discuss whether we're in the mood for playtime. Now, go upstairs and put clean clothes on that fine body while I get my briefcase from the car."

Perry didn't hesitate. They'd wasted too much time already. She and Julie were on the same page, which was the real reason their friendship and occasional sex arrangement had been so successful. Work always came before play. "I'll take these crates upstairs with me. Use the company credit card and order something to be delivered for lunch so we can get right to work."

"It's a plan," Julie said.

Perry felt better already. She hated confusion, confrontation, and drama. Having a plan was practical and efficient. That was her job, after all. As an efficiency expert, she evaluated the problem, developed an orderly solution, and installed order into business and industry workflows. Actually, her life's purpose was to bring order to chaos. Today, she and Julie would develop and initiate a plan for rehoming these dogs. But not too quickly. She'd keep them around for a bit, since they were a convenient excuse to see more of the enticing Ming.

Yes. Having a plan was good.

CHAPTER THREE

The gravelly voice of Louis Armstrong singing about a wonderful world begins to fade when an announcer starts the standing introduction to the next hour. "Somewhere along the way, our busy lives have become a relentless competition to do more in less time in order to meet others' measure of success rather than fulfill our own dreams. Many of the physical diseases, mental illnesses, and emotional breakdowns experienced in today's population directly result from the unprecedented pressure of those expectations. Dr. Lee, both a medical physician and licensed naturopath, discusses how to find a natural balance in your life between work, personal life, and yourself to take that first step toward holistic healing and achieving the goals you truly desire." The music comes up long enough for Louis to conclude before fading to the live podcast.

"Good morning. This is Dr. Lee. On our Thursday podcast, we talked about the slow return to normal, or what might be a new normal, as more of the population is vaccinated against the virus that caused the 2020 pandemic. This afternoon, many of us are preparing to head off to the office tomorrow morning for the first time after working from home for a year, so we want to discuss how we're feeling about that. And we already have our first caller. Hi. You're live on today's *Finding Natural Balance* podcast. Who are we speaking to, and where are you calling from?"

"Hi, Dr. Lee. This is Ramona from Tulsa. My company actually called us back into the office three weeks ago, and it's been rough."

"Hi, Ramona. Can you tell us what your expectations were compared to how the return to the office is working?"

"I thought when the pandemic restrictions eased, my life would be better without being cooped up with the kids while trying to work from home. But the stress is even worse with this mask-or-no-mask, vaccinated-or-not-vaccinated war raging. A lot of people have refused to come back into the office, and some have quit because they feel the company's rules that they must get vaccinated and wear a mask intrude on their personal rights. But what about my right not to sit next to one of those unvaccinated, unmasked people? I might not get deathly sick from their germs, but my ninety-year-old mother could if I carry their germs home to her. Others haven't returned to work because they're afraid to endanger their kids by sending them to school, and they have no other childcare options.

"As if that's not enough, the guy who oversaw special projects used his time out of the office to get a better job, so my boss has asked me to add his workload to my regular job until they hire a replacement. And my seven-year-old is so stressed about going back to school and maybe catching the virus, he's started wetting the bed at night. My sixteen-year-old, on the other hand, is happy I'm back at the office so she can bring this older boy she thinks she's in love with to the house while I'm still at work. How do I find my balance in all of this?"

"First of all, you should take your seven-year-old to his pediatrician," Ming said. "Bed-wetting is not uncommon at that age, especially in boys, but it could indicate a physical problem or an emotional upset that needs attention. Let's ask our listeners to chime in on the other two issues."

The chat thread began to fill with advice and questions.

Rick in Cincinnati: You shouldn't be expected to do

both jobs for the same money. You should get paid
more for the additional work or have your regular
job shifted to someone else for the duration.

Sarah in Texas: My son wet the bed for a while, but he
grew out of it. Don't worry about it.

Edna in Utah: If a boy came to the house to visit while
my parents weren't home, we had to sit on the
front porch where the neighbors could see what we
were doing.

A different chat popped up on her screen. Her assistant, Carl,
was signaling that a caller had some advice for Ramona.

"Hi. This is Dr. Lee. What do you want to say to Ramona?"

"Ramona should negotiate some flex time and work-from-
home hours if her boss wants her to take on extra responsibilities.
She also should ask him to commit to a date when he'll raise her
salary if her job or the other position isn't filled for a while. One
of my ex-bosses asked me to do two jobs until I was exhausted
from working seven days and nearly seventy hours a week. After
I took a job with another company, I found out he was holding
the other job open to improve his department's bottom line so he
could get his quarterly bonus."

"That's very good advice," Ming said.

Carl's chat popped up again. *Got another.*

"Hi. You're live on *Finding Natural Balance.* What advice
do you want to share?"

"My advice is about her sixteen-year-old. If this boy is
hanging around your house after school when you're not home,
don't take it for granted that your innocent little girl isn't having
or about to have sex with him. Sit the two of them down together
and talk to them about the responsibility of a relationship and safe
sex. Don't wait for his parents. Let the boy know that you will
hold him and his parents accountable if your daughter becomes
pregnant. The biggest problem today is that society still lays the
responsibility of unwanted pregnancies on the shoulders of the

girl, and the boy usually walks away free to brag to his friends and destroy some other young girl's future."

A third caller dropped into the queue.

"Another good idea," Ming said. "Shared responsibility is crucial to balance, something most societies lack. Assigning gender roles and responsibilities without regard to individual talent or personalities is our biggest failing. Boys need to take as much responsibility as girls, and the parents of boys need to get on board, too. Responder number three, what say you?"

A man's resonant voice filled her speakers.

"Looking at this from a manager's point of view, Ramona should regard these added responsibilities as an opportunity to show what she can do. She should listen to the *Timed for Success* podcast and read Dr. Chandler's books on making the most of every minute. If you try, you can find lots of wasted minutes in your day. That's time you can schedule to spend with your bed-wetter and the teenager. In fact, make a schedule for that teen. She won't get pregnant if she's too busy with after-school activities or a part-time job. Pay her to manage the household while you work. She can pick up your dry cleaning, clean the house, and learn to cook dinner. My sisters did that while they went to school."

The chat thread exploded with listeners adding comments too fast for Ming to read before the next popped in.

Amy in Michigan: What did Caller Three do while his sisters did all the work at home? Play sports? Carry out the trash, which takes all of five minutes?

Sandy in South Carolina: Caller Three is either single or has a wife that does everything at home so all he has to do is go to work. OR, he's divorced because his wife worked, too, and still had to handle everything at home.

Will in Maryland: This guy has never had kids, or if he did, they might as well be fatherless. I'll bet he schedules himself a morning on the golf course every week, but never helps with laundry or does the grocery shopping for the family.

Parker in New York: Don't knock it until you try it. Most people whining about not having enough time for everything are just poorly organized and easily distracted. Try a schedule for two weeks and see if it doesn't relieve some pressure in your life. Timed for Success has it going on. I've been to one of Chandler's seminars. It was life-altering.

Brenda in Atlanta: I read one of Chandler's books when it hit the best-seller lists. People are not robots. How do you schedule your life down to the minute without accounting for human variables? And kids, for God's sake. You can't tell a baby he has only five minutes to be fussy, or schedule what time and how long it will take a toddler to poop in the potty.

Ming groaned. Not this podcast poser again. Was Chandler paying these people to infiltrate her program because of the comment Ming had made a few weeks ago? And, why did her name sound so familiar?

The next caller had more to say about the *Timed for Success* podcast.

"What better way to see where you're out of balance? Chandler recommends charting what you spend your time on for a couple of weeks, then making a schedule to reach your optimum potential. It's as simple as that. No voodoo's involved. People are just afraid to exercise discipline in their lives. Hell. That's why the generations we're raising are dedicated to nothing but video games. They have no role models."

Ming glanced at the timer and the chat line that had frozen under the onslaught of comments. This was getting out of hand. It was time she checked out this rival who had managed to hijack her podcast.

"That last observation is a little harsh and a broad generalization about our younger generations, but we've obviously touched on a topic we'll want to explore further. Can running your life on a schedule help you balance it? While this might be the solution for trains, planes, or assembly lines, I'll remind you again that humans are not machines. During Thursday's podcast, we'll talk about why this is not a healthy approach for people. Until then, take a moment to close your eyes, breathe in, and slowly let it out as you visualize syncing your heartbeat with the earth's natural rhythm."

❖

Ming's blood was still pumping double-time when her phone chimed with a FaceTime call from Carl.

"Wow. That was incredible. The chat line is still burning up on the website. I've had to restart it twice because it froze." Carl's face was flushed and his eyes wide. "We've got people jumping on the website, rather than falling off like they usually do when the podcast ends. Mind-blowing."

"Go ahead and close the chat line for now. I'm only seeing back-and-forth among the chatters, and it's starting to get ugly. That won't help anyone's zen."

"I'm on it, Boss."

"I need to check out this podcast they were talking about so I can offer some real advice to keep that hack from infecting my followers any further with this life-is-a-schedule mantra."

Carl's babbling about comments coming over the chat line faded from Ming's attention as she googled the podcast. Her screen filled with findings from the search. Perry Chandler. What were the chances she'd run across two Perrys in the same week? Her gaze tracked to Wikipedia's entry with photos. Holy shit! Not two Perrys. The same Perry. Ming had saved Perry's phone number in her contacts as *Amanda's dogs* because she couldn't remember Perry's last name after she left her house Saturday.

Hmm. A double-doctorate in business management and industrial processes, a frequent speaker at business conventions, author of several best-selling business-management books. There was plenty of information about her reputation as a top efficiency expert, but very little about her personal life. Ming chuckled. Maybe she forgot to schedule a personal life for herself.

Carl pinged her chat window. *Check this out.*

The web address he sent led to a profile feature in an industrial publication that outlined how Perry Chandler timed her day down to the minute for optimal production. Ming scanned it, then slowed to read carefully. She was beginning to understand why Perry seemed so stiff on Saturday. She must have felt totally out of her element.

"Is this for real?" Ming muttered as she read. "This has to be contrived for publicity. Nobody could actually live like this."

The dogs would fix that. Or, at the very least, their cohabitation could be the experiment to top all experiments. Ming could see herself accepting a prestigious award after publishing the findings. *I'd like to thank Molly, JT, and Tucker for making this transformation possible...*

CHAPTER FOUR

The chime of the alarm set off a cacophony of barking that morphed into howls.

Perry rolled over and groaned. "It's not the doorbell. That's the alarm clock."

More howls. Well, from Molly and Tucker. JT sounded like somebody was choking him.

"Quiet, quiet. It's just the alarm."

The dogs stopped for a moment and stared at her, then Tucker—obviously unconvinced—jumped off the bed and ran downstairs to bark at the front door, which prompted JT to resume his noise from where he sat next to her shoulder and Molly to bay from the foot of the bed. "QUIET!"

Silence at last. Perry sat up and rubbed her gritty, burning eyes. God. She'd barely slept. She'd always thought her self-contained community of townhouses, apartments, and single-family homes was quiet. The dogs, however, had a different opinion, answering every barking dog, sitting up to listen after neighbors slammed doors, and growling at things Perry couldn't hear.

Julie had stayed over Saturday night, and the dogs had been relatively well behaved once the sleeping arrangements had been adjusted. The dogs hadn't been satisfied with the landing outside her bedroom. Molly wandered around the upstairs until Julie moved her bed into the master bedroom, which made the boys pace back and forth between Molly and their crates because they didn't want to be separated from her. Fortunately, her bedroom was large and easily accommodated the two wire crates and Molly's bed in the far corner. Once they had moved the crates into the bedroom next to Molly's bed, all had been relatively quiet until morning.

Last night had been a different story. Without Julie occupying the other side of her queen-sized bed, the dogs now thought the space was up for grabs. Molly grumbled and scratched at the side of the bed until Perry lifted her up, and then she curled next to Perry's legs and began to snore. She'd already lost twenty minutes of sleep time arguing with Molly over the bed, so she gave in and turned out the light.

She was almost asleep when the second dog jumped onto the bed and curled up next to the pillow where Julie had slept. Seconds later, the third joined them and chose his spot close enough to rest his chin on Perry's shoulder. She knew from his sigh it was Tucker. He'd barely let her out of his sight all day and had reluctantly let her comb the loose hairs from his wiry coat. Perhaps he was grieving more than the others. Deep down, she understood the longing for human contact, so she relaxed and allowed him this small comfort.

Strangely, Molly's warmth against her leg, Tucker's head on her shoulder, and JT's little snores comforted her, too…until the first car door slammed. She nearly peeled herself off the ceiling after furious barking inches from her ear shocked her awake. Then, again, a few hours later. And a third time when some cats had a witching-hour territory dispute somewhere nearby.

Perry groped along the bedside table, found her liquid tears, and squeezed the bottle until the drops filled her eyes and ran down her cheeks. Wiping her face with her T-shirt, she glanced at the clock. She was already behind schedule. "SHA, are you there?"

"Good morning, Perry. I am observing the order to remain quiet."

"I was speaking to the dogs."

"Should I add them to the list of household members?"

"No. They're temporary guests."

"Acknowledged."

Tucker reappeared at the bedroom door, and JT jumped down from the bed to greet him. Molly had already decided it was too early and was snoring again. Forewarned by Ming that the boys might pee in the house if she didn't let them out at regular intervals, Perry trudged downstairs and let them into the backyard. They would be fine there while she completed her morning routine. She was halfway up the stairs when she met Molly coming down.

"I suppose you need to go out, too." She turned around and let Molly join the boys.

Returning upstairs, she began her routine nearly ten minutes late.

Perry performed her usual ninety seconds of stretching exercises, then dropped to the floor and issued her standard command.

"SHA, four minutes. On my mark." She easily fell into the routine of counting out twenty-five push-ups. "…twenty-three, twenty-four, mark," she said, cuing SHA to signal when she'd achieved her four-minute plank.

"SHA, weather?"

She half listened to the daily weather report, then slipped her earbuds in and keyed her exercise music. She tried to mentally review material for the morning podcast, but the dark-haired beauty she'd met Saturday filled her thoughts. Maybe she should text Ming an update on the dogs. No. She didn't want to seem needy. She'd do that later in the week. Maybe Wednesday.

She yawned, and her stomach muscles screamed, but she welcomed the pain. She needed something to get that woman out of her head. She'd been slow to climax Saturday night with Julie until she closed her eyes and pictured Ming between her legs. That had never happened before.

"Four minutes," SHA reported. "There is a disturbance at the back door."

Perry rolled to her feet and dashed to the kitchen, where the three dogs were barking to be let in. "Geez. It's not even six o'clock, you guys. You'll wake up Mrs. Mayberry next door."

Molly sauntered in, giving her an it's-about-time look. The boys dutifully followed, and all sat next to the refrigerator, turning expectant faces toward her. Morning meds. Right. They watched as she peeled the plastic from a slice of American cheese, folded it over to conceal the pills, then tore off the appropriate section for each dog. Tucker's piece contained no medicine, but Ming had explained his portion would simply let him feel included.

She glanced at the clock while moving a prepared breakfast from the freezer to the microwave. "Start microwave in three minutes. Cook three minutes on high temp," she said as she headed back to the master suite.

"Confirmed," SHA responded.

She'd delay the extra three minutes she normally allowed for shaving on Monday mornings until tomorrow, after she'd adjusted her routine to incorporate the dogs' needs. She could do this. After all, she designed efficient workflows for huge manufacturing plants. A single household with one person and three dogs should be a breeze.

❖

Ming slowed her Mercedes as she approached the building owned by the physicians' cooperative in which she was a founding partner. The practice didn't open for another ninety minutes, but the parking lot was nearly full. She drove into the underground reserved parking and joined others arriving for the special meeting of the partners.

She crowded into the small elevator with five of her colleagues. Judging from the frowns that greeted her, she wished she'd taken the stairs, even though she avoided that route since walking in on a drunk using the enclosed staircase as his personal toilet—the stinky kind.

She smiled at Beth, the practice's gerontologist partner. Most of the five partners had gone to medical school or finished residencies together. She and Beth were among the few that had done both, and Beth was the only partner who encouraged Ming when she decided to add naturopathy to her general-medicine credentials.

"Morning," Ming said to the group. Four returned mumbled greetings, but Beth only glanced her way before rummaging for something in her large shoulder bag. She was not a morning person.

"I don't know why we couldn't meet over lunch or at the end of office hours," Philip, the ob-gyn partner, grumbled. "I had to deliver a baby at midnight and barely got three hours of sleep in an on-call room at the hospital." He glugged the last of his coffee and crushed the paper cup as if it were responsible for his exhaustion.

"You should have gone home." Margot, one of two internists, handed Philip her full cup of steaming java. "Oh, I forgot. You had to move to the suburbs so your trophy wife would be closer to her country-club friends." Her tone was as icy as the coffee was hot.

Philip glared at her. "It's not my fault that you live in the club's condos." Everybody knew about the off-again, on-again affair between the two. And there was the rub. The wife must have been alerted to the affair by her friends and was now close enough to make sure hubby was playing golf when he claimed he was instead of checking out the decor of Margot's bedroom. Karma had a way of coming back to bite you.

Ming didn't mind the early hour but was peeved to have the time stolen from her. She normally arrived between six thirty and seven but used the time before they opened at eight to review and prepare for cases scheduled that day. "I hope this isn't about another real-estate buy Lynda wants to add to our portfolio, or another partner wanting to buy in," she said. "We already need another floor and a parking deck for all the new patients."

Margot shifted her cold stare from Philip to Ming. "That's funny. I don't have a flood of new patients. Do you, Jessica?"

Jessica, their orthopedist, shrugged. "Probably a few less since Ming started offering acupuncture and osteopathic therapy." Her tone was matter-of-fact but not accusing.

"What?" Ming was surprised. They'd often collaborated on cases, and Jessica had never mentioned any problem between them. "I've taken only patients you've referred to me."

"I think we should save this discussion for the meeting." John, their psychologist, had been silent until now. "Everything will be addressed there."

The elevator dinged to announce their arrival, and the doors slid open to reveal the fourth-floor executive suites, effectively ending the puzzling conversation.

John was the only one who dared meet her gaze. Did they all know the reason for this meeting? John's eyes were kind as he gave her shoulder a quick squeeze, probably meant to be reassuring. It wasn't.

Ming grabbed Beth's arm as she moved from the back to follow the others out of the elevator. "Beth, what's going on?"

Beth stared down at the floor. "Some of the partners seem to feel you've outgrown the co-op, Ming. That's what they want to discuss."

Ming was stunned. "Outgrown? What does that mean? You guys want to throw me out? You can't do that. I'm a founding partner."

Beth finally looked up, her gaze swirling with a mixture of emotions. "I don't think you are the sole subject of the meeting. Lynda says the practice is headed for financial trouble if we don't make some changes. She said the growth surge in your area of the practice is just one factor affecting our bottom line."

"You didn't think I should be given a heads-up about this meeting?"

Beth shook her head. "I swear to you, they knew I'd warn you, so they didn't leak even a word of this situation to me until Lynda called me during my commute in this morning. I'm still digesting all this myself."

Ming nodded. That made sense. "Okay. I believe you. You would have told me, and they're apparently hoping to blindside me so I'll get angry and agree to something I'll regret later." She held up her hand to stop Beth's protest. She knew she had earned her reputation for having a rare but explosive temper. "I'm stopping off at the restroom. Tell them I'll be there in five minutes."

Beth glanced anxiously toward the conference room. "Okay. They'll take that long to get settled with coffee and whatever pastries Lynda's brought in."

Ming checked the bathroom stalls to make sure she was alone before pulling her phone from her purse and dialing Imani, her friend and attorney.

"This must be important for you to call this early. I might still be entertaining company."

"It is very important, and you never spend the entire worknight with your flavor of the month. Right now, you're in your office, prepping to be in court at eight o'clock, just like I'm in my office, where, on a normal day, I'd be getting ready to see patients when we open."

"You know me too well," Imani said. "Wait. This isn't a normal day? What's up?"

"I don't have details yet, or the time to explain what I do know. I just need you to get some people looking up answers for me that can be texted to me in the next hour."

"Give me the questions." This efficient, immediate response was one of many reasons Imani was a top lawyer in the state. Ming had no idea why she wasn't practicing law in Los Angeles or San Francisco, instead of Fresno.

"What's the current fair market value of the building my practice currently owns? And can you call my accountant and ask him to text me his latest estimation of the practice's real-estate portfolio minus the building we work in? Finally, can someone email me what information I need to gather to estimate the worth of my individual practice?"

"None of this will be a problem. I'll be in court all day, but I'll put my number-one paralegal, Sarah, on this."

"Thanks, pal. Hope I didn't take too much of your time."

"Not a problem. Today's case is open and shut. We have ironclad proof this East Coast company has been burying toxic waste on its property here for years, contaminating nearby farms, water sources, and residents. They'll be chum in the water for every lawyer shark in the state when I finish with them today."

"Go get 'em, courtroom warrior. I'll touch base with you later tonight about what's going on with me."

❖

Timed for Success opened with the chorus of Kenny Chesney's "Shiftwork," which faded into the standard introduction—a male voice-over with a ticking clock in the background.

"You're no longer spending two hours each day commuting to the office. You don't have to drive the kids to school or wait in line for an hour to pick them up in the afternoon. Time spent on laundry has been reduced by half since you and the kids can wear the same sweatpants and T-shirts for two days without anyone noticing. Your grocer and drugstore deliver. So why are you losing the race against time now more than ever? *New York Times* best-selling author and efficiency expert Dr. Perry Chandler has the answers you need to take control of the overwhelming demands of career, workplace, and home. Click on our *follow* button to learn how you can be *Timed for Success*."

"Good morning. I'm Perry Chandler. On our podcast today, I want to talk about determining your most productive time during the day and how to capitalize on it. This is a discussion, not a lecture, so you're invited to join in through the podcast's chat roll or call 1-8-8-8-S-A-V-T-I-M-E.

"Industries from restaurants to hospitals to automobile manufacturers work employees around the clock in three eight-hour shifts. Depending on the business, seniority normally wins you a spot on the day shift so you can be at home with your family on nights and weekends. Other companies rotate shifts so everyone gets a chance at the day shift every couple of months, and everybody does their turn on the less-desirable night shift. These practices, however, are not ideal for productivity. Any of you listeners want to tell us why?"

The online chat began to fill with responses. Perry read off the more interesting comments to those who might be listening to the podcast but not watching the website, and she interjected comments to remind followers she was still guiding the discussion.

"John from Missouri says, 'I can tell you why. By the time I adjust to sleeping in the daytime, I rotate to day shift, then to second shift. I hate second shift the most because my family is asleep when I get home and headed out to school when I wake up. I like having some work time where I get to see my family, but I'm so grouchy from lack of sleep, they probably wish I was at work.'

"But Sam from Georgia says, 'I know it's hard to rotate shifts, but I work in one of those "seniority" situations and never get to see my kids except on my days off because I'm stuck on second shift. I respect that those guys have put in the years, but their kids are grown. My coworkers on the second shift all have young families. Little kids need a lot more attention and time from their parents, but we're stuck at work while some daycare worker, spouse, or the kids' grandparents raise them. My little girl is four years old, and I'm missing all the big moments in her life. I'd gladly give up sleep to be on a daytime or even third shift so I could spend more time with her.'

"John and Sam have introduced very good points, which

could open an entirely different discussion on employees who are parents. But for this week's podcasts, let's keep to the theme. Finding your most productive time of day doesn't mean you have to spend that time at work. Being productive in your personal life can help you find more enjoyment time with your family and, therefore, enable you to be more productive at work."

But the listeners were like hounds following a scent.

"Also from the chat line, William from Detroit says, 'The day shift is filled with old white guys who would keep working until they drop dead on the line, just to keep any of us Black guys from moving up.'

"Obviously, this has to be a concern, as companies are paying greater attention to the diversity of their ranks," Perry commented.

"Rita from Illinois feels she's in the same predicament. She says, 'Same thing for women where I work. The day shift is the slowest of all because most of those guys are too old to still be on a production line. Every one of them has at least one artificial knee or hip. Most have several. They never meet quotas, but the union says they'll sue for age discrimination if the company tries to force them into retirement or move them to second or third shift.'

"Rita makes a good point about how unions figure into a company's attempt to become more productive and provide a better working environment for all employees." Perry was not a fan of unions. She agreed with their purpose—to protect employee rights—but they had not evolved with the workforce and were still too white-male oriented.

Her Google chat screen flashed with a message from Julie. *The phone board and chat roll are going crazy. I've pulled in Josh and Karen to help me screen. Sounds like you have several good starting points, but you need to move this ahead to talk about saving time at home, or you're going to get bogged down in the work complaints.*

She didn't need Julie's prompts like she had when she first

started the podcast, but she replied. *I'm going to let them talk for a bit. Could be good fodder for my next book.*

"Since the two subjects seem to be intertwined, how can you schedule your life better to be a success at home and work? Are you a morning person? Or are you a night owl? Maybe you like the second shift, but your spouse wants you home at night, and you're positive peace at home will make you more productive on the day shift. My advice to companies—and they pay a lot for it—is that they rely on empirical data rather than information from workers that may be tainted by the argument with their spouse that morning, a plea from a kid to skip a second shift to come to their ball game, or the possibility of missing a family pizza outing while the employee is at work. We'll also talk this week about how to collect empirical data on your time spent outside work so you can also be successful in your personal life."

Julie: Caller on line one.

"Caller One, you're live on *Timed for Success*. Who am I speaking with?"

"Hi, Dr. Chandler. Just call me Jane. I don't want to give my real name because I'm still employed by a company that hired you as a consultant during the year before the pandemic."

Perry was pleased Julie had found this caller for her. "That's fine. And, since we don't have permission to talk about your employer, let's be careful not to mention the company's name or identify any employees. I'm interested, though, to know how your experience went."

"Well, I was one of the employee representatives in the meetings to decide how the company would evaluate employees to determine when they were most productive. The company decided to consider two approaches. First, they had everyone fill out an in-depth survey, followed by a personal interview. But a lot of people felt the questions were too personal and invaded their privacy. The alternative was to compare detailed records of an employee's output as they were rotated through all three shifts, allowing a week of adjustment between each shift change.

Again, employees objected because they thought the bosses were trying to push them to work at unsafe and unhealthy speeds."

"Didn't your company explain that it was only trying to help each employee reach his or her full potential?" Perry asked.

"Since the company went public, management has been pushing to squeeze out more and more profits for the shareholders, usually at the employees' expense. Our raises, benefits, and staffing have been reduced. So, we have a lot of mistrust between the executives who are making those decisions and the workers. The middle managers, like me, are just caught between."

"So which method did the executives choose?" Perry asked.

"They decided to chart the production of workers as they rotate through different shifts. It took longer, and, truthfully, those results were also noted in workers' files that could be used when an employee is considered for future personnel actions."

"Like merit raises and promotions," Perry suggested.

"More likely for layoffs or denying promotions," Jane said. "That's what the workers suspect, and I agree with them."

The chat line was boiling over with comments.

> **Josh from Nevada:** Companies don't care about the workers anymore. They only care about lining the pockets of their rich friends who buy up their stock.
> **Martha from Texas:** If they can't find cheap enough labor in third-world countries to make their products, they'll charge consumers more so their fat-cat executives don't suffer like us low-paid workers do.
> **Tim from Michigan:** The only things they put in your personnel file now are things they can use as ammunition to fire you when they want. It's bullshit to say they might use that to give you a promotion or a raise. I'm a middle manager, too. I know what they do with that kind of info.
> **Boone from Georgia:** I was one of the employees

on the production line who were on the team that evaluated the results at my company after doing both interviews and the rotating shifts. We found most of the production-output evaluations matched what the employee said was his or her most productive time of day. Some had answered truthfully that their most productive time was not the shift they were currently assigned, but they requested that they not be changed because they had family responsibilities that prevented them from working their best shift.

Dr. Perry Chandler: Boone, can you call us at 1-8-8-8-S-A-V-T-I-M-E? I'd like to hear more about your experience.

Buck from Kansas: For every good company like Boone's, there are a thousand more where decisions are dictated by the nature of their work or profit margins. That's why we need unions to look out for the workers.

Sandra from Iowa: Union bosses remain corrupt and are still negotiating for the old white guys who elected them. Black and Hispanic workers—especially women of all colors—continue to be left behind because women have to stay home when the kids or the babysitter gets sick or their school switches to remote learning.

Betina from Indiana: You said it, Sandra. What have the unions done about demanding on-site childcare or a remote schoolroom so female employees can keep working? Women are also expected to take care of adult family members who need home care, and every time a woman misses a shift, she loses money and chances for promotion. We need to be talking about a way to balance work and personal responsibilities, not trying to increase our work production. Dr. Lee's *Finding Natural Balance* podcast talks about that.

Matt from Oregon: Whoa. Not all men dump everything on their wives. It kills me to miss my daughter's softball games, and I'd much rather eat dinner with my family instead out of a lunchbox in a grimy breakroom with my coworkers. I'd look for another job, but my wife has MS, and the health insurance where I work now is pretty good. Still, I don't want to work my life away and miss all the good times with my family. I'm going to check out Dr. Lee's podcast.

Julie messaged that she had Boone waiting on line two.

Thank God. Julie had been right. She needed to direct her audience's attention away from that other podcast. And fast. "Let's take our next caller. Hi, Boone. This is Perry Chandler, and you're live on *Timed for Success.*"

"Hi, Dr. Chandler. It's a pleasure to talk with you."

"Just for the benefit of our listeners who might be driving and not reading our chat feed, I'll read the comment Boone made on the chat line." Perry read Boone's comment for her listening audience. "It sounds like your company took the right approach. Once they did the research, how did they handle the results?"

"Well, a few guys were moved around, but most stayed where they were. My company has just one plant and is family-owned. The big boss knows the names of every employee, and most of the other bosses are members of that same family. They start as teenagers, working in every department when they're not in school, so they learn to respect the skill of the workers. After they graduate college, they're given supervisory jobs."

"And how did the older, experienced workers feel about being supervised by young, fresh-out-of-college kids?"

"We knew the score when we signed on to work there. We were paid well to be machinists. The family made it clear to their boys they shouldn't disrespect the workers. They kept up the paperwork from their section to the admin department—time sheets, maintenance records, orders filled. Stuff like that. They basically let us know when we needed to step up the pace on a big order or when we needed to shut down for full maintenance. Otherwise, they just let us work."

The chat roll lit up with women commenting about "good old boy" work environments, but Perry ignored them. This podcast was supposed to be a positive discussion about being more productive.

"So, most workers were happy with the study and actions taken?"

"Sure."

"Did production increase?"

"Not really. We were already producing at a high level."

"Sounds like your company is very efficient."

"We think so. The guys take pride in their work, and we have a bit of competition over who can complete the most of whatever we're making each day."

The chat comments were heating up with demands that their concerns be discussed, and the chatters were turning on each other.

> **Cathy from Virginia:** This is bullshit. Dr. Lee's podcast is much better.
>
> **Marlene from Detroit:** Yeah. I think this Perry person isn't really a woman. She talks like one of the suits in the executive suite, looking to get even more from overworked employees.
>
> **Mike from Boise:** You women are whiners who blame men for everything.
>
> **Glenda from Fort Worth:** Switch roles with your wife for one week, and we'll see who's complaining.
>
> **Tammy from Queens:** I read somewhere that she's a lesbo, so she might as well be a man.

Moderator: Please review the rules of our chat line. Bigoted comments will be removed from the chat and the writer banned for a minimum of thirty days for the first infraction.

Brooke from Atlanta: Check out Finding Natural Balance, Dr. Lee's podcast. She gives good advice for women and men. She cares about people, not just profit.

Christ. Now they were taking potshots at her. Perry messaged Julie to freeze the chat for five minutes so she could regain control.

"Let's address a few questions from the chat line now, Boone. How many of the workers at your plant are women?"

"All of the administration department—accounting, records, secretaries—are women, and the boss's daughter heads the department."

"Are any women on the production line?"

"Well, no."

"Can you explain why?"

"Those are essential jobs. Women call in sick too much. They have a sick kid or female problems, or they take pregnancy leave. Admin work can always wait another day or be split up between other workers when someone's out. You can't fill orders if a bunch of machinists call in sick."

"The men never stay home to take care of a sick kid or other family member?"

"No. Women are better at that sort of thing."

"Does your company offer any type of child care?"

"No. We can't have children running around a factory where machinists are working."

"One more question from the chat line—are the machinists paid at a higher rate than the admin workers?"

"Well, yeah. They're skilled workers. Any middle-school student can add and subtract numbers and file papers alphabetically. Plus, the machinists don't cost the company nearly as much for health care and paid sick time."

"Not good, Boone. I think your company, and the men who work there, should come into the twenty-first century. I'm surprised any women are still willing to work there."

Perry glanced at her watch. This hadn't gone well. Not at all. She messaged Julie to key up the closing music and began her sign-off. "That's all the time we have today, folks. This week's theme is about finding the time of day when you are most productive, but that's not necessarily at work. We also need to be productive in our personal lives, too. We strayed off course today when we talked about the work environment, so we'll move ahead and discuss being productive in our personal lives during Friday's podcast of *Timed for Success*. Thanks for listening and participating today."

Perry shut down the podcast and shoved her rolling office chair back so hard it banged against the wall behind her. "Who the hell is this fucking Dr. Lee? Is she paying people to hijack my podcast? Yes. That's got to be it. I bet she's some novice podcaster trying to steal my followers." Perry smacked her fist into the palm of her other hand. She should have checked her out when that remark came up in Friday's podcast, but that weird date and the arrival of the dogs had distracted her. "SHA, display today's schedule for revision."

This Lee person didn't know the chain she was yanking had a big dog at the other end. That's right. Perry Chandler was a big dog in the business world, and if Dr. Lee was running in that pack, Perry would have heard of her before now. All she needed was a little research time to put that puppy in her place.

CHAPTER FIVE

Ming paused at the door to the conference room and took a deep breath. Everyone was seated around the long meeting table. Lynda, hired to be their chief of practice operations and administration, was at the far end of the table, while Philip sat at the other end with Margot positioned on his right. Roger Walker, one of the attorneys from the firm that handled legal issues for the practice, sat at Lynda's right.

Ming, Beth, Philip, Jessica, and John were the original partners in the practice. Margot and Sandy, a pediatrician, worked under contract and were not partners. The partners also contracted Lynda to manage administration and operations so the doctors could spend all their time dealing with patients.

The others were silent as Ming deliberately took her time selecting a chia latte from the fancy coffee and tea machine and watching as it poured and frothed. Then she walked over to stand next to Philip.

"Since I'm apparently the main subject of this meeting, I believe you are in my seat," she said.

Philip started to protest, but Lynda intervened. "Philip, could you please sit on the other side of Margot?" She shot him a look that warned him not to antagonize Ming.

Philip huffed and seemed to deliberately slosh his coffee on the table before he moved to the other side of Margot. Ming stared at the puddle of coffee threatening to drip into the chair he'd vacated.

Beth frowned. "For God's sake, Philip. You are such a child. It's not our fault you can't fuck around with Margot while your wife is watching from the tennis courts." She jumped up and grabbed some napkins to mop up the coffee. "Ming. Please have a seat so the rest of us can hear what they have to say, then get on with our day."

Sandy looked confused, glancing from one partner to the next around the table. "What's this meeting about?"

Ming sat stiff and forward in her chair, resting her forearms on the table to make her small frame appear as large as possible. "Sorry, Sandy, but you weren't the only one kept in the dark as several of the partners conspired against me." She turned her most steely glare on the others. Well, the guilty ones. Lynda looked resigned but didn't flinch away. Roger shuffled paperwork so he didn't have to look up at her. John's eyes were as sympathetic as before, and Jessica stared nervously back, then dropped her gaze to the table, flushing red. Margot and Philip glared back, and Beth looked as irritated as Ming was with the group.

Lynda cleared her throat. "A financial analysis of the past eighteen months has revealed your venture into naturopathy and the popularity of your podcast have had an adverse impact on the other members of this practice."

Ming objected. "I was careful not to reveal my entire name to the podcast or give my physical location. Before I began airing *Finding Natural Balance*, I consulted our legal team and followed every one of their recommendations to keep that venture separate from our medical cooperative here."

Roger cleared his throat. "It appears we underestimated your followers. They tracked you down within weeks of the first installment."

"They're camping out in our damned parking lot...overnight because they come here without appointments and demand to see only you. And most of them don't have money or insurance to pay to see any of us," Margot said. She stood and began waving her arms as she elaborated. "Philip has called the police twice to clear them out, but, come sunrise, they're right back. Our paying patients who have legitimate appointments have no place to park and are canceling because so many of your patients are in the waiting room, they have no place to sit if they do find parking nearby."

Ming was incredulous. She turned on Philip. "You called the police? These people need medical help, not jail time."

"We don't have a license to run a goddamned campground in our parking lot. It had to violate a dozen city codes," Philip said, crossing his arms over his chest.

"Nobody was arrested," Lynda said. "They were simply told they were trespassing on private property, and they'd have to find different accommodations for staying in Fresno overnight."

"Doesn't the practice own other properties?" Sandy asked. "Maybe they could stay on one of those."

"Those are real-estate investments, and I'm not looking to get into the campground or motel business." Philip's acid response shut down any suggestions for a solution.

Ming's phone pinged, and she glanced down at the text from Imani's paralegal, Sarah, then opened the attachment. The worth of the building they were sitting in and their real-estate portfolio was larger than Ming had anticipated. Much larger. She struggled but managed to suppress her inner shark and keep her poker face intact.

"Let's cut to the chase, Lynda." Ming gestured to Philip and Margot. "I don't have time for their whining. What do you want?"

Lynda glanced at Roger. Her voice was even as she spoke and held no accusation or judgment. "While your popularity and patient list have grown, the other doctors have been seeing fewer new and returning patients. We began calling and emailing the patients who didn't come back to ask why, and more than half said the practice was too busy. They said they couldn't find parking and the waiting room was too crowded. They didn't feel safe, even though we mandate that every one of our patients be vaccinated—unless they have a valid medical reason—and wear masks while on the property."

"You're suggesting…what?"

"The majority of the other partners feel you have outgrown the practice and would like to buy you out or find a suitable doctor to purchase your share of the practice. I've had Roger run the numbers and prepare an offer from them."

Roger stood, gathered a handful of papers, and started toward Ming.

"Wait just a darn minute." Beth's shout rang out, startling Sandy enough that she nearly fell out of her chair. "I'm a founding partner, and I haven't voted on anything or seen any offer you intend to make." She pointed an accusing finger at Lynda. "You know that because you were the one who finally let me in on what you guys were doing…over the telephone…while I was driving in for this meeting." She turned to John. "You knew about this? I would expect this from Philip and Margot, who I will point out is not a full partner, but not from you, John. I've always trusted you."

John spread his hands out, palms up. "The numbers don't lie, Beth. We started this co-op as a balanced, holistic approach to patient care. Ming has become so popular, only her patients are being helped. We're not fulfilling our purpose."

Jessica ducked her head when Beth turned to her. "I argued against Philip at first, but what John says makes sense."

Lynda held up her hand, palm out. "You're not being railroaded. Nothing is official until Ming and all the partners sign it."

Ming clasped Beth's forearm. "It's okay. Let me see what they're offering."

Beth sat back in her chair with a sigh, then gave Philip and Margot another scorching glare. Ming scanned the contract Roger placed in front of her, then allowed her inner shark to surface and smile.

"You're joking, right?" She pulled up the attachment that came with Sarah's text and directed it to the conference room printer near Lynda's end of the table. "I was a few minutes late to the meeting because I put in a quick call to an old friend who is my personal attorney. You're familiar with Imani Harris, aren't you, Roger?"

Roger tugged at his necktie and nodded. Lynda gave him an inquiring glance, and he scribbled a quick note that he shoved toward her. Ming waited while Lynda read the note and the printer whirred. Lynda looked up quickly, as if Ming were a cobra about to strike. And she was.

"Imani had to be in court today to take down an international company that's been dumping toxic waste near here, so you'll probably see her on the national news tonight. Since she's busy, she asked her best paralegal to check the value of this building and our real-estate-investment portfolio." Ming pointed to the printer. "Her findings are printing for you now."

Roger grabbed the document from the printer, and his eyes widened at the figures he read, then handed it to Lynda.

Ming chuckled. "I was shocked, too. But not by those figures." She waved the contract Roger had given her at them. "I was surprised that you thought you could low-ball me with this proposal. You have sadly underestimated me if you think this ambush would rattle me enough to actually sign this embarrassing offer." She stood and leaned over the table, propped on her splayed fingertips. "And while you're double-checking the figures prepared by Imani's office, my people will also be calculating the worth of my part of the practice. Lynda, please have your assistant email me the patient flow and hours billed by each doctor over the past eighteen months. The partners should have been getting those reports every quarter anyway. Actually, copy that email to all the partners so I know I'll be getting the same information they are."

Lynda shook her head. "They aren't trying to cheat you, Ming."

Ming held up the contract Roger had given her. "This offer tells me that they are. And this ambush indicates you aren't above using shady business practices to make certain bosses happy." She straightened and picked up her briefcase. "Get ready to go into debt or dissolve the entire practice so you don't have to raid your kids' college funds to pay me off." She started for the door but turned back to them. "Until you figure out your next surprise attack, I'll be seeing patients in my office as usual."

❖

"Duh." Typing Dr. Lee into the search engine was a stupid move. Perry found about a million entries for Dr. Lee, and at least a hundred for Dr. Lee in Fresno. She didn't even know if this irritating Dr. Lee lived in Fresno. What was the name of that podcast? Perry texted Julie, who she knew would consult the podcast transcript.

Julie: Finding Natural Balance.

Perry: Thank you.

Julie: You're welcome. Preparing for battle?

Perry: You know it. This Dr. Lee person is an irritating fly I'm about to swat.

Julie texted back a thumbs-up emoji, and Perry typed the podcast name into the Google search engine. Bingo! Dr. Lee's *Finding Natural Balance.* She went to the website, but the bio seemed disappointingly vague. Dr. Lee's degrees and licenses were listed, of course, but included no year of graduation and no photo with any of the information. The website appeared to be recently updated. Had some of the personal information been removed?

In the meantime, she read through the philosophy behind *Finding Natural Balance.* While she wouldn't disparage naturopathy altogether, this "feel the earth's rhythms and follow your own circadian rhythms" sounded like a lot of hoo-hah to her. If clients didn't find balance in their lives, Dr. Lee could simply say they hadn't listened well enough. This con game was too easy to see through. She couldn't wait to roast this fake when the podcast invaded hers again.

❖

The cityscape gave way to suburbs, then long stretches of farmland and ranches as Ming drove with no destination, just a desperation to leave everything behind. She'd looked at the data Lynda had collected and analyzed. Her popularity had definitely hurt the practice. While she prospered, her friends had suffered. Of course, she had taken the initiative to add naturopathy to her medical skills and to develop her podcast. The other partners could have done the same. Instead, they chose to blame her for their stagnation. Well, not Beth. But the others did. Especially Philip.

Ming sighed. She was so done with the rat race. Oh, she'd managed very well. It seemed like she was nose-to-the-grindstone, trudging along with her friends to develop a holistic medical practice, and then she was suddenly worth millions, an internet phenom, and pursued by patients like she was some type of faith healer. She finally understood how overnight fame undid Hollywood and music stars. That fame came with a price—her friends, time for herself, and almost her sanity. What a joke that her acclaimed podcast focused on finding balance in life when she'd completely lost hers.

She slowed her Mercedes when she saw the sign—FOR SALE, 200 ACRES, 40 CULTIVATED FARMLAND, HOUSE, OUTBUILDINGS, NATURAL WATER SOURCE ON SITE. CALL 559-442-4876.

Pulling over and stopping, she jotted down the contact information and called the number on the sign.

A female voice, likely made husky by years of smoking, answered. "Cutter General Store."

Ming checked the number she'd punched in against the one

listed on the sign. "Uh, hi. I was calling about the two hundred acres for sale."

"You got the right place, honey. Hold on."

Ming could hear a cash register beep as items scanned, then a transaction being completed before the woman resumed their phone call.

"You aren't a real-estate agent, are you, because we're not interested in signing up anyone to market it for us. And we aren't going to sell to a developer, no matter how much money they throw at us. The family will only consider a buyer who wants to work the place and be part of the community here."

Ming brightened. "That's exactly what I'm looking for. When can I see the property?"

"Ben can show it to you today, if you can get here before dark."

"I'm parked by the for-sale sign right now."

"Then I'll have him out there in fifteen to twenty minutes. He'll be the guy in a blue Ford crew-cab pickup."

"I'm in a white Mercedes. Do you mind if I drive in and park at the house?"

"Go right ahead. Since we moved Mee-maw out last month, nobody's living there."

"Thank you. I'll keep an eye out for Ben."

Ming ended the call and drove slowly up the asphalt drive that was flanked by fields of alfalfa hay waving gently in the wind. The sprawling Spanish-style house needed a few small repairs to the stucco exterior and a fresh coat of paint, but the tiled roof looked fairly new, and the tile on the pergola-shaded terrace was gorgeous. She immediately fell in love.

She was about to check out the old barn behind the house when a blue pickup parked next to her car. A man, who appeared middle-aged and fit, stepped carefully down from the truck, pausing long enough for her to see his face before he slipped a mask over his mouth and nose.

"You called about the seeing the property?"

"Yes." Ming likewise gave him a look at her face before bringing her mask up to cover part of it. He limped slightly as he approached once her mask was in place, and she held out her hand. "Ming Lee. I already love the outside of the house, but I have a lot of questions."

He took her offered hand in his callused one, then offered her a squirt of hand sanitizer she gratefully accepted. "Ben Cutter. I reckon Hattie already told you we won't sell to a developer or sign with any real-estate people."

Ming nodded. "She did, and I respect that. I'm a physician and also a licensed naturopath."

He nodded. "Just so you know, our town is ninety percent vaccinated. The ten percent not vaccinated are children too young to qualify."

"That's reassuring because I'm tired of all the political interference in health matters like vaccinations, mask-wearing, and a woman's right to make her own decisions about her body. I'm looking for a property where I can find a better balance in my life. I want to see patients part-time, not seventy hours a week. And I want enough land to explore growing my own medicinal plants."

"You one of those marijuana farmers?"

"I might grow a little cannabis after I get the proper license, but only for medical purposes. I'll eventually market some of the plants I grow, I'm sure, on a very small scale. Nothing bigger than a pickup truck pulling a livestock trailer would be coming or going from here."

He grimaced slightly when he lifted his foot to prop it on the step. "I'm going to save us some time by telling you up front what stops people from buying this property."

"I'd like that," Ming said.

"Like Hattie told you, we won't sell to anyone who plans to cut the farm into pieces for resale or to put a hundred houses on. This land has been in our family almost a hundred and fifty years, since my great-great-grandfather filed his claim and began farming it. This is a rural community, and the folks here want to keep it that way. So, the family is insisting that the buyer also sign an agreement that the land will not be resold or developed for any purpose other than farming for the next fifty years."

"If I decide to buy it, I wouldn't have a problem with that."

"Our asking price is three and a half million dollars, but by the time it's split up among the family members, we probably won't get more than a couple hundred thousand each. We could get five times that amount if we weren't making demands along with the sale, but we all have homes around here and care about who we bring in to be our new neighbor."

"The price is not a problem either, Mr. Cutter. Now I have some questions for you."

"Shoot."

"How open is this rural community to people of color? Frankly, I'm extremely tired of being judged because of my name and my Asian features. My parents were born in this country, and so was I. The recent pandemic has fueled a lot of unmitigated racism, and I won't live among people with small minds."

He grinned at her. "My wife is African-American, Dr. Lee, and Mee-maw, the matriarch of our family, is seventy-five percent Shoshoni. The biggest ranch on the other side of Cutterville is owned and run by a gay couple. Nobody minds that, so I'm sure nobody will have an issue with you unless you're a racist."

Shame heated Ming's face. "I'm sorry. I didn't mean to sound defensive. I've just had a very long, very bad day."

Ben pulled off his Stetson and rubbed his hand along the stubble of his buzz cut. "How about I show you the property before it gets too dark and hopefully make your day better?" He waved his hat toward the door, indicating she should go first.

Normally, Ming refused to go into a house with a strange man, but she sensed nothing malicious in him. Still, since she'd twice been mistaken as an easy mark because of her small stature, she was careful around any strangers. Her cousin, who trained US Army Rangers, had taught her how to always position herself so it'd be hard for a stranger to grab or attack her before she could defend herself with the slim knife custom-designed with a two-inch, spring-loaded blade so it was barely a bulge in her trouser pocket.

Ming was always careful—with her money, with her friends, and with intimate relationships. So how did she let her partners blindside her today? That ambush bothered her more than leaving the practice. Although she hadn't consciously thought about it, she'd been restless for a while and ready to move on to a new adventure. Even the podcast was beginning to bore her.

"Dr. Lee?"

Ming shook herself from her musings. "Lead on, please, Ben."

An hour later, they'd toured the house, livestock barn, and several hay barns and equipment sheds along the tractor path that wound between the fields and led to an overlook in the foothills rising close behind the barn. The property included a small pond next to the house fed by a creek created from the overflow of a small lake a bit farther away. The land was perfect for her plans. The house and barn needed some repairs and updates, but the bones were good, and she loved the hacienda feel of the farm.

Ben switched on the outdoor floodlights as Ming scribbled down Imani's name and phone number on the back of her own business card.

"My number is on the front, and my attorney's is on the back. She's more of a corporate-trial lawyer, but she'll arrange for one of the real-estate attorneys in her firm to handle the paperwork. Have your attorney call her, and they can work out the details."

Ben stared at her. "So, doctors really do make that much money?"

Ming laughed. "No. It's complicated, but the short version is that I invested in something a while back with several partners, and they're going to be paying me a lot more than the price of your farm to buy me out." She cocked her head at him. "I, of course, can put up substantial earnest money to take the property off the market until we can close the deal. I hope that will be soon because I'll be paying cash, so we won't have to go through the loan process."

"No worries. We've already turned down five proposals to purchase, so I reckon we can wait, since you appear to be the buyer we've been looking for. You've got my vote, at least, but you'll need to meet the rest of the family for a consensus."

"Just name the time and place." Ming held out her hand again, and Ben took it to shake on the deal. This time, she offered him sanitizer from the small bottle in her pocket. She liked the odd familiarity of the ritual, like smoking a pipe next to a teepee to seal an agreement. "It's been a pleasure, Ben. I look forward to meeting your wife and becoming neighbors." She opened her car door, then turned back and called to him. "One more thing, please."

"Sure."

"I'm going to be honest with you and hope you'll honor my privacy. I'm making this career change partly to escape some internet fame. Too many of my podcast fans have tracked down where I live and work and invaded my life. I plan to legally change my last name to Davis, which is my father's first name, so that's the name that will appear on the contracts and property records. Hopefully, none of those people will be able to find me here if you tell people your family is selling to Dr. M.L. Davis."

"I'll have to explain the whole situation to Hattie, but you don't have to worry, Doc. Your secret is safe with the folks around here if it keeps gawkers and stalkers away."

Chapter Six

Perry yawned and stretched her back. It felt way out of alignment after sleeping with her legs pushed to one side by Molly's compact cannonball body. "SHA. Remind me in three hours to call my chiropractor for an appointment." The appointment would require another change to her schedule.

"Reminder noted. Shall I adjust your schedule to begin your morning exercises?"

The three dogs looked expectantly at her. "No. Start shower to acclimate water temperature."

"Starting shower."

With a heavy sigh, Perry stood and pointed to the bedroom door. "Okay. Time to go out."

She helped Molly down from the bed, and the dogs barked happily as the boys raced and Molly waddled to the back door. Perry trudged into the kitchen, opened the sliding-glass door for them, then shoved her premade breakfast into the microwave.

They had totally screwed her schedule. She had to make time to let them out several times during the day, prepare their dinner, and watch them as they ate because Molly and Tucker liked to share between bowls, but JT refused to share and tried to eat all the food in everybody's bowl if possible. Also, Molly ate very slowly, walking around as she chewed each mouthful and giving JT plenty of opportunity to poach her dinner after gobbling his.

When the microwave indicated her breakfast was ready, she realized that she'd zoned out and the shower was still running upstairs. Geez. Now she'd be more behind. She gave herself a mental shake. The dogs were busy sniffing at something in the back corner of the yard, so she left the door open wide enough that they could squeeze in when they were done.

She sprinted upstairs, took an extra three minutes to shower since it was Thursday and she still hadn't made time for her Monday shave, then left her hair to dry naturally and pulled on shorts and a T-shirt. No video-log or podcast today so it was definitely a no-bra day unless the chiropractor could see her later. She was checking the mirror as she finger-combed her hair so it wouldn't dry weird when Tucker appeared, agitated and whining. Perry had learned he was the Lassie of the group, coming to her any time the others were doing something they probably shouldn't or found themselves in trouble—like Molly accidently getting shut in the downstairs bathroom. "What's up, boy?"

Tucker paced from her to the stairway and back. She needed to get her breakfast anyway. "I'm coming. I'm coming." He sprinted down the stairs, then paused. "God only knows what they've gotten into now," she grumbled. "SHA. Reactivate microwave for ninety seconds."

The dogs stood grouped around something on the kitchen floor as Perry approached, and she screamed—actually shrieked like a prepubescent girl—when Molly moved back to sit and proudly present the gift they'd brought inside.

A fat mole with huge front claws twitched on the kitchen floor. JT sniffed at it, and Molly grabbed it, gave it a hard shake, and flipped it into the air.

"Shit!" Perry climbed onto the kitchen island as though the mole might take flight and target her like a heat-seeking missile. At least she yelled like a butch, rather than screamed. "Watch where you're flinging that thing."

The mole lay motionless. The dogs and Perry stared at it for a long minute.

"SHA, call Ming."

Ming picked up after the second ring. "Well, hello. I didn't expect to hear from you before Saturday."

"I have a dead animal in my kitchen."

After several long seconds of silence, Ming responded. "I'm coming over."

If it were possible on cell phones, a click and a dial tone would have followed.

"Ming?"

"Your call has disconnected," SHA confirmed.

Barely five minutes later, Ming banged on the front door. "What have you done? How could you kill one of them after only a few days?" Molly and JT rushed forward to greet her, while Tucker retrieved his ball to show her. She knelt to pet them. "Thank God you all are okay."

Perry threw her hands up. "Why would you think I've done something to the dogs? They're the killers. They brought a rodent into the house and dealt the death blow right in front of me." She pointed to the dead mole, and the dogs returned to sit proudly by their kill. "I don't know what to do with it. Hide the body?"

The microwave pinged again because she hadn't retrieved her breakfast after its second heating. She opened its door, then slammed it shut to stop the insistent noise. She couldn't even look at the eggs. Her stomach was attempting a slow crawl up her throat because Molly's hard shake and the faint crunch of bone were running on a loop in her head. Maybe if she kept talking, she wouldn't think about the scene. "Do I make a little rodent casket, hold a rodent funeral, and bury it in the backyard? I have no idea what to say at a mole funeral, and these murderous dogs will probably just dig it up again. What if it has a little mole family waiting for it to bring home grubs and worms for the baby moles? Do I have to support them now that my guests have killed their breadwinner, uh, worm-winner?" Perry literally began wringing her hands and pacing the kitchen...avoiding the unfortunate carcass, of course. "I know I complained about the mole, and I might have shown one of its tunnels to the dogs. But I didn't mean for them to catch and slaughter it. My neighbor Mrs. Mayberry said moles are not on the list of game animals legal to hunt in this state. If she gets wind of this, she'll call a game warden and have me arrested."

Laughter burst from Ming before she clamped her hand over her own mouth to stifle it. "Oh my God. You're hilarious when you're freaked out."

"This isn't funny. I have a dead rodent in my kitchen, and I think I'm going to throw up."

"You need to get over that weak-stomach thing." Ming's tone was amused rather than scolding.

"You didn't witness the death blow." Perry covered her eyes. "Oh, God. I can't unsee Molly snatching it up while it was still twitching." She shuddered. "Or unhear the tiny bones crunching."

Molly shifted her front feet and gave a sharp bark for emphasis.

"Yes, you did very well," Ming said, laughing. "That mole must have been tearing up the yard, and you stopped it. Now, you've brought the evidence to your alpha for a reward. Good girl. You deserve a treat."

Tucker danced in a circle and barked sharply at "treat."

"Oh, you boys helped?" Ming pointed to the bits of dirt clinging to their front paws. "Yes. I can see that you did. I'm sure your alpha has treats for you, too."

The dogs all looked at Perry.

"I'm supposed to reward them for bringing vermin into the house?"

"Yes, you are."

"Don't you have patients to see?"

"I stay late on Thursdays, so I go in later." Ming gathered four paper towels from the kitchen dispenser. "Get three of their favorite jerky treats to give them while I dispose of the deceased."

Following instructions, Perry handed out the jerky, along with congratulations, as Ming scooped up the dead rodent and deposited it in the trash. She tied up the trash bag and handed it to Perry to deposit in her large rolling garbage bin. But when Perry took the trash-filled bag, its weight strained her back muscle made sore by her poor sleeping position. She dropped the bag, grabbed her back, and groaned. "Oh, shit. That hurt."

"You injured your back?" Ming circled around to slip her hands under Perry's T-shirt and read the taut muscles with her fingertips. "Hold still."

Her hands were warm on Perry's skin but changed too quickly to fingers tapping along her spinal column. Ming stopped and pressed her fingertips hard against one vertebra. The painful muscle spasm immediately released, and Perry moaned at the relief.

Tucker whined and touched his nose to Perry's leg.

"I'm okay, buddy." Perry instantly admonished herself for speaking to the dog like he was concerned about her. "What am I thinking? You probably just want another treat."

"You're wrong," Ming said. "Animals are very intuitive and empathetic. While we use language to communicate, they read body language and facial expressions. The pain he reads in your expression upsets him."

Perry looked down at him. "Sorry. I'd reach down to pet you, but I'm afraid to bend over."

"I want you to wait here, please. I'll be right back."

"Okay. Could you…I hate to ask this…" She was afraid to move and trigger another painful spasm. She swallowed when Ming stepped close and took her hand.

"I won't report you to the board of independent lesbians if you ask," she said softly.

Their gazes locked and held.

"Thank the goddess. I was worried about that," Perry said. "I've probably already been reported for being a softy and taking in the dogs."

"Actually, you get points for that. It's in the lesbian handbook."

"I didn't know."

"I used to be on the board."

Perry laughed. "Used to be? Did you get kicked off?"

Ming's look of horror was obviously overly dramatic. "What? No! They have term limits. But I still have influence with the board. I could probably get you an updated handbook so you could study to be a better lesbian."

"I would be indebted if you could."

Ming smiled but gently released Perry's hand. "I'll see what I can do. But for now, what was your question?"

Perry could think only about how much she missed Ming's hand in hers until Ming bent to pick up the abandoned bag of trash. "Oh, could you wheel the trash out after you put that in it? The bin is in the garage, through the door next to the front door. I'll show you."

Ming picked up the bag of trash containing the dead mole.

"That's not too heavy, is it?" Perry asked as she—with Tucker at her heels—limped behind Ming to the front of the condo. Ming stopped, turned, and gave her a clear give-me-a-break expression. Perry looked down at Tucker. "What do you think, buddy?" She glanced up at Ming again. "Yeah. You're right. She thinks I'm stupid for asking."

Ming then pointed to Perry. "Exactly. See? You *are* learning something from them." She opened the door to the garage, and Perry followed. "My grandmother could lift this bag, and my lesbian card has never been in doubt. So, no. It's not too heavy."

Perry blocked Tucker from following them and closed the door before activating the lift on the door to the two-car garage so Ming could roll the bin to the street. She waved at Mrs. Mayberry, who was also rolling her trash bin to the curb.

"Oh, good morning, Perry. Did you hear that pack of coyotes prowling early this morning? My Gracie was so terrified, she hid under the bed."

"Uh, no. I'm afraid I didn't." She grinned at her neighbor.

"Maybe it was me singing in the shower. I've been told my singing sounds like howling dogs."

Mrs. Mayberry chuckled but shook her head. "You are incorrigible, Perry Chandler. But why are you limping, dear?" She eyed Ming. "Is that why your friend is pushing your trash to the street?"

Heat suffused Perry's neck and ears. "Uh, I twisted my back. Ming is actually my doctor and was gracious enough to make a house call on her way to her office."

"Hello." Ming waved a greeting as she rejoined Perry.

"Nice to meet you," Mrs. Mayberry said. "I didn't know doctors still made house calls. I can hardly even get an appointment with my doctor at his office. Are you taking any new patients?"

"No. I'm sorry. I'm actually about to move my practice outside Fresno. I was with a group, but we've outgrown the largest building we could lease, so several of us are going out on our own."

"You are?" A million internal questions battled for Perry's voice.

"I'm sorry, but I'll be late for office hours if I don't get my patient inside for her treatment now."

"Of course." Mrs. Mayberry waved a farewell. "Perry, dear, call me if you need anything. I'm right next door, you know."

"Thank you so much. I will." Perry limped inside and hit the button to lower the garage door. "When pigs fly. That old biddy has been trying to wheedle her way into my house for years."

"Maybe she's lonely or really just wants to be a good neighbor."

"Or maybe she's the neighborhood gossip and wants to dig up dirt on the lesbian next door."

"Do you have dirt to dig up?"

"Of course not." Perry hesitated. "I mean, I'm single, but I rarely have sleepovers here."

Tucker was waiting just inside the condo, but the other two dogs were nowhere in sight.

"Can you make it up the stairs?"

"I think so. I've been up and down several times this morning, but I'm a lot sorer after that episode in the kitchen."

"Probably because you were very tense over the dead mole."

"When I saw it, I thought my heart would stop."

"Do I want to know how you injured your back initially?"

"You can blame...oh." Perry gritted her teeth when she started up the stairs and a new spasm gripped her lower back. Ming reacted quickly, pressing her thumb against the vertebra she'd pinpointed earlier and massaging the spasmed muscle with her other hand. After a moment, it eased, and Ming drew a plastic bag from her pocket. She extracted a yellow gummy candy and held it out to Perry.

"Are you allergic to any fruits or medicines?"

"What? Oh. No fruits, but I'm allergic to penicillin."

"Chew this then."

"Is that marijuana candy, Doctor?"

"It's regulated medicinal cannabis, containing precise doses. It is not the marijuana gummies sold for recreational purposes. Cannabis is legal in this state and is one of nature's natural muscle relaxers and pain relievers, and does not have the addictive side effects of opioids. Eat it so we can get you upstairs. I wasn't lying when I told Mrs. Mayberry that I might be late getting to the office."

Perry chewed the gummy and did her best not to tighten when Ming wrapped an arm around her waist to help her one stair at a time. In the bedroom, Molly lay stretched out on the bed, snoring loudly while JT watched them from his crate.

"Morning naptime. They definitely have a daily routine." Perry was already feeling a bit fuzzy. "I respect that about them, but we're still struggling to mesh our separate schedules."

Ming gently moved Molly to the other side of the bed and helped Perry lie on her back. "Speaking of schedules, did you have any appointments this morning that you need to reschedule?"

Perry apparently was still thinking about the dogs' schedule. "I should have my people call their people to smooth it out. But their people, uh, person jumped in the rainbow river."

Ming never would have guessed that this stoic business-woman was hiding such an adorable bumbling comedian inside. She chuckled as she corrected Perry's confused euphemism. "Crossed over the rainbow bridge."

Perry gasped, her blue eyes wide with some sudden realization. "YOU speak dog language. You can be their people, uh, person."

"Right." Ming placed her hand on Perry's right shoulder to hold it in place, then gently hooked her other hand behind Perry's right knee. "Close your eyes, take a deep breath, and let it out slowly."

Perry sucked in a breath and blew it out noisily as Ming slowly drew Perry's right knee across her left leg, holding it there to stretch the muscle. But Perry wasn't relaxing. "SHA, call Julie."

"Calling Julie."

"I need you to concentrate on what we're doing," Ming said.

"I'm multitasking. It's a more effi, more ficent, more…"

"Efficient."

"Yeah. Use of time."

"Whose time are we using, Boss?"

JT jumped onto the bed, and Tucker whined at Julie's disembodied voice.

"Julie is my people, my person. She's, um, um, my right hand." Her words were slightly slurred, and she held up her right hand to stare at it. "Not that right hand. It does things she doesn't." Her face flushed as she glanced sheepishly at Ming. "Well, sometimes she does. But we're just friends."

Laughter came over the hidden speakers. "Are you high? On a Thursday morning?"

Ming repeated the stretch from left to right and held it. "Hi, Julie. It's Ming. Perry had an emergency this morning when her doggie warriors slayed an enemy mole in the yard and brought it in the kitchen as proof of their bravery. She called me when she panicked over the disposal of the body, and I discovered when I arrived that your accident-prone boss has injured her back as well as the hand she scraped Saturday. I'm treating her back now, but I've had to medicate her. I don't know if it's in your job description, but can you see that someone reschedules her appointments for the rest of the day?"

"Sure. Her back problem comes up at least once a year. It's an old sports injury from our college days. How bad is it this time?"

"She'll be fine if she takes care of it today and is careful tomorrow."

"I can come over and work from her home office to make sure she doesn't fall down the stairs and gets lunch and dinner."

"That would be perfect. I'll leave some instructions with the medication and for using ice packs."

"Great. She has some in her freezer, but I'll bring the ice packs I have, too."

"Ming is Tucker's person." Perry gasped again. "What if they start killing something every morning as part of their morning routine? No, no, no. They can't do that."

Ming chuckled and shook her head. "Relax, St. Francis of Assisi. I'm sure your very small yard does not have enough wildlife to sustain a daily hunt."

"What's she mumbling about?" Julie asked.

"She called because she thinks you and I need to negotiate with the dogs to combine her schedule with theirs."

"No hunting furry things in the new schedule," Perry said loudly.

Laughter again. "Is that a rule for you or the dogs?"

"What? I don't kill things."

"Well, that went right over her head," Julie said. "I'll look to see what needs to be rescheduled for this morning, then take care of the afternoon stuff after I get over there. It'll be about twenty minutes."

"I probably won't still be here because I have patients to see." Ming didn't mention that she'd posted a last-minute note canceling the morning's podcast after Perry called. She couldn't blow off patients waiting at the office, too—especially with tension still high among her partners. "I'll leave the instructions and medicine on the desk in her office."

"Thanks, Ming. I'll have to buy you a drink soon so I can hear all about the dead-mole crisis."

"Call disconnected," SHA announced.

Ming released the second cross-stretch, then climbed onto the bed to push both of Perry's knees up to her chest for a final stretch. A satisfying series of pops sounded along Perry's spine as Ming leaned all her weight onto her folded legs, and Perry moaned in relief.

"O-o-h-h, man. That felt so-o-o good."

Perry was totally pliant, indicating the medicine had reached full effect, so Ming pressed a little harder into the stretch, bringing their faces inches apart. Her blue eyes were glassy, even in the dim light of the bedroom, but her full lips were puckered into a pout. "I want to buy you a drink. Not Julie."

But it wasn't a drink Ming wanted. Planting her arms to transfer her weight, she slowly kissed the pout from Perry's mouth. She went willingly when Perry dropped her knees to the side, cradled Ming's hips between her thighs, and curled her hands around Ming's waist to draw her closer. So much passion was leaking around the dam that was Perry's self-control, but not even the cracks made by the cannabis had broken all the way through.

Ming caressed her cheek as she withdrew. "You need to rest, and I have patients waiting at my office." She climbed off the bed and straightened her clothes. The dose of cannabis was strong, so she was surprised when Perry spoke rather than drifting off to sleep.

"Ming?"

"Yes?" How Perry could still focus was beyond Ming's comprehension.

"Thanks for everything this morning."

Ming's smile was more for herself than Perry. "Totally my pleasure."

"I was thinking the pleasure was mine." Perry licked her lips. A dry mouth was a common side effect of cannabis. "Thai and a dog walk on Saturday?"

"Yes. I'll be here around noon."

"Good." Perry's eyelids finally drooped as her last words trailed off to a whisper. "I like your bedside manner."

Ming opened a few doors to find Perry's home office, scribbled some notes for Julie on the notepad she found in the desk drawer, and laid the small bag of cannabis gummies next to the note. She paused at the top of the stairs to take one last look at her patient. Perry hadn't moved, but Tucker had jumped onto the bed and curled next to her. If anything could widen the cracks in Perry's considerable restraint, it might be that little dog's unconditional devotion.

CHAPTER SEVEN

This is *Timed for Success*, and we're talking about timing your life to make the most of both your work and personal time. On Monday, we were discussing how to find that time of day when you are your most creative and productive, but we got bogged down in work situations. We all have to work to pay our bills, but few of us think about making the most of our time at home. What do you spend the most time doing that you wish you didn't have to? I'm asking our listeners."

The chat roll immediately lit up.

Ryan from Toledo: If I had my way, we'd get rid of the dog and pave the front and back yard so I didn't have to mow every damned weekend.

Penny from the UK: I wish the lazy bloke I live with would clean the loo at least half the time. I'm tired of wiping up where he splashes pee everywhere. I even have to keep my toothbrush in a drawer so he doesn't drip on it.

"Okay. We've got the battle of the sexes cranking up on the chat line, but how about we save the discussion on the division of labor for next week. Today let's talk about two things—what do you have to do and what do you want to do during your personal time? Looks like we have some good talking points on the chat line already, so let's address these before we add new ones.

"Candace from South Carolina writes: 'My husband and I both work full-time during the week, so on the weekends we have to mow grass, do laundry, and buy groceries. Also clean the pool and dust and vacuum the rest of the house. Then we always have some small job that takes up time, like fixing the handle on my daughter's car door, washing the RV, and trying for the hundredth time to organize the garage. We'd like to kayak with friends, cook out, and enjoy the pool we spend so much time cleaning, or go RVing with our best friends, Danny and Michelle, so we can watch the sun set over the lake.'

"I think Candace has a lot of options here. I'd look at two possibilities—hire a teenager to take care of the lawn and clean your pool. Better yet, try to interest your daughter in starting a small business recruiting her friends she can hire out to do laundry, yard work, and even organize closets and garages for busy people. She would be putting money in her friends' pockets and taking some off the top for managing the work. It'd be good practice for any future career. That should free up your time to camp and kayak at the lake with your friends. Or you could schedule one task each night during the week, so your weekend isn't packed with work. Clean one room every day. Clean the pool every Wednesday evening. Make your daughter and husband responsible for their own laundry, and do yours on Sunday night to get ready for the work week.

"Barry from New Mexico has a different problem. He says, 'Since my wife died, I'd like to spend more time with my buddies, watching sports and going fishing. I pay a woman to clean my house, or else my adult daughters would be underfoot all the time. I like to cook, too, but my daughters keep my freezer filled with precooked meals and make a fuss if I don't eat them. Honestly, the meals aren't that great. I prefer my own cooking, and I'm thinking about taking a culinary class at the community college. Also, in return for the meals, they keep wanting me to fix things at their houses. They have husbands who can get off their lazy asses and do that.'

"Barry, you're wasting time dealing with your daughters who are really serving their own purposes. If Daddy fixes everything around the house, then they don't have to nag their lazy husbands to do it. Tell your daughters to back off and let you manage your own life. Everyone should take my advice. The first step to optimizing your personal time is to not let other people dictate what and when you do things. It's *your* time to schedule, not theirs.

"Next up, Heather from Oklahoma says, 'I feel like I work all week, then spend my weekends working at home—doing laundry, cleaning the house, and going grocery shopping. My husband is a high school coach so he spends his Friday night coaching, then the rest of his weekend watching football or basketball on TV to get ideas for new plays. I actually love sports, too, and would like to have time to watch some games with him.'

"I'm a sports fan, too, Heather, and I can tell you that unless he's watching old taped games, live ones don't normally start until the afternoon and on the weekends. In the mornings, your husband can mow the lawn and do the grocery shopping while you clean the house. Then you both can fold laundry while you watch sports together all afternoon and evening. Share the load. Hubby might find out you have a good eye for plays and sign you up as an assistant.

"Last, but not least, Matt from Illinois writes about a common problem among married couples. He says, 'My wife and I work at the same company, and everyone tells us how lucky we are to work together, but we hardly see each other on the job or at home. We're both managers in different departments and mostly eat lunch at our separate desks while we work. After business hours, I take our son to football practice, and she drives our daughter to gymnastics lessons. On the weekends, she goes to gymnastics meets, and I go to football games. Then I have yard work, and she has housework. We share cooking and laundry responsibilities. The only time we have for us is when we crawl into bed together exhausted.'

"Matt, Matt, Matt." She repeated his name in a scolding tone. "First of all, you and your wife should schedule a day to have lunch together each week, and let your assistants know the time is sacrosanct. Secondly, you are letting your children run your life. Your bosses apparently feel you have some management skills, so use them. If your kids are old enough, don't be that parent who sits through every practice. Your budding athletes have coaches to supervise them. If they're really young, set it up with some of the other parents to trade off who watches practice, then text an alert when the kids are ready to be picked up. Use the time when it's not your turn to take care of those weekly household chores or to have some private time with your wife. It's all about scheduling. Sit down with your wife, and maybe the kids, too, and plan it out.

"Now, I have a few general suggestions to get things going. First, take a few weekends and keep a diary of everything you do, including how long you do it. If you stare at the ceiling for ten minutes after your alarm goes off, then write that down. Nothing is too small to note. If you multitask—fold laundry while you counsel your daughter on the dynamics of high school dating—write that down. This should give you an accurate picture of when you're making good use of your time and where you're wasting it."

This was so easy. Why couldn't people solve their own problems?

Julie messaged that she had a caller waiting on line one.

"Hello, this is Perry Chandler, and you're speaking live on *Timed for Success*. What do you want to say about managing your personal time?"

"This is Frieda, and I want to say that you obviously don't have children. During this formative time of their lives, some are independent enough to be left with other parents or on their own, where another child needs to know you're there to boost their self-confidence. And scheduling a kid is nearly impossible. A seven-year-old can never remember where she put her gym tights, a twelve-year-old will leave his cleats in the other parent's car, or the teen is still sprawled in bed although you've yelled at him three times to get up."

This woman's superior air irritated Perry. "No, I don't have children of my own, but I was the child of busy medical researchers. Their work was very important to the lives of many people, so I was taught from an early age that wasting time had consequences. Teach your children to choose their clothes for the next day, including gym clothes, prior to going to bed the night before. It will reduce their stress and yours the next morning when you're both on time for school and work. If they haven't learned to do this themselves after a few months, then let them miss a few gymnastics classes or other after-school sports because they didn't have their tights or cleats. Don't wreck your work schedule to fix their mistake, or they will go through life doing whatever because you'll step in and fix it. As for the teen, hit them where it hurts. Teens' phones are where they basically live, where they hang out with friends and keep up with everything that's important to them. It's the only thing you can use to fully get their attention."

"It sounds a bit harsh, but I'll try your first suggestion."

Perry was teetering too close to child rearing, which wasn't her specialty. Hell, she'd flunk the lowest level of that class. She didn't have siblings or even cousins to learn from.

Julie's text confirmed her deficiency. *Whoa. Maybe you should back off giving advice on how to raise children. Especially since your only experience is your biological units' failure at parenting. I'm still amazed at how well you turned out. Buckle up, because the chat roll is heating up.*

Nelson from Down Under: Righto. I train dogs for a
living, and children aren't much different. Reward
and consequences. Give them the chance to make

the right choice, but don't let them manipulate you and waste your time.

Cindy from Kentucky: These are children, not dogs. Their brains aren't developed enough to make adult decisions. If they were, we wouldn't have to parent them. You should listen to Dr. Lee's podcast on helping children find balance.

Albert from France: They are children. Let them be children. Americans spend too much time organizing their children's lives. Then they grow up and become parents who organize their children's time. It is no wonder we are constantly remaking old songs and old movies. Children are growing up with no imagination, no ability to create. They only know how to schedule. Dr. Lee is a real doctor and has a much better outlook on dealing with people.

LaTasha from Atlanta: Seems like to me Dr. Chandler has done all right for herself. Her parents raised her to be tough. That's what a woman has to be to get ahead in the world because too many men would pat us on the head and promote their incompetent male friends.

Perry sighed. Sometimes this podcast felt like managing children. She planned to ignore the Dr. Lee references. She really did need to take time to listen to one of those podcasts and dig deeper into the host's background. She'd been surprised to see female pronouns for the infamous Dr. Lee. She'd figured it was one of those doctors who spent all their time looking up other people's asses and was now selling shit in his podcast. Focus. She needed to focus.

"Let's don't slip back into the men-versus-women discussion again. We're going to save that for later. Let's stay on target. Our goal is to find where we can take charge in our personal lives so we can find more time for ourselves to recharge or to spend with our partners, families, and friends."

> **Evan from Arkansas:** I save time by wearing clothes more than once before I throw them in the laundry. Saves wear and tear on the clothes, too. Most things can be worn more than once unless you spill something on them. Jeans can last three to five days, a shirt—if you wear an undershirt and use deodorant—at least two or three days. And get an extra day out of your underwear by turning them inside out.
>
> **Edith from Homer, Montana:** The cowboys up here wear their long johns a week or more before they launder them.
>
> **Ramona from Alabama:** I'm guessing the cows don't complain about their smell?
>
> **Dr. Perry Chandler:** Can you arrange to work from home at least one day a week? Unless you're handling laundry for a family of five, a few loads timed so that you can fold them during your breaks would cut down laundry time on the weekends.
>
> **Ralph from New Jersey:** I saw something on the internet where a guy made little dust-mop booties for his dog so they could keep the wood floors clean.
>
> **Vonda from Savannah, Ga.:** Dumb ass. That's not real. Just buy one of those Rumba things that vacuum for you.

Julie messaged: Caller on line two.

Perry: Thank God. Save me from this chat-roll disaster.

Julie: People feel strongly about this stuff. You've hit a nerve, and our page views are rocketing. Keep it up.

"Hi. You're live on *Timed for Success*. Who am I speaking with, and can you tell us where you're calling from?"

"I'm Adam, and I'm in Sacramento."

"What would you like to tell us?"

"This podcast on saving time is wasting my time. The commentors obviously aren't serious. Just work more so you can make more money, then pay other people to mow the lawn, clean the house, and chauffeur the kids all over the place. This plan creates jobs and relieves your stress. Trickle-down economics is the American way. Unless your son has the potential to play in the NBA or NFL, teach him to play golf. That's the only sport he'll need in the corporate world. Also, pinch those pennies early in your career, and invest everything you can. Let your money work for you now so you can retire early and take the wife on that cruise she's been nagging you about."

Perry sighed. "I'm going to ignore for now that you completely eliminated any girls when you said NBA and NFL, then suggested that fathers needed to teach only their sons to play golf. But I agree with other parts of your recommendation. Being more productive and putting in the bit of overtime to get ahead of your peers could get you up the ladder quicker. Also, clamping down on expenses now to invest some money is a great idea. Do you really need that second ski trip this year? Don't run to the Apple store every time a new iPhone comes out with an incremental improvement. Make that money work for you in the stock market."

Julie: Caller on line one.

"Hi. You're on *Timed for Success*. What would you like to add?"

An unidentified female voice answered. "I think Adam is full of it. When he has a heart attack on the golf course before he's fifty, I doubt he'll wish he'd spent more time at work. Dr. Lee says work becomes our home when we don't have balance. Work is a temporary situation until we retire. Family, friends, and the nest we build for retirement are the forever in our lives."

"But without success at work, you might not have a retirement to look forward to," Perry said. "Maybe balance isn't simultaneous but something that evens out over time. You spend more time working now but just enjoy the benefits of your earlier success when you retire."

"Dr. Lee offered this eye-opening scenario on *Finding Natural Balance*," the caller said. "When you're single and in your early twenties, it's fun to go with your office buddies to the local sports bar for burgers and a beer after work. Then you're over thirty, and most of your pals are married with families. Sure, you're their boss because you put in the extra hours, kissed a few extra rings, and climbed the ladder. Only now you're in your office alone, working late because you don't want to go to the bar by yourself. Or you do go because nothing's waiting for you at home but a clean apartment, and you end up eating dinner at the bar, pretending to watch a football game on one of the screens while you're really watching a table full of young hires from your office sharing stories and beer and eyeing women. They won't invite you to join them because you're the boss and, in their eyes, the old guy who works and drinks too much. Then you're almost fifty and you're looking up at the ceiling of your hospital room, listening to your heart monitor beep. The office manager sends you the customary flowers with a card signed by a bunch of people, many whose names you don't even recognize, because they passed it around the office for all to sign. But nobody comes to visit. Your boss calls. He spends about thirty seconds asking how you feel and assuring you the office misses you. Then he spends thirty minutes asking about projects with upcoming deadlines and telling you who will take over your job while you're out, which nearly causes you to have a second coronary. Life sucks, but you have plenty of time now to think about how things could have been if you'd had more balance in your life."

Perry mentally shook herself after several long seconds of podcast silence. Julie would have to edit that out before she posted the recorded version.

"Wow. This Dr. Lee sounds depressing. I wonder how many calls the suicide help line received after that podcast." The unprofessional and inappropriate remark slipped out of her mouth before she could bite her tongue. "Sorry. Let me back up. That wasn't a fair response, but her example is overly dramatic. And I certainly don't want to make light of the very serious issue of suicide. I agree we need balance in life, but balance doesn't mean the same thing for everyone. It's not a black-and-white, fifty-fifty deal. Some areas are gray, and the ratios should be flexible, depending on where you are in your career and personal life. Thank you, though, caller. Wait. Your last name wouldn't happen to be Lee, would it?"

But Julie had already ended the call, and the chat line was bloody again with the parent-versus-childless and men-versus-women battles. Perry glanced at her watch and dropped her chin in relief. The stretch of her neck and shoulder muscles felt good. The temptation to end the podcast clawed for attention. She didn't need the money from it. Her teams were busier than ever, and she could use the time to write her next book. But she couldn't end the podcast now. It would look like this notorious, vicious Dr. Lee had chased her away. Nope. She'd return to fight another day.

"We're out of time now, but let's track our time usage over the weekend and write it down. I think the results will surprise you."

Julie cued the podcast closing, and Perry snatched her headphones off.

"The cyber crowd is vicious these days."

Three furry faces looked up at her in agreement for a minute, and then Tucker ran to the top of the stairs and barked.

"I know, I know. I forgot to let you out after breakfast. Just give me a few more minutes. I've got to dig into this damned Dr. Lee."

Molly barked sharply and lumbered down the steps with Tucker in tow. Shit. They weren't going to wait. Perry had already typed a long note of ideas for how to dig into Dr. Lee's dirt, uh, life when JT walked to the doorway and lifted his leg. She sprang from her chair.

"No, no, no. Bad dog. No peeing in the house."

Lovable, fun-loving JT just stared at her. He did lower his leg, but only after he was done and she was already there, throwing tissues onto the urine pooling on her gleaming hardwood floor. She emptied the entire box of tissues, then stood up to glare at the soggy mess. No way she was going to pick that up with her bare hands.

"Damn it! Bad dog."

The label didn't faze JT, who was hop-stepping to the stairs and yipping like they were playing a game. Tail held high, he waved it with each jaunty step down the stairs.

"That dog must have a pea-sized brain." Actually, that wasn't true. She'd seen him figure out how to retrieve a bone or a ball that had rolled behind furniture when the others had given up. Even as angry as she was about the pee, his glass-half-full personality, comforting cuddles, and super-cute face made him impossible to hate. She stomped down the steps after him. One thing was certain—she wouldn't get lost in work and delay potty break again.

FOREVER COMES IN THREES

CHAPTER EIGHT

"Hey, Danny. How's everything going?" Ming set the Thai takeout on the floorboard, then settled into the driver's seat of her Mercedes convertible. She missed his first words as her phone synced with her car's system.

"...doing fantastic. The weather is perfect, and we've already adopted two cats and a dog in the first hour. Another couple is looking seriously at the St. Bernard, and Bonnie is talking with them. Are you still bringing those three small dogs?"

"I am, but it will be at least an hour, maybe even two before we get there. The foster is a first-timer, and I want to make sure she understands our requirements for adoption. Also, although I'm acquainted with these dogs because I knew their deceased owner, I'm not sure how they'd be around children and cats. They still have to be tested. They definitely wouldn't be suited for a home where a kid might have a pet rodent, reptile, or bird. These are terrier mixes and have proved their hunting skills."

"Gotcha. I'll inform the other volunteers that people can put in applications to adopt them, pending further testing."

"Excellent. See you in a bit." Ming felt to her core that someone different lurked behind Perry's façade of indifferent efficiency, and she'd seen the signs of bonding between Perry and the pups. But after listening to yesterday's *Timed for Success* podcast, doubts niggled at her earlier, maybe too quick, conviction that fate had already matched the trio with their forever home. Pets, like children, needed time and attention, not workaholic owners. Besides, wasn't Perry expecting her to help place the dogs with someone else? She parked in the short driveway in front of Perry's double garage, checked her watch, and smiled. Ha. Five minutes early.

Perry sprang down the walkway, her grin a reflection of the bright sun, and retrieved the takeout bag from the car before Ming could open her door. "It's an awesome day, isn't it? Perfect for a walk to the park."

Ming returned her enthusiasm. The adoption event was happening in the dog park about five blocks away, so they could take the dogs there soon. "It's perfect for after we eat."

Perry set the bag on the kitchen island and opened the refrigerator. "I have water, beer, green tea, sweet tea, and soda. What would you like to drink?"

"Green tea would be wonderful." Ming opened the food containers while Perry gathered some small plates and serving spoons.

"That smells great. I love Spicy J's. What'd you get for us?" Perry asked.

"Fried rice, the appetizer trio, and mango shrimp."

"All of my favorites," Perry said, unwrapping the disposable chopsticks provided by the restaurant. "Dig in." She snagged some calamari to transfer to her plate but froze when Ming didn't join her. "Uh, did you want to say, um, a blessing or something?"

Ming startled herself with an eruption of laughter at Perry's caught-in-the-headlights expression. She was sure Perry had no clue she was so expressive, but the real shocker was how these small cracks in the self-confidence of this international businesswoman made Ming want to hug and protect her. She tucked that thought away for examination later. "No. I'm not religious. I might want to compliment the chef, but I don't generally bless the food."

Perry looked relieved. "But you're not eating."

"Could I have a fork? I've never really mastered the whole chopsticks thing." She choked back another burst of laughter when Perry's cheeks flushed like cherries.

"I wasn't…I didn't assume…I mean…just because…"

"Relax. I'm one of probably only a handful of people in the entire state of California who can't eat with chopsticks." She spread her fingers and held up her hands. "You would think fingers skilled enough to stitch a wound, wield a scalpel, and manipulate acupuncture needles should be able to use chopsticks." She shrugged. "But not me. I secretly suspect my grandmother isn't as fond of Mexican food as she claims. She's just too embarrassed to go to an Asian restaurant with me where people would see me eating with a fork."

Perry retrieved one and handed it to Ming. "You do acupuncture? Why didn't you use that on me Thursday? I've always wanted to try it, and I wouldn't have been too drugged up to work."

"You needed to relax and rest. And acupuncture sessions can leave you feeling woozy or fatigued, too."

"Still, if I hurt my back again, I want to try that."

Ming started to explain that she wouldn't likely be making house calls in Fresno as soon as she untangled herself from the co-op practice and her property purchase was finalized. She planned to move out of the city as soon as possible. Before she told anyone, though, she wanted to nail down a few more boards in the new life she was building. So, she nodded and chewed some calamari.

❖

The metal loop for connecting the leash to the harness stuck out next to JT's elbow as he twirled and danced, clearly excited. Perry shook her head. The harnesses were the old type that came apart if you weren't careful when you removed them, and putting them back together correctly on the dog was like working a Rubik's Cube. Scratch that. She could solve the cube in under fifteen seconds, but these harnesses seemed like they clipped together differently every time. She was tempted to sit one dog down and practice until she solved the trick to sorting them out. Or she could just buy three of those easy-on, easy-off new harnesses. Yet they were a bit pricey for dogs she didn't plan to keep.

She threw her hands up. Obviously, she'd put this one on wrong. That loop was supposed to be on top, between his shoulders. "I can untangle parachute lines, so why can't I figure out how to put on a stupid dog harness?"

"Well, these old-style harnesses are much more adjustable as your dog grows or ages and gains weight, but they can be the devil to buckle on correctly." Ming clipped the leash to the harness as Perry removed it. "It's easier if you leave the leashes attached when you take them off, so you know which part goes between the shoulders and don't get it turned inside-out. Can I show you?"

"I need to do it." She refused to admit defeat, especially in front of this woman she wanted to impress.

"I agree. I meant that I can instruct as you do it."

"I can do it."

"I know you can, but you're the alpha, and you need to make him be still."

"He's too excited."

"Give him a command."

"He's not going to listen."

"Do your employees listen, even when they're excited about something?"

"They better. I'm the boss." Okay. She got it. She was a big dog in the business world. It was about time she started acting like it at home. "JT, sit."

JT immediately sat and stared up at her. She held the harness by the leash and realized it was clear how to slip it over his head, tug one foot through, and close the clasp to secure what had a moment ago appeared to be a puzzle of random straps. She grinned at Ming.

"Good job." Ming returned her smile.

They stared at each other through a heavy haze of expectation. Perry's head was going to explode if Ming didn't repeat Monday's kiss or at least hug her before they left for the park. Instead, Ming held out Tucker's harness and cleared her throat.

"Um, this is Tucker's harness. I'll get Molly."

She would get that kiss. Yes, she would. She would put that harness on Tucker like an expert and impress the giver of kisses, then steal one of those knee-melting smooches if it wasn't immediately offered. After all, Ming had kissed her before. Wasn't it her turn to make the move? Visions of that kiss when Ming knelt to check the fit of Tucker's harness burst when Ming reached down and neatly clipped the teal leash to Molly's matching collar.

"Hey. Where's her harness?" Why did she get the easy dog?

"Molly doesn't need one. JT and Tucker have slender terrier heads. They could easily slip a collar by backing up and twisting a bit. As long as Molly's collar is properly tightened, she'd have a hard time slipping it over her big, chunky head. She's also better trained to a leash than the other two."

Well, no worries. She'd get this harness on Tucker faster than her Rubik's Cube record. She found the leash ring and clipped it on, then used it to hold up the harness. Yes. She could easily see how the straps should go and, after a small adjustment, gave the command.

"Tucker, sit."

Molly and JT sat in a show of pack solidarity, but Tucker lay flat on the floor and rolled onto his back. She tried to sit him up, but he was as limp as a debutante pretending to have the vapors.

"Christ almighty." Swearing under her breath wasn't helping, but at least it drowned out small snorts of laughter coming from Ming, who had clamped her hand over her mouth when Tucker flung himself to the floor.

By the time she managed to get the harness on him anyway, she was chuckling too at his antics. And when she rubbed his chest and announced "all done," he jumped up and led the stampede to the front door, ready for wherever they were going. Perry laughed. "You little shit."

She checked that she had her phone and house keys, then joined Ming and the dogs at the door. Ming handed her Molly's and Tucker's leashes.

"I'll take JT," Ming said. "He tends to wander back and forth and get everybody crossed up." She handed Perry a small plastic bag of soft dog treats. "Use these to reward good behavior or to distract them from situations that could become difficult. I'll tell you when to hand them out."

Perry put her hand on the door, stopping Ming from opening it. "I think I deserve a treat for my stellar dog-harnessing performance."

Ming's posture went from friendly to sultry. "Do you?"

She inched into Ming's personal space. "I am the alpha in this house. Ming, kiss." Her command was soft instead of forceful, her lips intentionally light on Ming's. She ran her tongue along Ming's lower lip but withdrew without deepening the kiss. She wanted to savor each tiny step with this woman in a way she never had, never wanted before. Then she reconsidered and had dipped her head for a second serving of those tasty lips when a sharp bark caused them both to flinch. Perry looked down, and three furry faces stared back. Then JT barked to back up Molly's interruption.

Something odd flashed in Ming's velvet-brown eyes. Indecision? Regret? God, Perry hoped not. Then it was gone as quickly as it came. The corner of Ming's mouth quirked up, and amusement filled her eyes. "Your pack grows restless."

Perry heaved an overly dramatic sigh. "Okay, okay. We're going."

Though Perry tried to play their kiss off as casual, Ming's warm lips and peppermint breath plowed through her like a six-foot, tractor-drawn tiller, digging up long-buried desire and emotions. She was so engrossed in puzzling out how her forward advance in their flirtatious tête-à-tête had left her feeling like the sacrificed lamb, she was surprised to look up and see the park teeming with pets and people as they neared. Molly barked and strained against her collar to join them. JT hesitated, apparently torn between his duty to be at Molly's side and his desire to hide behind Ming and Perry. Tucker reversed course and headed for the security of the condo. When his leash pulled him up short, he jumped against Perry's leg in a frantic pick-me-up-now dance while keeping up a running commentary of sharp whines and worried grunts.

Perry stooped to reassure him with quiet words, but he was clearly determined, so she wrapped her arms around him and picked him up as she stood. "What's going on? The dog park is never this busy."

Ming cleared her throat. "I meant to tell you, but we sort of got off track when you waylaid me at the door. A big adoption event is being held today. Several of the rescue groups I work with are here."

Something inside Perry stuttered. "So, these guys could go home with someone else today?" She'd be glad to get rid of them, right? She didn't have time for one dog, much less three. It was just, well, she'd kind of gotten used to talking to someone other than the smart-house computer. And who knew that dogs had an internal clock like she did? They woke her at the same time every morning, exactly two minutes before her alarm. They expected their daily bite of cheese, even though they watched her conceal pills in it, right after they went outside to pee. And they politely waited for her to sit down with her dinner plate before they dove into the food she put down for them.

"They might meet some potential adopters but won't be able to go home with anyone today because we have to get their veterinary papers in order and test them for compatibility with children, cats, and other pets that could be in a household," Ming said. "And if the potential adopter hasn't already been cleared, the sponsoring rescue group would want to check out their home situation to make sure they could care for them appropriately."

The pinch in her gut eased, and she realized she had Tucker in an iron hug, so she relaxed her arms, and he gave her a grateful lick on the chin. "Okay. I mean, you know, we don't have any of their stuff here for anyone to take them today."

Ming turned to her, and Perry froze, caught in the middle of planting a kiss on the top of Tucker's head to reassure him. Heat suffused her neck and cheeks.

"You could always change your mind and keep them," Ming said. "They are comfortable with you. Tucker has obviously bonded with you."

"No, no. Can't. I'm too busy. I don't know anything about keeping dogs. Besides, when things fully reopen, I'll probably be traveling at least two weeks out of every month again. Who would take care of them?"

Ming nodded but didn't appear convinced. "Of course, we're all assuming life will someday go back to the way it was before the pandemic." Her eyes glazed, as if her thoughts were far away for a moment. "The impact on so many things could be devastating—like performance arts, sporting events such as the Olympics, and international tourism. It's hard to imagine never going to a local arts festival, a concert or a movie theater, a Broadway play, or a March Madness college basketball tournament." She looked at Perry. "You are vaccinated, aren't you? Did I already ask?"

"I don't think you've asked, but I am. I required everyone in my company to be. Luckily, I had no objectors. And, since you're a doctor, I'm taking for granted that you are, too?"

"Of course."

Molly's sharp, happy bark cut through the cacophony of conversations, yaps, and cat yowls coming from two semi-trailers, where crates of potential feline adoptees were stacked for viewing. JT was quiet but constantly wound between their feet, so walking without stumbling required a lot of concentration.

"You can make Tucker walk. He'll be okay after a few minutes," Ming said.

Although Perry's arms were tiring, Tucker's heart pounded against her chest, and he pressed his head into her shoulder at the slightest indication she might be about to put him back on the ground. She couldn't bring herself to let go of the terrified little guy. "He's fine. Light as a feather," she lied.

Ming didn't look convinced, but before she could respond, a young man approached with a middle-aged woman in tow. He waved at Ming.

"There you are," he said. "I've been looking all over for you. Are these the pups?"

"Yes," Ming said. "The happy barker is Molly. We estimate her age at thirteen years. We feel pretty accurate about the ages of the two boys since they were puppies when they were rescued." She pointed to JT, who was sitting quietly at her feet. "This is JT, and my friend, Perry, is holding Tucker. JT is nearly eight years old, and Tucker is around ten."

"Hi, Perry. It's nice to meet you," Danny said. "So, no spring chickens here."

"The boys aren't that old." Perry squatted to scratch Molly's ears while still holding Tucker. "Sorry, Molly. Didn't mean to put you in the old-folks category."

"Unfortunately," Danny said, "she does fall in that range, which will make her hard to adopt. Few people want to take a dog they know they'll have only long enough to become attached to, then lose them to death. But then we do have some kind souls and some fosters who are willing to give these old dogs a loving and comfortable home for their final years."

She still objected. Sure, Molly needed help getting onto the bed, and she had a bad knee on her right hind leg. But she was a great huntress, and when she was feeling playful in the evenings, she could throw her bone almost waist high in the air. This guy made it sound like she was ready for hospice care.

"There are a lot of people and animals here," Ming said, eyeing clusters of both.

"I have a quiet spot for you guys over behind the cat trailers. There's a bench, and it's enclosed with a temporary fence, so you can let these guys off leash. I'll send some potential adopters your way and let Ming handle them." He looked at Perry. "She knows what questions to ask."

"I have my iPad to add any remarks on the people who come to look at them," Ming said.

Danny gave her a thumbs-up. "Go right around that trailer, then. Your spot has the green ribbon tied to the gate."

Behind the two large trailers, they found a series of portable wire pens, most eight feet by eight feet, with a couple of folding chairs inside. The one with a green ribbon tied to its gate was eight by thirteen, about three feet high, and had been put together around a park bench.

"I guess we get the big pen because we have three dogs," Perry said.

"I'm sure." Ming opened the gate and led all of them inside. She unhooked Molly's lead, then JT's, and they began exploring the grass and fence. Perry unhooked Tucker, but he still sat next to her on the bench until curiosity got the best of him, and he hopped down to explore with his packmates.

A young couple with a boy about four or five years old approached, but the child cringed against his mother's legs when Molly barked her happy greeting.

"Hi." Ming stood and acknowledged the couple. "Were you looking for a dog to adopt?"

The father answered while the mother spoke softly to the kid. "Yes. We were thinking a medium-sized one. Something sturdy that would bond and grow up with our son. I had a dog when I was a boy, and he was my best friend." He pointed to JT. "How old is that guy? He looks friendly."

"Actually, he's almost eight years old and the youngest of the three. But he's very friendly," Ming said.

The mom finally convinced the boy to come to the fence, and he giggled when he stuck his fingers through the wire and Molly licked them. JT wagged his tail and stood on his hind legs so the man could reach over the fence to scratch his ears. But when the child approached, he dropped to the ground and backed away.

"They haven't been tested around children yet," Perry said. "So he's probably just not used to them. JT will growl at other dogs if they come near his food, but he hasn't growled at me. I'm not sure what he'd do around a kid. Their owner was a single, older woman who didn't have children."

"Why'd she give them up?"

"She died unexpectedly. She was a colleague of my mother, so I'm trying to help find them a new home."

"Oh, that's so sad," the woman said. "That one is so cute. You said his name is JT? Is he housebroken?"

Perry shrugged. "Yes and no. He has peed in my house several times but never pooped."

The woman nodded. "That's why we should either get a puppy we can train early, a female dog, or a larger male dog," she said to her husband. "The smaller and older the dog, the harder it will be to train him if he isn't already fully housebroken."

"You're right," he said.

"There's a litter of Labrador-mix puppies over that way." Perry pointed helpfully to the far corner of the adoption area where a small crowd was gathering. "You might want to hurry over before they're all claimed."

The man looked where she pointed, then grabbed his son and swung him onto his shoulders. "Thanks. I think we will." He trotted off, his kid squealing in delight at the impromptu ride, and his wife jogging to keep up while her warnings that a Labrador puppy might not be a good idea fell on deaf ears.

An older woman, her leathery skin covered with tattoos,

hurried over and greeted Ming. "The guy from the Fresno shelter is here and wants to talk to us about a couple of dogs he thinks are worth pulling before their time runs out. Can you bring your iPad, and let's see if we can place them with a foster?"

"Sure." Ming turned to Perry. "Cheryl, this is Perry. She's fostering these three while we search for a home for them. Perry, this is Cheryl. She heads up the rescue group for the fiercest and hardest to adopt of all breeds."

Perry's brain immediately went to pit bulls, because Cheryl reminded her of one. She probably had a leather jacket adorned with gang colors draped over a Harley parked somewhere nearby. In the small Southern town where Perry had spent summers with her grandparents, pit bulls were called junkyard dogs because they were favored to patrol junkyards and construction yards to keep thieves out at night. Cheryl must have read her mind, because she pointed her finger at Perry.

"Nope. Not pit bulls. Everybody thinks that." She slid a backpack carrier from her shoulder and set it on the ground to free a tiny chihuahua.

The small dog immediately poked out his chest and strutted over to pee on the enclosure near where JT sat. JT jumped to his feet, tail high, and stood very straight and tall, his ears pricked in a surprised, who-is-this-interloper expression. He approached the chihuahua to sniff where he'd peed, then immediately urinated on top of it. This got Tucker's attention, who came over to add his contribution. Molly wasn't interested in their male show of marking territory. She strolled over and thrust her nose through the wire to sniff the little invader. Dog or odd-looking rat? The miniature Godzilla didn't wait for introductions. He roared like a tiny lion and nipped Molly's nose, which transformed the benevolent queen into an oh-no-you-didn't attack ninja.

"Killer, you little shit, come here." The chihuahua dodged when Cheryl tried to scoop him up and defuse the confrontation, then made the bad decision to take another run at Molly, who grabbed his ear that poked through the fence and hung on. Luckily, the fence prevented a melee when the boys jumped in, barking ferociously to defend their queen.

Perry jerked Molly's collar and shouted above the dogs' frantic barks and Killer's howls of pain. "Molly, leave it. Sit." No one seemed more surprised than Perry when Molly immediately released the chihuahua's ear, and the three dogs Perry had already dubbed The Terrors all sat and looked up at her.

"Damn. I'm sorry about that. You see why chihuahuas are so dangerous," Cheryl said. "The little shits have a St. Bernard-sized temper and the arrogance of a chow. People get them because they think a little dog will be easy to care for, but they're the toughest to housebreak, incredibly territorial, and not good around children because they bite a lot. So, a lot of them end up in shelters."

What the hell? Perry stared at the biker woman. "You run a chihuahua rescue?"

Cheryl stuffed Killer back into his backpack carrier. Perry could see now that it was mostly made of black mesh that the dog could see through. "Yep. Got the bite scars to prove it." She held out her tanned hand, which was dotted with white puncture-wound scars.

Ming fished her iPad from her messenger bag. "Do you mind if I go with Cheryl for a few minutes?" She took a small note pad and pen from the bag and laid it on top. "If anyone comes by, just answer any questions they have about the dogs, and get their name and phone number so I can call them later if they're truly interested in the dogs."

"No worries. Go. And take that killer dog with you before Molly has to teach him another lesson." Perry put her hands on her hips in mock indignation, and Molly gave a sharp bark for emphasis. This warning inspired JT to bark at Molly, his signal to start a victory sing-along. Molly lifted her nose to the sky and gave a full-throated howl any beagle would be proud of, while

Tucker added his less refined tenor, and JT joined in with his strangled attempt. Perry was tempted to add her own deeper howl, just for harmony, to the ruckus, but other dogs around the adoption area were starting to bark and join the noise, so she quieted her charges.

"Do you want us to get arrested for starting a riot?" she asked the dogs. Molly seemed to consider this possibility, but JT hopped around barking. He was evidently eager to restart the fun chorus, but Tucker used his body to push JT away and growled. "It's okay, Tuck. Let's all sit down." When did she begin talking to the dogs like they were people? Perry shook herself, then looked up to see a young woman approaching.

"Hi. I'm Gigi."

Perry shook Gigi's offered hand, and then they laughed when they both took small bottles of hand sanitizer from their pockets to squirt onto their fingers. "Always pays to be safe, even if the pandemic is supposed to be under control now."

"I agree," Gigi said.

"Are you looking to adopt?"

"Yes. I graduated from Stanford last year and have been working for a local programing company. I wanted to wait until I was sure my job was stable, and it is. Now I'm ready to add some companionship to my life."

"These are active guys. Do you live in an apartment?"

"No. I rent a really cute little house with a fenced backyard and have the option to buy it if I want."

When Gigi bent over the three-foot fence and held her hand out, Molly and JT rushed to greet her. Tucker held back, ducking behind Perry's legs.

"Aw, are you being shy?" Gigi squatted to put herself more on Tucker's level, but he looked away, rejecting her overture.

Perry liked her gentle voice and the way she greeted the dogs. "Would you like to come inside the fence to get to know them better?"

"Yes. If you don't mind."

Perry nearly tripped over Molly and JT as they enthusiastically escorted her to the gate to admit Gigi, who plopped down onto the grass and let them crawl and lick all over her. Her gaze, however, followed Tucker, who continued to hang back, adamant in his rebuff. She sat up when Molly and JT calmed and gestured to him.

"I had a rough-coat Jack Russell terrier like him when I was a kid. He went everywhere with me, even walked me to the school bus every morning and was waiting when it brought me home. Mom used to worry he'd get in the road and tried keeping him in the yard or house, but he'd find a way out and be waiting at the bus stop anyway. So, she gave up. Just like she gave up making him sleep somewhere other than in my bed." She held out her hand to Tucker again. "Hey, handsome. Won't you come over for just a minute?"

Tucker turned away, refusing to look at her.

"Just ignore him and give him time. He's slow to warm up to new people." She sat on the ground, too, and snagged Tucker to bring him around in front of her so Gigi could scratch his ears and talk to him.

"Hi. Can we look at your dogs, too?" A middle-aged couple stood outside their fence. The woman was making the inquiry, but the man looked like he'd rather be anywhere but at the park. "We're looking for an older dog for my father-in-law. He's pretty much housebound, and I'd like to find a companion for him. I think an older, calmer dog would be best."

The man pointed in the direction Ming had gone. "The Chinese woman said yours are older dogs."

Perry wanted to grind her teeth. How could people be so clueless? "You must be referring to Ming. She's not Chinese. She's one hundred percent American."

"I'm so sorry. My husband didn't mean to offend. He meant the woman with Asian features."

"Well, we're trying to place all three of these dogs together. Their owner died unexpectedly. They're a bonded pack."

"They're dogs. They'd adjust."

Perry didn't like this man's attitude. Did he treat people at his workplace with that same arrogance?

"You said the same thing about your father when you insisted on moving him here, away from his friends," the woman told her husband.

"Molly's almost deaf, and the two boy dogs help her compensate for her hearing loss. They nudge her when I call them. Or if she's stuck under a bed or accidentally becomes closed in a room, I just have to ask Tucker to find her, and he will."

JT had settled on Gigi's lap, and Molly was licking his face so that his beard poked out in wild directions. The woman smiled at the dogs' interaction. She had kind eyes and deserved better than this arrogant, selfish husband.

"Why don't you give me your name and phone number? I'll pass it on to Ming because she's the coordinator between a lot of the rescue groups here today, and if we're unable to place these three together, then maybe JT or Molly would work out for you. Or Ming could find your father-in-law just the right pup from some other foster home." Perry held out the notepad and pen.

"That would be really great. Next time, I'll bring my father-in-law, Russell, with me instead of Harry to look at dogs." She scribbled her name and cell number on the pad.

"Dogs can be a lot of company," Gigi said.

The woman smiled as she handed the pad back to Perry. "Perhaps a dog a bit larger would be good. We got Russell into a nice senior development, and having a dog to walk could help him get out and meet some of his neighbors."

"Good idea," Gigi said.

They waved good-bye to the couple, well, to the woman, and Gigi held out her hand for the notepad.

"I need to go. I can see why you'd like to place these three together, but I can realistically afford to care for only one. I refuse to be that person who has so many pets they can't pay for vet care. Even annual shots and a checkup can cost hundreds of dollars. Three together would probably be nearly two thousand. And they will surely have some health issues that come with age."

"I admire you for thinking ahead like that and admitting limitations. All three are great dogs, and I'm going to put a star by your name, so you'll get first choice in case we do have to break up the pack. That is, if you haven't already adopted some other dog."

"Thank you…"

"Perry." She took the pad from Gigi. "Sorry. I'm a little off balance still because we had a throw-down between Molly and a bad-tempered chihuahua right before you showed up."

Gigi laughed. "I can imagine. Those can be nasty little dogs. But, like the terriers I love, some people understand and love chihuahuas too."

Perry waved good-bye to Gigi and let out a relieved breath when she spotted Ming heading back. After Ming arrived, Perry handed over the notepad and offered unsolicited commentary on both prospective adopters.

"You've been busy. It sounds like either one of these could be a good placement."

"Maybe we should keep looking. This is only the first day. We could still find someone to take all three." Perry envisioned orphans being torn from the arms of their siblings. "They really do depend on each other. Although the boys act jealous of each other, they wrestle and play together several times a day. They're sort of fun to watch."

Ming hooked her arm around Perry's and closed the gap between them. Her petite but strong body felt good pressed against Perry's side, and she wanted so, so much to draw Ming closer for a kiss. But those lips were moving. What were they saying? "Keep it up, and somebody might think you're getting attached to them."

"Nope. I do like the little buggers, but I just don't have any time for them. I work too much."

"Maybe you need them to show you how to find a better balance between work and your personal life."

"Now you sound like that crazy Dr. Lee podcast." The second the words were out of her mouth, Perry wanted to take them back. She didn't know Ming well enough. She might really like that podcast, and it was rude of Perry to criticize a rival openly. Not just rude. As a well-known—in business circles—personality, making rash statements of any kind could always come back to haunt her. "Sorry. I shouldn't—"

"Hey. The guy over there said you have some pups we should meet." The couple appeared to be around retirement age but in good physical shape. "I'm Tom, and this is my wife, Roberta, but everybody calls her Bob." The man shook hands with Ming and Perry. "I'll shake hands for both of us. Bob finished chemotherapy a year ago and has been declared cancer free, but we're still cautious, with the pandemic and all."

Perry took out her hand sanitizer and offered him a squirt, too. "Can't be too safe," she said.

"So, Tom, do you guys live in Fresno?"

"We did, but we just sold our house and bought one of those bus-type RVs. We plan to become full-time travelers. We decided to go with an RV so we could take our dog with us. Unfortunately, Bandit was diagnosed with lymphoma about the same time Bob got her diagnosis for breast cancer, and he didn't make it."

"I'm so sorry," Ming said. "What kind of dog was he?"

"Just a mutt," Bob said, her eyes welling with tears. "Our best guess was boxer-beagle, if you can envision that. He weighed about forty-five pounds before he got sick. We still miss him."

Tom pointed to Tucker. "That rough-coat guy there would be about perfect for us. Wire-haired dogs don't seem to bother my allergies much."

Perry shook her head. "Tuck wouldn't do well. He's nervous around strangers, and traveling would put him constantly in new situations and around new people. Actually, the three of them are very dependent on each other, so we were hoping to place them together."

Tom shook his head. "You might place two of them together, but good luck with finding someone to take all three."

Bob folded herself over the fence and was petting Molly and JT. "I just love this little guy. Is he a schnauzer mix?"

"Yes," Ming said. "He's a really sweet cuddler, too."

"JT? He's shy in new situations, also, unless he's with his packmates," Perry said. "Molly is the brave one. She loves going on a walk and greeting everyone she sees. But the two boys do better at home or together when they're out in public."

"Are they housebroken?"

"Yes," Ming said.

"Well, Molly is," Perry said. "But the boys are hit-and-miss. And if one of them pees, the other one has to add to it. They'll mostly go out to pee, but if it's raining or they get anxious because I've been gone too long...look out. I hate to think what they might do if we break up the pack. Being with each other is their security."

"They were accustomed to having a pet door and going out whenever they wanted," Ming explained. "But they're adjusting. Both are very smart dogs and anxious to please."

"They also are good about not chewing up things if you keep some bones around for them," Perry said. "I mean, mostly. You don't have any stuffed animals or dolls in your house, do you? Those things are toast if the trio of terrors is around. Their hunting instinct kicks in. I had a pair of slippers made from real rabbit fur and didn't close the closet door all the way one morning. After they sniffed them out, I was finding bits of bunny everywhere for days. I had to laugh about it because they were very proud of their kill. I didn't like the slippers anyway. A girlfriend who was kind of a stalker gave them to me."

Ming was looking at her like she'd grown a second head, while Tom and Bob were discreetly backing away.

"Like I said, good luck. I do hope you can place them all together since they're so bonded," Tom said before they both turned and fast-walked to the pen of Labrador-mix puppies.

Ming, hand on her hip, whirled on Perry. "If I didn't know better, I'd think you deliberately ran them off. They could have been a good option for one of the dogs, maybe even Molly."

"I didn't get a good vibe from them." That was a lie. They seemed like very nice people, but Perry was sure Bob had already zeroed in on JT. Everybody did. He was the cutest, the friendliest, and the youngest. But he was Tucker's only playmate and Molly's wingman. He also was the conductor of their three-dog choir. Taking him would be like removing one leg of a three-legged stool and expecting it to still stand.

"They were perfectly nice." Ming's expression softened. "Of course, the dogs are already living with their ideal owner."

"Don't even start with that." Perry didn't need to hear why the dogs should stay with her. They were wrecking her schedule.

Ming was not dissuaded. "Tucker bonded with you right away, and all three obviously listen to and recognize you as the alpha. I couldn't believe Molly let go of that chihuahua when you told her to leave it. And JT crawls into your lap every chance he gets."

"JT pees on my floor."

"You can order a pet door online that fits in your sliding-glass door with no major construction."

"No. No, no, no. I'll find them a home. Not just an option, but a really special home for all three of them." She couldn't keep them. She was too busy. They needed someone who had time to take them on walks and play with them. But she couldn't deny that she identified with their situation, left adrift without an alpha presence for security and guidance—just like she'd been as a child. She wanted, needed to make sure they landed in the right place.

"Okay." Ming's smug expression made it clear she wasn't buying Perry's story. Ming looked around at the crowd that was beginning to thin. "Are you ready to head back? I have a meeting with my lawyer at five thirty."

Disappointment instantly drained Perry's enthusiasm for the day. She could barely call their outing a date. Lunch had been rushed in their hurry to get to the park, and once they got here, Ming had spent most of the time with other rescuers. The only highlight was a chaste kiss that the dogs interrupted before it could go further.

"I thought maybe we'd go out for dinner. Or order in, if you prefer. Netflix premiered several new movies last night that look interesting."

Ming looked truly regretful as she clasped Perry's hand and squeezed it. "That sounds wonderful, but I really need to be at this meeting." They walked in silence for several blocks before Ming spoke again. "I have to work a few hours in the morning, but if my meeting goes well this evening, I'd like to show you something tomorrow afternoon. And perhaps we could have dinner together. The pups can come, too."

It would mean another wrecked schedule, but she'd make that sacrifice for a chance to kiss Ming again. Perry couldn't stop thinking about this woman and wanting to be near her, or just hear her voice. "Sure. That sounds good. I'll add you to my calendar."

That comment earned her a playful jab in the ribs. "Just make sure your calendar is free until Monday morning."

❖

"Wonder Woman has nothing on me." Imani's bragging was unnecessary as Ming scanned the second pile of paperwork her friend and attorney laid in front of her.

"Woman, you are preaching to the choir. I've always known you could move mountains, but this is miracle work, even by your high standards."

"Well, I can't take all the credit, but I have been smart enough to partner with and hire the very best people possible.

And I called in a few favors, especially to get your name change through in record time and under confidentiality rules. I might have laid it on a little thick about the internet crazies stalking you and you having to sell your home and practice because of them. I might have also insinuated that a couple of the nutcases might physically harm you."

Ming shuddered. "That's actually crossed my mind when I've walked out to my car at night."

Imani studied her. "I'm sort of puzzled about why you're moving out to a remote farm where it would make it even easier for some mental case to—" Imani imitated Ming's shudder. "I can't even think about it, much less put it into words."

"First of all, this incredible deal you negotiated for me will pay for major upgrades to the property I'm buying, one of which will be a top-of-the-line security system. Secondly, the people in that small town mind everybody else's business, so word spreads fast if a stranger is hanging around, and the residents never give out information to people they don't know. Instead of the clerk at the general store saying, 'Yeah, she lives just a mile down that road,' I'd get a phone call from the store owner to let me know someone was in town asking about me."

Imani laughed. "I hear you. I grew up in a town like that. If I misbehaved at school or anywhere else, my mama knew about it before I got home to confess." She edged forward in her chair and held Ming's gaze. "Seriously, Ming, have you really thought this through? You won't find much in the way of dating prospects out there in the wilderness. You're a young, attractive woman— too young to become a hermit."

"Actually, I have." Ming relaxed into the comfortable, high-backed conference-room chair. "I need peace and to feel…I don't know. My life has gotten a little out of control, so I'm making some changes to get a firm grip on the reins again. The best times of my life were the summers I would spend with my grandmother. She had a greenhouse and a huge garden, and would teach me how to grow all kinds of things. I want to feel that way again—my hands in the warm dirt, coaxing living plants from dry seeds to make medicines that will help people."

"I hope it's everything you want, not just a childhood memory you're trying to recapture."

Ming placed a reassuring hand on her friend's forearm. "Everything in my life seems to have led me to this moment, and that includes giving me the resources to do this. How quickly will my soon-to-be former colleagues' money be in my account?"

"Let's see. Their offer proposes three payments. The first payment, which would transfer upon signing the agreement, will cover the purchase of the property you want. If you agree to their proposal and sign the papers today, that could be as early as Monday. The second payment will come in sixty days, which will give them time to sell some of their real-estate portfolio to pay out your share. The final payment will be due to you in ninety days, basically allowing them time to reorganize and find someone to buy into the practice and take over your open slot."

"I think their offer is reasonable."

Imani nodded. "It is, or I wouldn't have brought it to you. But I could get more if you want. You guys probably paid more for the properties in the practice's portfolio than you should have because your guy is a limp dick when it comes to negotiating."

Ming had to laugh at Imani's crass reference. "Maybe you should tell them that after they sign under my signature on the agreement." She was already thinking ahead as she picked up the pen Imani had laid on the table and began to sign the papers every place Imani indicated. "When can we close on the property?"

Imani consulted the calendar on her iPad. "Today is Saturday. Since you're paying cash and foregoing an inspection of the house, then we only have to research the title, which should be easy since it's been in the same family for so many years. We could set something up for Wednesday, if the seller agrees."

Ming wanted to clap her hands in glee. She was so close to fulfilling her dream. "Excellent."

They both stood, and Ming gave her friend a firm hug. "Thank you. You have no idea how much this means to me."

"Seeing you happy will make it all worth my time."

CHAPTER NINE

*F*inding *Natural Balance* seems to be getting a lot of attention on an unrelated podcast, where they're talking about being more efficient to achieve more during your personal time. The host of that other podcast is a recognized expert in the field of business and industry efficiency. She's also single, without the responsibilities that come with dependents." Ming could no longer ignore comments made on *Timed for Success*, because the sniping had nearly doubled her own pageviews and subscriptions. "So, she seems to be struggling with the discussion that keeps circling back to managing shared personal time. The two biggest things that affect our personal time are spouses and dependents, which could be children, an aging or disabled family member, or even pets. Let's talk about spouses first.

"This struggle of shared personal time is wrapped up in so many other things—religion, tradition, gender roles, and our historically patriarchal society. The generation who raised our parents were well rooted in gender roles. The father was the primary breadwinner, while the mother tended the brood and homestead. But society really began to change during the Second World War, when women were asked to fill the jobs men left behind to go defend the free world.

"The war ended, the men returned home, and the women received a pat on the head and were sent back to their housewife duties. But some of them refused and stayed in the workplace, even though they were relegated to lower-paying jobs that most men didn't want. So, while the workplace was beginning its transformation, not much changed at home. Even when women worked outside the home, they were still expected to shoulder most household and child-rearing chores.

"More experienced in business supply and demand, their male counterparts helped by responding with innovation. They invented, produced, and marketed an array of time-saving devices to make a housewife's life easier—electric mixers, toaster ovens, Crock-Pots, vacuum cleaners, ice makers, better washing machines and dryers, and handheld hair dryers and curling irons.

"Now, what about children?" Ming might not be any more qualified than Perry to address this subject, but child-rearing seemed to dominate family schedules.

"Our parents also still adhered somewhat to their parents' 'children should be seen, not heard' philosophy. The parents didn't go to every one of their kids' after-school activities. Coaches, as well as art and music teachers, were responsible adults in charge of the children. Mom dropped the kid off, then ran errands until it was time to pick the kid up, making the most efficient use of her time. Children didn't meet with special coaches and teachers to improve their skills. Parents recognized that every kid wasn't going to play in the NBA or be a concert violinist, so the youngsters played outside with siblings or neighbor kids after school. Mom tended to work part-time, and Dad got off work at five o'clock every day. The neighbors came over, and you grilled out on Saturday afternoons.

"Today, both parents work full-time. Dad, and maybe Mom too, works late, and they call in a pizza or some other unhealthy fast food to be delivered. They pay someone else to chauffeur the kids to practices and lessons. They might even bring work home for after dinner. The kids don't care because they're entertaining themselves on their phones, electronic tablets, and laptops with games and social media. They need those devices, you argue, to keep up with schoolwork and technology and the pulse of the society they'll need to interact with as adults.

"But these things—high-speed internet, video games, phones, laptops, tablets—cost money. Kids break the devices, and new, updated versions come out every year. So, you work more overtime to pay for them and all the other security and time-saving innovations technology has provided. In the end, you have to ask yourself whether these purchases are helping or tipping the scales of your life even more heavily toward hundred percent work. In fact, the tentative reopening after the pandemic shutdown has a lot of people reevaluating their work situations. More than three percent of the American workforce quit their current jobs last month to begin a new job or search for one with improved working conditions, more pay, and better benefits.

"Let's hear your ideas about finding balance in your life."

The chat line was humming with responses, and the phone board had calls waiting as Ming's crew scrambled to screen them for the best responders.

❖

Perry and Julie stared at the long, blue feather tangled in JT's mustache.

"I'm afraid to look in the yard," Perry said. The mole was bad enough. She felt no regret over the unattractive creature that had been digging up her and Mrs. Mayberry's yards, but she didn't want to think about JT dispatching one of the songbirds her neighbor lured with feeders full of tasty seeds and colorful little houses nailed along her fence, where they raised their springtime broods. She enjoyed the birds, too.

"You should do it before Mrs. Mayberry spots the body when she's filling her feeders," Julie said.

Perry suspected the diminutive Mrs. Mayberry had purposely positioned her bird feeders on high posts so she needed a tall stepladder to refill them, which allowed her to look down into

Perry's yard. She was tempted to sunbathe nude just to rattle the nosy old lady. Her condo was on the end, so she didn't have a neighbor on the other side to spy on her from a second-story window, and Mrs. Mayberry's windows were positioned so she couldn't see Perry's small, square patio. "You go first. I'll get the poop-scooper from the garage to pick his victim up."

The dogs seemed puzzled over the search but joined in to sniff every corner and around every bush, obviously intent on finding whatever the alpha sought. Alas, their search produced only a second feather.

Julie examined it. "Blue jay or a bluebird. Maybe they ate it. Or maybe the bird just molted a few feathers in your yard, and JT sniffed one out."

JT sidled up to Julie at the sound of his name, and she took the feather from his mouth.

"It was just tangled in his beard and not really in his mouth," she said.

Perry was so relieved. She just couldn't imagine the sweet-tempered JT killing something. He had a goofy side, barking at the clouds when he heard thunder and jumping high in the air to try to catch bumblebees. Fortunately for him, his lunges were wildly off target, and the bees never seemed aware of his pursuit. "Okay. Everybody back inside." Molly had found something interesting and was intent on digging under one of the shrubs.

"I think she's losing her hearing," Julie said.

Perry snorted. "Her hearing is selective. Watch this." She spoke in a normal conversational tone. "Do you guys want a treat?"

Molly's scamper across the yard to be the first to the door belied her age.

Julie laughed. "That little stinker."

"Yep. The queen pretty much does what she wants, when she wants."

Treats were handed out, and Julie grabbed her laptop. "You want to work down here or up in your office?"

"I don't really want to work at all on a Sunday."

Julie put her hand on Perry's forehead. "You must be sick. You always want to work, and you blew off our normal run-then-work Saturday routine yesterday because of that dog-park thing." Her eyes went wide, and she slapped her hand over her mouth in a dramatic display for a few seconds. "Oh my God. I almost forgot to tell you."

"Tell me what?"

"I think your Ming might be the infamous Dr. Lee."

"What? Why would you think that?"

"What has your digging turned up on Dr. Lee's background?"

Perry was reluctant to admit her epic failure to fully research Dr. Lee's background. Perry's *Timed for Success* stats were increasing, but mainly because Dr. Lee's followers were now joining her podcast so they didn't miss the back-and-forth argument between efficiency and balance. She'd effectively lost control of her own podcast to the participants who had turned it into a forum for their own issues.

"I haven't had time to do much research on the mysterious Dr. Lee."

"What? This person who is targeting your podcast and the series on personal efficiency that you planned to use for your third book? Tracking down information on this person should be a priority. I know you like Ming, but have your ovaries short-circuited your brain?"

"No. It's just every time I start to look into it, the three terrors here pee on the floor or bring their latest kill into the house or have some other crisis that diverts my attention. But you didn't answer my question. Why do you think Ming is Dr. Lee? I don't even believe Dr. Lee is a woman. Only a man could be that arrogant."

"I found some message boards from her followers speculating that she's a doctor right here in Fresno, which makes sense because her podcast website says she's licensed in California."

"That's circumstantial."

"Do you know Ming's last name?"

"No. It hasn't come up."

"You slept with her, but you don't even know her last name?"

"I haven't slept with her."

Julie sat back, her face a classic display of shock. "You haven't slept with her yet?"

"Don't look so surprised."

Julie opened her laptop and began typing.

"What are you doing?"

"You might be avoiding it, but I'm going to find out everything this woman's been doing since she enrolled in kindergarten."

"For heaven's sake—" Perry's phone buzzed with a text.

Ming: Do you like sushi, and can you and the pups be ready in twenty minutes?

Perry: Yes! And yes. Where are we going?

Ming: It's a surprise. Jeans and a T-shirt. Might need a jacket for after dark. And pack an overnight bag for you and the dogs. I'll have you back early enough for work tomorrow.

"Okay," Julie said. "From that big grin on your face, I'm going to guess that was a text from a certain doctor you seem gaga over, and we're not going to be working this afternoon."

"Nope. We won't." Perry didn't try to hide her glee. "She's picking up me and the dogs in twenty minutes. AND, I've been told to pack an overnight bag." She jumped off the bar chair she'd been sitting on and performed a brief, hip-rotating dance while chanting, "She likes me, she likes me, she likes me."

Julie ignored her premature victory dance, peering at her laptop as she maneuvered her cursor and clicked several times. "Hey, look here. Does this look like Ming?"

Perry looked over Julie's shoulder at a college-yearbook website. The photo Julie pointed to was a young woman with Asian features, long, straight bangs that almost hid her eyes, and dark hair that hung forward to obscure the contours of her chubby face. It could have been Ming, about fifty pounds heavier. "No. That's not her."

"The caption says Ming D. Lee."

"Lee is like the most common Asian name ever. Anyway, what does it matter if it is her?"

Perry could see that Julie was making a decision as she stared at her.

"Are you familiar with *Podcast Prattle*?" Julie asked.

"That podcast that talks about other podcasts? Of course. Rayna Shine—is that a fake name or what?—is the host. Getting a mention on that woman's podcast is money in the bank."

"She wants to have you and Dr. Lee on her podcast. The fuss between your followers has caught her attention."

"Hell, yeah. Book it. Any time, any place."

"What if Ming is Dr. Lee? You wouldn't want to get blindsided."

"She's not."

"This student fits the timeline of the credentials listed on Dr. Lee's podcast website."

"I'll ask for her last name today, okay? But that's not her."

"Why don't you just ask if she's the host of *Finding Natural Balance*?"

"She knows my last name and what I do. If she was my evil rival, don't you think she would have said something by now?"

"Maybe, maybe not."

Perry stared at Julie. Why was she pushing this? "Are you jealous?"

"I'm just trying to save you from getting hurt. I've never seen you so enamored with anyone."

Julie was right, but she wasn't about to admit it. She'd completely lost focus at work because all she could think about was Ming. And, to be truthful with herself, she'd discouraged potential adopters for the dogs yesterday because, once the dogs were gone, her excuse to see Ming would disappear, too.

"I've posted the dogs' photos on a bunch of social-media

platforms. JT has received lots of pings. Tucker got a handful. Molly, not so much. Her age puts people off. As soon as you're ready, we can set up a day of meet-the-pets to decide who will get them."

"Nobody wants all three?"

"A few said they could maybe take two, meaning the two boys."

"Put the responders in a spreadsheet, and I'll look at them."

Julie closed her laptop. "Will do, Boss. I'm going to head out and work from my own home office."

"Take the day off. You deserve it."

"Thanks, but all this work will just be waiting for me Monday...on top of the usual hectic Monday workload." Julie gave her a brief hug. "You have fun."

CHAPTER TEN

It's not officially mine until my former partners add their signatures to the contract and transfer the first payment into my account so I can close on this property Wednesday, but all the pieces are lined up to fall into place." Ming watched the emotions battle across Perry's expressive face and wondered again if she was aware how much her features revealed.

"It's beautiful property, Ming. But I see a lot of work here."

"I see a lot of potential and, finally, a labor of love instead of just labor. Because that's what my life has become, Perry. I've been going to work every morning lately because I have patients scheduled, not because I look forward to seeing them."

They both turned as a dusty pickup came slowly down the drive toward them.

Perry spun around, scanning the yard. "Where are the dogs?" The words were barely out of her mouth when a chorus of barks and yaps drew their attention to three dogs speeding their way from the barn.

"Doing what that pack does best. They were hunting for vermin in the barn." Ming laughed when Perry put one hand over her chest and the back of her other hand against her forehead. "They're going to be my death if they keep killing things in front of me, but I wouldn't want them to get run over."

She waved at Ben as he stopped and grinned at her before climbing out of his truck. Molly and JT raced to him, but Tucker took up position halfway between Ben and Perry. Ben removed his Stetson and carefully let them sniff his hands, then scratched ears until everyone was satisfied that he was a friend. He finally stood and pulled up the gaiter around his neck to mask his mouth and nose.

"People are careful around here, so you'll want to put your mask on," she told Perry. They both had masks in their pockets because they were careful, too.

Ben approached slowly with one eye on Tucker, and Ming knew he was reading the same body language she was—Tucker was intent on protecting his alpha, and a nervous dog was like a scared young soldier with a quick trigger finger. "Call Tucker to you and slip his harness and leash on him until we're sure he won't go after Ben."

"Thanks," Ben said. "I've got a Jack myself. They can be fierce protection against strangers, and I'd like to leave here with my saggy butt in one piece." Ben stepped closer once Tucker was leashed, his smile showing in his eyes. "Come out for a last inspection before the closing on Wednesday, Dr. Davis?"

"Please, it's Ming." She shook his offered hand. "We'll be neighbors in a few more days. This is my friend, Perry Chandler. I'm so excited that everything is working out, I wanted to show her the property. I hope you don't mind."

"Not at all. I'm glad I caught you. I've got a few messages I can give you now instead of Wednesday." He shook Perry's hand, and they laughed as they both pulled hand sanitizer from their pockets. "I guess we could forgo the handshakes, but that just doesn't feel natural to me. I'd rather go ahead and shake, then sanitize."

"I'm with you," Perry said.

Ben took a plastic Ziploc bag from his pocket, opened it, and offered it to them. "Turkey jerky. Make it myself. If you don't want to try it, I won't be offended, but I'm thinking it might help me make friends with your guard dog here."

They each accepted a piece, and Ben took one himself before squatting and offering a small bit to Tucker, who refused until

Molly and JT both ate a piece and looked for more. He chewed and swallowed it, then edged closer for seconds. "Like that, did you?"

"Yeah. That's really good," Perry answered.

Ming and Ben laughed, but he gave her another piece before handing out seconds to the dogs. He stood after Tucker sniffed his hand, looking for a third piece, and licked it. They were friends now.

"Your limp is almost gone," Ming observed.

"Yeah. My back feels so much better. You're pretty good with those needles, Doc. And I'm happy that soon I won't have to drive to Fresno when I need a treatment."

"You won't have to drive to Fresno ever again if all goes right tomorrow. And there's no reason it shouldn't. They just have to put their signatures next to mine on their own offer." She wanted to hug him because she could feel the open-armed welcome of this community deep in her core. This place, these people felt so...right. "You said you have messages?"

"I do." Ben replaced his hat to shade his eyes from the sun. "My cousin, Ross Cutter, is a contractor. He says he can meet at your convenience to give you an estimate on renovations to the house and get a team right on them. I'm not saying this because he's my cousin, but he's in such demand he's been turning down projects." He gestured to the house. "He'd be honored to be the one to update the old family homestead, though, just so he'd know it was done right. He'll give you a good price, too."

"That would be amazing, Ben. Tell him I'd be willing to drive out tomorrow afternoon or anytime Tuesday or Wednesday after the morning closing. I saw my last patients Friday in Fresno, so getting this place up and running has my full attention now. I also need to talk to whoever has been maintaining the fields."

"That would be Collin Cutter."

"Another cousin?" Perry asked.

"Actually, my youngest brother. He's one of those college-educated farmers. He worked on this farm with Papa as a kid and gradually took over managing it when Papa got sick shortly after Collin finished his master's degree. He also manages two other small farms and leases some acreage that he uses for crop testing for the state agriculture department. So, he'll be okay if you two don't hit it off or you want to manage things here yourself."

"I'm sure I'll need his help, at least initially, and maybe permanently. I need to talk with him to see if he's interested in staying on board, given the changes I want to make, starting with putting up a series of greenhouses next to the old barn."

Ben laughed. "I mentioned that to him, and he's already got sketches and ideas he wants to share with you. Here's his business card with his cell number. He said to call him when you're ready to talk."

This was music to Ming's soul. "Fantastic. I look forward to speaking with him."

"Well, I'll let you ladies get on with your tour." He held out the keys to the house. "The key to the Gator, that's the utility four-wheeler in the barn, is hanging just inside the back door of the house. It'll be better for driving Perry around the farm than that fancy car of yours. You're welcome to stay the night if you want. Just leave the keys under the frog by the back door. Electricity comes primarily from the solar panels on top of the barn, and since nobody has been living out here for a month, the batteries should be fully charged." He tipped his hat, and Ming snagged the collars of JT and Molly to keep them from following as he turned his truck around and drove away.

"He seems nice," Perry said, releasing Tucker from his harness after Ming let go of the other two dogs.

"He really is. It seems a little sinister that most of the people in the town are related, but they are the nicest people I've met, and very diverse. They are accepting of same-sex couples and mixed-race couples. Many of the adults and almost all the children are bilingual. The town actually has a civil- and social-rights board, where people can bring complaints if they feel they've been subjected to racism or any type of discrimination."

"Wow. I can't believe some *New York Times* reporter hasn't found this town and written a story on it."

Ming could feel Perry close behind as they walked across the terrace to the back door. "The people in this community wouldn't talk to a reporter. They're very private." She'd barely put the key in the lock when she was spun around and pressed against the door. Perry's tall body was hot against hers, her breath a caress against her cheek.

"That's good, because I've been craving some private time with you, Dr. Davis."

Her new name sounded strange, yet comfortable spoken by Perry, and Ming wondered briefly if Perry was mocking...no, teasing her. She had to have figured out that Ming was Dr. Lee. But she couldn't dwell on that subject now, not with Perry's lips brushing, tasting, then capturing hers. Not with Perry's tongue, thick and hot, pushing into her mouth and sending tingling jolts of arousal to every sensitive part of her. Perry disengaged, and they gazed at each other with hooded eyes and heaving chests.

"That should hold me until after our tour and dinner," Perry said.

Ming closed her eyes and groaned, barely resisting the urge to grab her own crotch to calm the throb of her sex. Actually, she'd rather grab Perry's and drag her inside. Hopefully there was still a bed there. The anticipation, however, was delicious, so she would hold out a few hours longer to savor it. "You'll definitely pay for that later," she said, touching her lips one last time to Perry's.

❖

Only sex could be better than this. Sitting in the Gator, Perry closed her eyes and imagined the sun-warmed breeze caressing her face was, instead, the soft fingertips of a lover trailing along her cheeks and lips. Without opening her eyes, she could feel the breeze cool slightly as they crept closer to the small lake.

The scent of honeysuckle was heavy in the air, and she sucked in a lazy breath, envisioning how it might feel to stroke her hand down the satin skin of Ming's bare back—until the cannonball named Molly stepped firmly on her aching crotch and she nearly fell out of the vehicle.

"Ow, ow, ow."

Their transport was like a gasoline-powered golf cart with a small truck bed where the back seat should be. The two boys rode in the bed of the vehicle, with the picnic basket and a thick quilt. After a few false starts where Tucker, then JT was intent on leaping out once the vehicle began moving, harnesses were again deployed and leashes anchored short to a tie-off in the center so they couldn't jump out or into the front seat, where Molly sat in Perry's lap. The boys finally relaxed on the blanket and turned their noses to the breeze to sniff the tantalizing scents of forest and wildlife as Ming drove very slowly, which was a good thing because Perry's near-tumble could have ended her hopes for tonight—a fate more painful than any injury.

She was injured enough without falling out because Ming was laughing as Perry clutched her throbbing—but not in a good way now—lady parts while holding Molly partially aloft so she wouldn't step down again. Molly licked her face, but her gaze held no apology.

"I'm sorry. I don't mean to laugh." Ming half covered her mouth with her hand. "It's just your expression was so serene one minute, and so horrified the next."

"I might be really injured. I think she put all of her thirty pounds on that one foot." Perry preferred to think her voice was tight with pain, not just whiny.

Ming parked in a clearing next to the small lake. "You're in luck, because I'm a doctor." She trailed the fingertips Perry had been daydreaming of earlier along her cheek. They were as soft as she'd imagined. "I promise to give you a full exam later and kiss it better if needed."

Perry groaned. "We could spread the blanket out on the

ground over there, and you could check now. It feels all wet down there. I could be bleeding." All is fair in war and flirtation.

"Nice try. You can spread the blanket over there, but you'll have to wait to spread yourself or me," Ming said. "I slaved over multiple online menus to put this lunch together, and I'm starved. It's almost two o'clock." Her finger burned a hot trail along Perry's cheek, down her neck, and into the deep V-collar of her T-shirt.

Perry swallowed hard. She was normally a top, but this woman was dominating her at every turn. And it felt fantastic. Ming was freeing the boys from their harnesses, so Perry took a deep breath, squeezed her thighs together to calm her libido, then set Molly on the ground and grabbed the blanket. The quicker they ate lunch, the sooner they'd get to tour the house where they would hopefully find a bed, or a table, or…hell, even a floor would do. She just needed to be skin to skin with Ming, to inhale her, absorb her. She made Perry ravenous in a way she'd never hungered before.

She bent to put her mouth next to Ming's ear. "Then let's eat. I'm anxious to sink my teeth into dessert." She nipped Ming's earlobe, then her neck, before bathing her tongue over the pink mark she'd made. She was rewarded with a discernable shiver and a slight hitch in Ming's breath.

Ming closed her eyes for only a second but pushed Perry back. "The blanket?"

Perry inclined her head, along with a very slight bow. "Your wish is my command."

"I'll keep that in mind," Ming said.

❖

Ming shoved their entire picnic basket into the farmhouse's empty, but running, refrigerator, then pinned Perry against the kitchen cabinet. She'd been patient throughout the hour-long lunch, where they fed each other sushi and cubes of juicy melon, talked about how Ming had turned her co-op partners' mutiny around to her benefit, and, much to Tucker's dismay, had a splashing contest in the spring-fed lake with water so clear you could see the sandy bottom. But she could wait no longer.

She captured Perry in a hot melding of lips and tongues, then kissed her way along Perry's angular jaw and down her tasty neck until interfering cloth thwarted her. She peeled the still half-soaked T-shirt from Perry's lean, sculpted body and accepted Perry's hummed moans as permission to peel off the underlying sports bra. Her breasts were small and high, with dark-pink nipples and no tan lines. *Mental note: Perry sunbathes topless.*

"You, too." Perry's words were hoarse, her tone urgent. "I want your skin against mine."

As Ming yanked her own damp T-shirt over her head, her skin pebbled at the touch of Perry's cold hands searching for, then finding, the clasp on her lace bra. When the bra joined the other clothing on the floor, she pressed her chilled skin against Perry's warm body. Because of their difference in height, her nipples rubbed against Perry's ribs, so she curled her shoulders forward to tease Perry's breasts while she drew her into another deep kiss. Perry tasted of sweet ginger, salty soy, and hot wasabi. Pleased that Perry sounded as breathless as she felt when she withdrew from their kiss, Ming clamped her teeth gently onto her earlobe for a few seconds before releasing it.

"Bedroom," she whispered as she took Perry's hand and tugged her through the living room.

❖

Perry was stunned, uncertain, delighted, and powerfully aroused by Ming's commanding advance. The bedroom appeared recently cleaned, with a colorful quilt covering the four-poster bed. In a martial-arts-style move, Ming tugged Perry's hand to spin her around and trip her with a well-placed leg behind Perry's knee so that she flopped faceup onto the bed. Perry did not resist when Ming yanked her shorts and briefs down her legs and dropped them on the floor, then stepped back and dropped her own shorts to step out of them. She stood there for a minute, allowing Perry a good, long look.

Ming's skin was flawless—smooth and unblemished by scars or birthmarks. Perry widened her legs as Ming crawled onto the bed between them and drew her knees up as she settled her sex against Perry's. They were both wet when Ming rubbed against her, then captured her breast in her mouth. Perry arched upward when Ming's tongue flicked against her hardening left nipple, then bit hard before abandoning it to the cold air. But only a second passed before her right nipple received the same treatment, accompanied by another hard rub.

"God, Ming. Please."

Ming abandoned Perry's breasts to hook her arms behind Perry's knees to curl her long torso up. Perry started to protest, but the only sounds out of her open mouth were moans as Ming's hot tongue teased her sex, lingering to massage her clit, then backtracking to plunge into her. Stars! How could that small mouth contain such a tongue? Perry squirmed as a tingling sensation traveled from her breasts to her toes. Ming rose again to spread their folds and rub their slick, hot sexes together. She held Perry in a curled position and pumped against her as she kissed her neck, then captured her mouth in an aggressive kiss. Perry moaned at the taste of herself on Ming's tongue, then moved with her, grinding against Ming as her climax began to coalesce low in her belly.

"Let it go," Ming demanded. "Let it go now."

And she did. She gasped as she bowed taut when the orgasm gripped her and every muscle in her twanged with sharp pleasure. She let out a long exhale as her orgasm began to recede, but Ming, eyes closed in concentration as she ground against Perry's sensitive clit, was yet to reach her own pinnacle. Perry tightened her legs around Ming's hips and rolled both of them.

Frustration, surprise, then hot, melting desire flashed in

Ming's eyes when Perry reversed their roles, showering kisses, teasing nipples, and tonguing deep into her sensitive navel before shouldering Ming's legs. She sucked her clit, scraping the bundle of nerves with her teeth as it swelled to rock-hardness under her tongue. So deliciously salty-sweet. She plunged two fingers inside her wet, slick warmth just as the spasms began, thrusting hard and sucking forcefully. Thrusting and sucking. Thrusting and sucking. Ming rose off the bed, a primal scream bursting from her throat and blasting toward the ceiling. Perry consumed all she gave her, then crawled up to guide Ming's hand inside herself and pumped her way to a second orgasm against Ming's thigh.

Sweat-soaked and sated, Perry flopped onto her back and felt for Ming's hand. They entwined fingers while they waited for their pounding hearts to calm so they could draw more than a pant of air.

At last, Ming let out a long, satisfied sigh. "Wow."

"Yeah. Wow," Perry echoed.

Ming disengaged her hand and rolled away from Perry to the edge of the king-size bed as something scratched the floor nearby. She looked back over her shoulder when Perry gasped. "What is it?"

"My God, Ming." Perry had caught a glimpse before, but this was her first real look at the tattoo covering nearly every inch of Ming's back. She'd never seen anything so beautiful. She traced her finger up the trunk of the cherry tree that appeared to grow along Ming's spine, then outlined the branches laden with pink blossoms that spread outward across her slender shoulders. Some of the blossoms drifted down onto a strange dragon with huge butterfly wings and gold scales that nearly glittered. Tail curled protectively around the tree's trunk, the dragon clutched a yin-yang globe in its claws. Only a master artist could have created this work of genius, and only someone with immense patience could have borne such long hours under the tattoo needle. Perry was torn between reverence for the artistry of the work and wanting to cry for the harm done to the satin-smooth skin of this woman to whom she'd just made love. "This is...it's incredible...amazing. How long did it take to finish?"

"Two years. My grandfather was the designer and tattoo artist. I could explain the images to you if you don't care about sleeping any tonight, but honestly—" Ming yawned. She squirmed around until she was nestled in the soft bedding. "You've exhausted me, and Molly is trying to make a nest out of our clothes we dropped on the floor. You need to bring their beds in."

Perry was exhausted, too, so she grabbed a furry throw from a wingback chair in the corner and spread it across the other side of the bed, then lifted Molly onto it. The boys hopped onto the bed, and Tucker promptly claimed a spot next to the pillow, while JT took several minutes to arrange his portion of the throw to his satisfaction before flopping down to sleep. Perry slid under the covers on the opposite side, planting a few kisses on the cherry blossoms inked across Ming's sexy shoulders and then settling on her side as a barrier to keep the dogs from disturbing Ming.

CHAPTER ELEVEN

Ming was not Dr. Lee. She was Dr. Ming Davis. So why did every mention of Dr. Lee send Perry's thoughts directly to Ming?

Perry had awoken earlier to Ming spooned in her arms, a contented cuddle that stirred a longing she'd buried deep many years ago. Then shower sex that was a hot, panting flurry of mouths, hands, fingers, and teeth fed rather than quenched that yearning, and the memory was making it difficult to concentrate on her podcast.

Julie: You need to cut that guy off, or he's going to rattle on all day. You've got a new caller on line two.

Perry: Okay. Sorry. Having trouble focusing today.

Julie: You need to shake off that sex-on-the-brain fog. Five minutes to go, and then you can lose yourself in wet dreams until eleven, when you have an international call with the Baldoura Corporation.

She ignored Julie's snipe and waited for her current caller to take a breath. "I hear you, Ray. To get a better-paying job, you might need some specific training. Contact your local community college. They should be able to tell you what jobs are in demand in your area and what training you need to qualify. Industries will often work with the local colleges to set up abbreviated programs to train workers for their specific needs.

"Now let's hear from the caller on line two." She cut off the first caller and clicked on the virtual button for line two. "Hi. You're live on *Timed for Success*. What do you have to add to our discussion?"

"Hi, Dr. Chandler. This is Rayna Shine from the vlog *Podcast Prattle*. How the recent pandemic has changed the workforce's priorities is a hot topic across a wide spectrum of media, but topping the chatter stream is the podcast battle between *Finding Natural Balance* and *Timed for Success*. I'd like to invite you and Dr. Lee to debate the subject face-to-face on my vlog. My legal people would get with your attorneys and Dr. Lee's to work out the details."

As she'd told Julie before, she was already on board but wanted to drag this conversation out a bit to tease her listeners. "Well, Rayna, that's an interesting proposal. To be honest, I hadn't heard of Dr. Lee until that podcast's followers infiltrated my podcast and have been trying to dominate my subscribers' conversation on how to use our time more efficiently. Dr. Lee's podcast website is pretty skimpy on information. It lists a lot of degrees and accomplishments but doesn't even give the host's full name so you can cross-check whether that information is accurate."

"So, you think Dr. Lee is an impostor? A poser selling snake oil to the public?" Rayna asked.

"I'm simply reminding everyone that because of all the bad information and conspiracy theories out there, you should be suspicious if you can't confirm the source is qualified to be commenting on the subject." Perry hadn't intended the conversation to veer in this direction, but she couldn't resist airing this pet peeve. It constantly amazed her how gullible the public could be, especially how often people even refused to accept the truth when presented it.

"That's an excellent point," Rayna said. "I'd love for you to repeat that concern on my vlog."

Julie was signaling that time was up, so Perry let her know to start the closing music.

"That's all the time we have today, folks. Rayna, please stay on the line so my assistant can trade information with you. This is Dr. Perry Chandler of *Timed for Success*, looking forward to this time on Friday, when we'll chat more about being efficient in your personal life."

She tossed her headset onto the desk, sat back in her chair, and closed her eyes. She was instantly back at the farm with Ming's lithe body curled against hers. She wanted to feel their hearts beat in sync again, trace the delicate cherry blossoms adorning Ming's delicious shoulders, and rub her aching clit against Ming's firm ass. God. She was turning into a puddle.

Her computer pinged repeatedly with a string of insistent messages.

Julie: What are you thinking?

Julie: Answer

Julie: Me

Julie: If you're masturbating, STOP.

Julie: STOP RIGHT NOW.

Julie: I'm going to call

Julie: and you better pick up.

Perry shook her head but answered on the first ring. "No. I'm not masturbating, you idiot. Do you have sex on your brain? Do you need to get laid more often?"

"No. But you need to shut down the teenage boy that's taken over your brain. What are you thinking? Are you still going to do that vlog? I'm telling you that Ming is Dr. Lee, so you'd better get in all the sex you can before she finds out that you're the Dr. Chandler whose followers are invading her podcast."

The anger rising from Perry's gut and heating her ears was unreasonable, but she was tired of Julie's apparent jealousy. "First of all, she is Dr. Ming Davis. Second, my photo is all over my website and my book covers, so if she were Dr. Lee, I'm sure she would have looked me up and already know *Timed for Success* is my podcast. Third, if she is Dr. Lee and knows who I am, she wouldn't be dating me."

An uncomfortable silence loomed before Julie spoke again. Her voice was soft but unapologetic. "I think you're wrong but hope you're right. I just don't want you to get hurt."

Perry relented. She did realize Julie was only trying to protect her. "I know. I'm sorry. But I'm a big girl, so it's on me if I get hurt. Okay? You've done your best to warn me."

❖

The terrors scrambled out of Perry's office and down the stairs when the doorbell chimed and SHA announced someone was at her front door. Perry groaned. She had so much work to catch up on since she'd basically blown her weekend schedule to spend time with Ming. She was tempted to ignore the summons. She didn't need religion or a security system or cookies. Wait. Cookies might not be a bad idea.

"Hola," Ming said when Perry opened the door. She held up a grocery bag. "Authentic Spanish paella and salad. Had dinner yet?"

Molly barked joyfully, while Tucker and JT raised their noses to sniff at the dinner offering. Perry grinned and wrapped one arm around Ming's shoulders to draw her into a kiss. Way better than cookies.

"My neighbor is going to think you're one of those food-delivery services."

"Driving a Mercedes?"

Perry shrugged. "Those businesses saw profits soar during the pandemic."

Molly's barking stopped, and she scampered down the steps and across the yard before her escape registered and they sprinted after her, Tucker and JT on their heels. Fortunately, Molly's target was Mrs. Mayberry, who was watering her flowers next door. Tucker hung back while Molly and JT greeted her enthusiastically.

"Hello, you little darlings. How are you today?" Mrs. Mayberry crooned as she bent to pet each on the head.

Perry picked up Molly, and Ming snagged JT. They never needed to corral Tucker because he was always at Perry's heels.

"I'm sorry, Mrs. Mayberry. They slipped past me when I opened the door for Ming."

"Oh, it's no problem."

"I'm just fostering them until they can be rehomed. Their owner, one of my mother's colleagues, died unexpectedly."

"Oh, I'm so sorry." Mrs. Mayberry's sympathy was directed at Molly, who licked her hand when Mrs. Mayberry gave her head another pat.

"I hope they haven't been bothering you too much with their barking."

"Oh, on the contrary, dear." She turned to Ming and touched JT's name tag. "I cheered when this brave fellow grabbed the tail feathers of that irritating blue jay that's been dive-bombing the chipmunks I feed in my backyard. It's amazing how high he can jump—JT, not the pesky jay. That nuisance bird hasn't been back, and I've got this handsome boy to thank."

"He is up for adoption," Ming said. "He's the sweetest cuddler of the three."

Perry froze, a vision of dead chipmunks lined up on Mrs. Mayberry's patio filling her head. "Uh, that might not be a good idea. He'd probably chase away the other birds that Mrs. Mayberry feeds. I'm sure he doesn't know the difference between a cardinal and a blue jay. Dogs see only in black and white, don't they? I think I read that." She was babbling, but she had to stop this idea before Mrs. Mayberry bought into it.

"I suppose you're right. Anyway, my daughter and her husband just bought a big house with a guest cottage out back, and they've been after me to move. I'm finally considering it because I don't get to see my grandchildren enough. I don't think they figured a dog into the picture."

The tightening in Perry's chest eased. She'd been afraid she'd have to confess the mole murder if Mrs. Mayberry had seriously considered adopting one of the dogs. And her neighbor was sharp enough to instantly translate mole-killer to chipmunk-hunter.

"I'm sure you'd make a great pet mom," Ming said. "But Perry's right. I'm afraid your bird friends wouldn't be safe from the dogs' natural instinct to hunt."

Ming was impressed that the dogs obediently followed Perry inside after they said good-bye to Mrs. Mayberry. Did Perry realize the bond she'd established with the little pack? Once it was clear they weren't being invited to share the food Ming brought, Molly and JT gnawed on their chew bones. Tucker lay on a nearby rug, clearly so he could watch Perry's every move before nodding off for a dog nap.

Perry set out plates and opened a bottle of wine, while Ming warmed the food. As they worked, they laughed about Perry finding JT with the feather stuck in his beard and calling Julie to help her search for a bird body before Mrs. Mayberry found out, only to discover today that she'd witnessed the entire event and approved of JT's well-timed leap that scared the pest away for good. The easiness of their conversation and the domestic feel of dining together in Perry's kitchen felt very much like the many happy evenings she'd spent with her grandmother. She loved her parents, but their expectations for her and her need to please them was a constant undercurrent in the time they spent together.

Actually, an undercurrent of expectation bounced around in this room. Sex. Later. Dinner was the appetizer. That was why Ming was there instead of accepting Imani's offer for dinner to celebrate Ming's success today.

Still, more than sexual tension engulfed them. Shy glances of something peppered their comfortable conversation. They certainly had no trouble being sexually suggestive, even occasionally aggressive with their flirty looks and comments. But this seemed different. Could these glances be...affection, perhaps?

"So, how was your day?" Ming abandoned her deep thoughts before Perry noticed she'd gone quiet.

"Busy." Perry held her gaze and raised a suggestive eyebrow. "I was having trouble concentrating."

Ming swayed toward Perry. "Really? I had you figured for someone who could shut everything else out when it was time to focus on work."

"Normally, I can. But I kept straying off course every time I thought of this." Perry closed the distance between them. Her lips were soft as they caressed Ming's, and her mouth tasted of the spicy paella with a hint of the salad's raspberry vinaigrette. Ming held her gaze when Perry withdrew. She was a split second away from demanding they abandon dinner for the bedroom when Perry's question derailed her.

"Tell me about your day."

Ming mentally stutter-stepped as she switched direction from lascivious to victorious. Her predator side, the tiger, licked its huge white teeth.

"The signatures of my former partners in our cooperative made me a multi-millionaire today. I mean, I was already worth several million on paper, but this deal handed me over ten million dollars in liquid assets. They had to sell off some of the portfolio properties and let two new doctors buy into the practice just to pay me off." She suspected Perry's bank account matched or exceeded her own, so she would understand Ming was bragging about turning the tables on her traitorous coworkers, not her wealth.

Perry sat back in her chair. "Wow. That's incredible." She poured more wine and held her glass up. "Here's to one smart

businesswoman's victory and her many successes still to come."
Perry sat forward again, eyes gleaming. "So, how'd that one
bastard look with crow feathers stuck in his teeth?"

Ming couldn't stop her giddy laugh. This woman got her.
They were so in sync. It was a silly mental thing she'd done
since childhood, but she imagined Perry as a wolf. Her gleaming
eyes were golden, and her tongue was lolling over sharp canines,
eager to share a taste of Ming's kill.

"His face was so red, I thought he might blow a major artery
when Imani asked them to show identification to her notary
before each of them signed the contract. Then he turned green
when the office manager came in and whispered a little too loud
that someone from the IRS was there to see him."

"No. You're kidding." Perry laughed. "What great timing."

"I'm pretty sure he's the one who started this whole business
to kick me out. He didn't know I was already restless and ready
to leave." Ming thought back to that morning when they had
blindsided her with the news they wanted her gone. "I'm still
stung about how they planned this attack behind my back. I
thought those people were my friends. I guess some of them still
are. But I might not have let Imani clean them out so badly if they
hadn't tried to take advantage of me first."

Ming drank the last of the wine in her glass while Perry
dumped the scraps of their dinner into the trash and dropped
the plates into the sink. She barely had time to set her wineglass
down before Perry stepped behind her and circled her arms
around Ming's waist, feathering kisses down her neck.

"Actually, I'm hoping to take advantage of you, too." Perry
nipped her earlobe, then held it gently in her teeth, pressing on
nerves that sent tingles down her neck to her breasts. "But I'll be
happy to let you make me pay for it. Instead of draining my bank
account, you can indenture me as your sex slave."

Ming twirled in her arms and bit down hard at the base of
Perry's neck. She was the tiger, and talking about her financial
victory fed her hunger for this prey. "You'd better rethink the

order of that plan." She dug her nails into Perry's scalp, then pushed her away. "Upstairs. Now."

Their first coupling was fast and rough, fueled by flaming passion, and then, after a short respite to catch their breath, they made slow, sensual love. When the sweat of their exertions had dried and their hearts slowed, Perry tugged the blanket up to cover them. Ming settled her head on Perry's shoulder and snuggled against her long, sexy body, listening as her heartbeat and breathing slowed into slumber. Sex with Perry was beyond incredible, but the constant desire to be with Perry worried her. Was this more than just fun?

Had she found the yin to her yang, or yang to her yin? This possibility scared her in light of all the other changes currently in her life. Deep down inside, she was worried that Perry had never mentioned their dueling podcasts after the one time she'd alluded to them at the adoption event and something had interrupted Perry's reaction.

"Maybe you need them to show you how to find a better balance between work and your personal life."

"Now you sound like that crazy Dr. Lee podcast."

Had Perry been teasing with the crazy comment? It was great if she could compartmentalize work so that it didn't taint their personal relationship. Ming had read that some political couples did that. But what else could Perry be capable of sealing off from their relationship? Another lover? A secret, kinky sex life? An illegal enterprise? She couldn't shake the feeling that she was hurtling down a freeway with no brakes.

CHAPTER TWELVE

Who knew an arthritic thirteen-year-old Lhasa-apso mix built like a waddling cannonball could turn into a guided missile when she spotted a cat? Or that the cat would be a personal friend of the goofy but protective half-grown, sixty-pound Labradoodle racing across the dog park to intersect Molly's strike path?

The morning started out bright and sunny enough. Well, from Perry's point of view, waking up with Ming in her arms made everything sunny and bright. She was riding so high on pheromones that she cut her morning team meeting short and decided to take her trio of terrors to the dog park. She should be searching for more information on Dr. Lee and preparing for the upcoming vlog her people had worked out with Rayna Shine's people, but she didn't care. She just wanted to wallow in this euphoria Ming brought into her life.

She was checking to make sure she had an adequate supply of poop bags when Tucker whined, then sounded the alarm in his sharp, incessant, Timmy-fell-down-the-well—or more precisely, Molly-sees-a-cat—bark.

Molly shot forward, yanking Perry off balance and causing her to drop all three leashes. She silently congratulated herself for not falling flat on her face when the leashes were torn from her grip and yelled at Molly to stop. Molly, however, was an activated nuclear weapon with no code to disarm.

A dog-park melee of shouting, arm-waving, barking, and pet retrieval ensued.

A woman was screaming at Puddles, the pursued cat, to run when the half-grown Labradoodle she was leading homed in on Molly and yanked the woman off her feet to intercept.

As Molly's self-appointed bodyguard, JT took note of the Labradoodle's intent and revealed that the twenty percent of his mixed DNA that wasn't cocky schnauzer was apparently Chicken Little. He turned tail, ran back to circle around Perry's legs, and begged to be picked up out of danger.

Surprisingly, nervous, paw-wringing Tucker drew on his Jack Russell terrier super-hero genes and rose to the occasion. He circled behind the unsuspecting Labradoodle and latched on to his left hindquarter just as the larger dog bowled Molly over, diverting her long enough for the cat to escape to the safety of a nearby tree.

The cat, when finally retrieved from her perch, was indignant. The goofy Labradoodle joyfully licked the hands and faces of everyone who came by to exclaim over his heroism. The owner of both animals was aghast at a single, small puncture mark on her dog's leg.

Meanwhile, Tucker stood bravely by his packmate and gave the dumb 'doodle pup the stink eye in case he got any ideas about coming after Molly again. Molly the Missile had run out of fuel and forgotten all about the cat, focusing instead on a good roll in the sun-warmed grass. JT, now that the threat level had been downgraded to DEFCON 5, strutted over in his big-dog stance to take up sentry with Tucker.

After many apologies and a promise to pay any veterinary expenses, including therapy for the traumatized cat, Perry took her pack home. It was almost time for their afternoon nap.

❖

"I'm the one who needs therapy after that catastrophe. Was that woman neurotic, or do they really have therapists for pets?"

Ming laughed, and Perry loved the sound. She wished it wasn't coming through a video call. Ming had spent the day arranging for her move to the farm and had dinner plans with her lawyer to tidy up last-minute legal stuff for the closing tomorrow morning.

"They actually do have pet therapists."

"So, they sit on those little couches you see advertised as dog beds and whine complaints about their owners?"

Ming shook her head, still chuckling. "The therapists are part vet, trainer, and animal naturopath. They listen to the owner, observe the animal's behavior, then maybe coach the owner on how to deal with unwanted behavior—theirs and their pet's. They also might utilize medicine, massage, or alternative practices like acupuncture to improve the animal's situation," Ming said. "Animals can be hyperactive or suffer from neuroses just like people. Sometimes, they're simply reflecting their owners' problems. But some animals have suffered severe trauma that can't be healed by a warm bed, daily feedings, and a kind caregiver."

Perry could understand. Even her growing feelings for Ming weren't healing her pain of having disengaged parents raise her. She'd been like a puppy left alone in the yard with a water bowl and a bag of food. "Okay. I understand. But being treed by Molly, who didn't come anywhere close to catching her, couldn't have been very traumatizing for the cat."

"Maybe a dog had grabbed and injured her before, so, as harmless as today's incident was, it could have brought up her past trauma."

"You're saying she could have kitty PTSD?" Perry kept her tone light and teasing, but she made a mental note to call the contact information the woman gave her and ask if her pets were okay or needed further treatment. Wait. When did she become an animal lover?

"You're incorrigible."

"I'm just kidding. I'm going to check in with their owner."

The affection in Ming's smile warmed Perry.

"I'm going to miss my bed warmer tonight," Ming said.

"Your bed warmer is going to miss you, too."

"Then tell sweet Molly I will be back for more cuddles." Ming dramatically slapped a hand over her mouth. "Wait, you thought I meant you?"

"Yeah, yeah." Perry smiled and shook her head at Ming's teasing before she grew serious again. "Will I see you tomorrow? Can I take you out to celebrate the closing or cook dinner for you here?"

"Hmm. Dinner at your place sounds perfect."

"Good. I can't wait to hear more about your plans for the farm." She paused. "Ming?"

"Yes?"

She wanted to say more, but it was too soon, and she was too scared. "Pack an overnight bag."

"I was hoping you'd say that."

They stared at each other over the video link, both awkwardly searching for how to end the call. Finally, Ming touched her lips, then the screen. "Sweet dreams, Perry."

A flirty reply about sexy dreams tripped over her tongue, but her mouth formed different words. "Always when they're about you." She mirrored Ming's virtual kiss. "Until tomorrow."

❖

The sun crested the mountain and outlined Dr. Lee's slim figure in a starburst of light as she completed a series of excruciatingly slow tai chi moves before extending her arms skyward to welcome the new day. She rotated so the warm sunlight illuminated her face, then smiled up at her second camera and greeted her audience.

"Good morning. Celebrate with me the awakening of this

day, because each one brings fresh strength, new possibilities, and the opportunity for deeper understanding." Ming closed her eyes, face still upturned toward the sun as she sank into a lotus position. "We must begin by opening ourselves to unclutter our minds and find our balance."

And cut.

Ming marked the end of the video, satisfied with the edit of the intro for what might be the new video log to complement her podcast, which had been gaining subscribers hourly since the debate began between her podcast and Perry's. The scene had been shot in Sedona several months before her life turned upside down at her practice and in her personal affairs. Now, she wasn't sure she wanted a vlog. It would mean being recognizable to the general public after she'd scrubbed her website of all photos so her subscribers couldn't find her. She was looking forward to the privacy of the farm, and sticking with only a podcast would ensure that reality. And did she really need the podcast any longer? She was certainly wealthy enough to live off her investments for the rest of her life. On the other hand, the podcast could be a valuable tool in launching her business farming medicinal plants for naturopathic medicine.

She glanced at her watch. Podcast. Right. She scrambled to acknowledge the chat message from her production assistant, Carl, advising that she had fifteen minutes until airtime. Water, bathroom, notes. She smiled to herself. She would have plenty of time if she could stop daydreaming about last night's dinner and lovemaking with Perry. She didn't have words for the depth of their connection because she'd never experienced anything like it before. She wanted to close her eyes, hit rewind, and experience every second—from the passionate kiss at the front door until the ten-minute good-bye make-out session before SHA alerted Perry of an incoming international call early that morning.

Not a fancy Smart Home Assistant, but a simple ping from Carl's incoming chat let her know she had one minute for a quick sound check, so she donned her headphones and finished running through the checks just seconds before the opening music and intro began.

"Good morning. Today, I want to talk about changes. Life circumstances are never constant. A new pet, child, or love interest may be added to your household. You could lose a friend or family member through death or estrangement. Coworkers leave and new ones are added. Your health, finances can improve or decline. So, maintaining your natural balance will always require adjustments. Some will be small, but others could be huge.

"Why are we talking about change now? Because the so-called Great Resignation—workers quitting their jobs in search of better ones—is still happening a year after medical breakthroughs reduced the coronavirus threat to a manageable level. Federal supplements to state unemployment gave the working poor a glimpse of what it was like to be able to feed and clothe their children without having three jobs. When the pandemic restrictions lifted, those workers refused to go back to their old jobs with low pay and no benefits. Other workers balked at returning to long daily commutes. Basically, American workers said 'no more' to companies making large profits while refusing to pay a living wage or provide benefits like paid vacation and sick days, health insurance, holidays, and retirement plans. Salaried employees are tired of working sixty- and eighty-hour weeks so the boss can get a bonus for making or exceeding production goals.

"So, today, I want to hear about changes you've made to find or keep your natural balance. Also, we'll talk about what questions you should ask if you're considering a big change in the near future."

Carl signaled a caller on line one.

"Hello. This is Dr. Lee. What did you want to share about change in your life?"

"Hi, Dr. Lee. I am Sonya from Miami. I was working two part-time hotel-housekeeping jobs during the day and waitressing at night, seven days a week. I never had a day off, and none of the three jobs offered benefits. When my mother died before the pandemic, I wasn't paid for the three days I was off to travel and attend the wake and funeral. And when the pandemic closed everything down, I lost all three jobs. My kids and I would have starved without the churches and charities that offered groceries and gas money during the months it took to get my unemployment application through the crappy state government. So, when my benefits came through, I took classes online so I could get better employment. I don't mind hard work, but I deserve a decent paycheck and health insurance for my children."

"I agree with you, Sonya. According to reports, a lot of people aren't going back to their old jobs because they also decided to use their months of unemployment to train for something better. Let's see what our next caller has to add."

Ming's subscribers had a lot to say about making changes, so she let the podcast run ten minutes over the normal hour before she signaled Carl to start the closing music.

Carl: One more caller. You're going to want to talk to this one.

Ming: Put it through, but this is absolutely the last.

"Hi, Dr. Lee. I'm Rayna Shine from *Podcast Prattle*, and I've been monitoring the apparent rivalry that has fueled the meteoric rise of your podcast and Dr. Perry Chandler's *Timed for Success*."

"Any debate, Ms. Shine, has been between our subscribers, who chose to air it on the two podcasts. It's my understanding that Dr. Chandler uses her doctorate degree in business to help factories increase their production. I use my medical doctorate and naturopath license to help people achieve a more wholesome and satisfying life. I don't see how you can compare the two."

"Have you listened to Dr. Chandler's podcasts?"

"Part of one when her name came up in a discussion during mine. I'm not really interested in how to squeeze more profit from a production line."

"Were you listening when she told her listeners that an

example you used was so depressing that it likely generated calls to the suicide hotline?"

"No. If she said that, I wasn't listening." She didn't know whether to laugh at Perry's overly dramatic statement or be angry at the obvious insult. "Did you have a question or something to add to our current discussion, Ms. Shine?"

"Some people are saying the conflict between the two podcasts is staged to suck in more listeners. I wanted to invite you to appear on a *Podcast Prattle* vlog with Dr. Chandler to make your separate cases so people can see your differing points of view are real, not scripted."

Ming considered this proposal. Their competing podcasts had started to feel like an elephant was in the room no matter how much they ignored it. Maybe it would be better to talk openly about them, with the agreement they wouldn't let work bleed into their personal lives. "Stay on the line, Ms. Shine, and my assistant Carl will get your contact information."

CHAPTER THIRTEEN

D r. Chandler, if you'll come with me, please." A young woman wearing a headphone and mic set beckoned from the doorway.

Perry checked her reflection one last time and shifted her shoulders so that her blazer hung perfectly. She'd decided on business casual—a white, button-down Oxford and dark-blue chinos and blazer—hoping to give the impression this vlog was just another day at the office. She smiled at the mirror and gave in to the mesmerizing memories constantly invading her conscious thoughts. While work had been routine, the past month of long dog walks, dinners, and sleepovers with Ming had been spectacular. Perry's interest in a woman usually fizzled after a few steamy nights, but each date with Ming was fuel to her burning desire to spend every minute of every day with the distracting doctor. The very thought of her left Perry breathless and her underwear damp.

"Dr. Chandler?" The production assistant's query pulled her back to the dressing room and the vlog at hand. Focus. She needed to focus on the present.

She'd expected to be taping in a bedroom-converted-to-studio at Rayna Shine's residence and was surprised to find Rayna had rented an auditorium owned by a local community-theater group. Although her dressing room was simply a space blocked off by eight-foot-tall, sound-softening partitions, it held a small, worn sofa and a hair and makeup station.

"Right behind you."

The woman led her through a maze of theater set pieces, talking rapidly the entire time.

"We have a small audience of about a hundred. They've been warned they are only allowed to applaud and that hecklers will be immediately removed, but Rayna may take questions from a few if time permits toward the end of the vlog. You'll be introduced first since your face is well known, and Rayna will chat with you for a few minutes. Then the mysterious Dr. Lee will be introduced and join you two. Rayna will chat with Dr. Lee for a few minutes, then draw you into the conversation about your competing podcasts."

"Got it."

They stopped just offstage, and Perry watched Rayna settle into the middle of three director's chairs positioned in front of a huge projection screen. The theater setting made sense now. They were going to actually have a live audience. In fact, everything seemed like a real television set except for the iPhones fastened atop tripods and placed at strategic angles instead of huge television cameras on dollies. A second production person stood behind a podium covered with papers, an iPad, and two digital timers—one set for an hour, the other counting down to airtime. A stage manager? Did Rayna's vlog generate enough revenue to pay all these staff members? The woman who led her from the dressing room seemed to read her thoughts.

"I'm one of Rayna's two assistants. The rest of the staff belong to the theater group that owns this venue. They come as part of the rental fee, probably because they don't want strangers breaking something in the expensive lighting or sound systems." She handed Perry an earbud. "You'll be able to hear the production chatter until you go onstage and are switched to a private channel so you'll hear only stage directions intended for you."

"Stage directions?"

"Maybe nothing, but you could hear instructions advising you to shift in a certain direction because you're blocking a camera view." She paused to giggle. "Or a warning that your hair dye is running down your face. God. Somebody should have handed Rudy Giuliani a handkerchief."

Perry chuckled. "That was embarrassing. You have to feel bad for the guy, even if you don't like him."

The stage manager murmured instructions into her headset, and the theater lights blinked twice. "One minute, folks."

Perry almost jumped when the warning came through her earbud even though the stage manager was only a few feet away.

"Ready checks. Lighting?"

"Ready."

"Sound?"

"Yo. We're good."

"Guest number one?"

Perry gave a thumbs-up, but the assistant answered.

"Ready in the wings."

"Guest number two?"

"Ready," another voice answered.

"Stage?"

"All set." Rayna flashed a thumbs-up while she adjusted her blouse.

"Live in five...four...three...two...cue curtain." The stage manager reset both digital timers on her podium to zero.

Gears whirred and the heavy curtain lifted, exposing Rayna to the audience and an explosion of applause. The screen behind her showed the *Podcast Prattle* name and logo.

"Thank you, thanks." Rayna smiled as she quieted the applause. "Hello again and welcome to a special episode of *Podcast Prattle*, being taped for the first time before a live audience. I'm excited today to introduce the hosts of two popular podcasts that have nearly tripled their subscribers over the past two months. A lot of other podcasters want to know their secret for rocketing from successful to incredible, and that's what we're here to talk about today.

"Our first guest is Dr. Perry Chandler, recognized internationally as an expert in work-flow efficiency in both a factory and a white-collar office environment. She's also the author of two best-selling books and host of the very popular *Timed for Success* podcast." During this introduction, pictures of Perry talking with workers on a production line, speaking at a conference, and signing books flashed on the large screen.

"Cue Dr. Chandler," the stage manager murmured into her mic.

Perry stepped out onto the stage, waving at the enthusiastic crowd. She shook hands with Rayna, who had been warned that Perry wasn't the hugging type and wouldn't cooperate with a façade implying she and Rayna were friends. When the applause quieted, she spoke to the crowd rather than Rayna. "It's awesome to be here today and actually see some of the faces behind the calls and chat remarks I get on *Timed for Success*." She settled in her designated chair and looked to Rayna to begin.

"You started your own company while still studying for your graduate degrees at Columbia University. Is that correct?"

"Actually, I began while I was an undergrad. I was a business major and interned the summer before my senior year at a manufacturing company to get some experience in the field. After a few weeks, it was clear to me that their shipping-and-receiving department could be more efficient and cost-effective with just a few modifications in their workflow. I had a good boss, who was willing to listen to a college kid's suggestions and try out my ideas. That department had been a constant problem for customer service, and when complaints dropped and their backlog of shipments cleared up, he rotated me through other departments for suggestions. After that summer, word of mouth spread to a few other companies, and I had several offers for jobs and internships when I finished my undergrad degree. That's when I got the idea for starting my own consulting company."

"Wow. You must have been a really busy student."

"I was, but the experience helped me become more efficient with my own time. Also, my best friend and college roommate was a marketing major, so I hired her to take charge of my new company's social media and marketing. Over the years, she's evolved into basically my second-in-command, assisting me with correspondence, multimedia presentations, and a million other things."

"Now you have a thriving company with several consulting teams you personally manage and two best sellers under your belt. You also have a full schedule of engagements as a public speaker. Why add a podcast to your already full work schedule?"

"The pandemic lockdown multiplied the need for an efficient lifestyle tenfold. Companies scrambled to modify their workflow so their employees could work from home. Other companies had to figure out how to accommodate pandemic protocols on their manufacturing lines, as well as find new sources for raw materials and ways to distribute their finished products as domestic and international shipping slowed to a crawl. Workers suddenly had to make workspace in their homes, parents became de facto teachers when schools had to go virtual, and many adults became overnight caregivers for virus-stricken family members.

"Basically, the traffic that had filled our streets and stores moved to the virtual world online. I'd been reaching thousands in the physical world but discovered I could influence millions in this virtual world. The podcast, where listeners can call in or join the chat line, also has become a great source of material for the book I'm working on now."

"And what's the subject of this new book?" Rayna asked.

"Thirty seconds until commercial break." The stage manager's voice came through Perry's and, judging from her glance offstage, Rayna's earbuds.

"Blurring the line between work and home revealed a lot of things we didn't expect. For example, many were surprised they miss their hated commute because they'd unconsciously used that time for much-needed self-reflection, problem-solving, or just simple relaxation. I'm writing now about how we can get that time back by becoming more efficient at home as well as at work."

"Balancing your work life and your personal life is the basis for our next guest's podcast," Rayna said. "We'll discuss *Finding Natural Balance* with Dr. Lee and talk about why the rivalry between these two podcasters has caught the attention of millions of new listeners…right after this commercial break."

"And you're out. You have ninety seconds to relax," the stage manager said.

"So, you've never met Dr. Lee?" Rayna asked.

"Not that I'm aware of," Perry said carefully. The hair on her nape was beginning to rise as the gleam in Rayna's eyes warned her something was afoot. "The voice is sort of androgenous. A lot of people seem to think Dr. Lee is female, but I'm convinced only a man could be that narcissistic."

Rayna's eyes grew even brighter after the declaration. "Well, you're about to find out."

"Back in five, four, three, two, one," the stage manager announced.

The main camera person pointed to Rayna, and she began the introduction.

"Dr. Lee is both a general-practice physician and a licensed naturopath, augmenting her Western medical training with natural treatments common in Eastern medicine and alternative therapies such as acupuncture." She read the definition off prompt cards held up by an assistant. "Her podcast *Finding Natural Balance* has drawn millions of listeners as pandemic shutdowns and workarounds magnified daily stress in most households around the world. So many followers, in fact, that she had to quit her practice, remove all photos from her podcast website, and relocate her home after hundreds of people found out where she lived and worked in Fresno, California, and camped out in her office's parking lot and outside her home in hopes of seeing her. Although she agreed to appear here today, she's asked that we not reveal her real name in the hope it will prevent stalkers from tracking her down again. Please welcome Dr. Lee."

Ming walked out from the wings to enthusiastic applause and whistles and gave Perry a wink before turning to quickly hug Rayna.

Perry's stomach twisted, and her thoughts raced. This had to be a joke. Ming's last name was Davis. Okay. So maybe she used an alias for her public persona. But she'd never mentioned having a podcast. Was she afraid Perry might be a very clever stalker? No. What was between them was real. Wasn't it? She thought back to the last time they were together. They hadn't declared love or made plans for a future, but she'd had felt it in every kiss, every caress, and every time Ming gave herself to her.

She saw Rayna's and Ming's lips moving, but she felt like they were on mute or that she was underwater, watching them. The only voices registering in her head were her own thoughts... her fears. Ming smiled at the audience when one guy yelled out, "We love you, Dr. Lee." A camera person shifted his tripod to get a better angle on Ming's face, and the movement jerked Perry back to reality.

"Why did you study naturopathy after completing your medical degree?" Rayna asked Ming.

"I think a lot of people, because of my Asian features, expect me to say some elder member of my family taught me the value of natural remedies," Ming said. "Actually, I became interested in naturopathy because many of my patients confessed they'd been self-medicating before finally coming to me. I get it. Doctors are expensive, and prescription-drug prices are soaring. The patients were going online and reading about natural remedies they already had in their pantries or could grow in their gardens. With all the publicity about opioid addiction, I found more patients were willing to see me because I was also a naturopath and wouldn't dismiss their cheaper home remedy. I might adjust the dosage or recommend a different natural remedy, but I wouldn't prescribe an expensive drug without first considering a cheaper natural course of action."

"That's so very interesting. But what led you to start your *Finding Natural Balance* podcast?"

"The pandemic lockdown." Ming cast a glance at Perry. "Americans were already caught up in a pressure cooker. The working class has been shouldering the bulk of the workload in our country's drive to achieve more and produce more, but without adequate compensation. Home was no longer a refuge from work stress, because the pandemic forced people to take work problems into their homes, where that stress mixed with any personal family stresses. The podcast was a way to reach millions, rather than a few patients in my office, and help them find their balance in this unfamiliar crisis situation."

Rayna sat back in her chair to include Perry in the conversation. "That sounds a lot like Dr. Chandler's motivation and goal. So, I have to ask why your podcasts are caught up in this duel that has tripled your audience. Is this a calculated marketing ploy, as some online chatter suggests? Or are your methods actually at odds?"

The question hit Perry in the gut. This certainly wasn't a ploy on her part. Had it been a stunt that was a piece of Ming's plan to sell her practice and become an herb farmer? Suspicion and embarrassment roiled into a growing ball of anger. She wanted to grind her teeth. Had she been played all along?

"That would be impossible since I had no clue that—" Perry caught herself before she said Ming's name, remembering the contract she'd signed earlier that contained a codicil specifying she would not reveal it if she recognized her. She started over. "I don't enter into business agreements without a complete background check, so there absolutely was no such collaboration on my part since I had no clue to Dr. Lee's identity before she walked onto the stage a few minutes ago."

"How is that possible, given the two of you have been seen all over Fresno together?" Rayna asked. A series of photos flashed on the screen behind them—Ming and Perry dining together at a variety of restaurants, them at the pet-adoption event, and Perry stealing a kiss from Ming as they walked the dogs together. "Are you saying your podcasts never came up in conversation?"

"Given my recent problem with stalkers, I try to keep my work separate from my personal life," Ming said. "That's impossible to do all the time, so I googled Perry Chandler after we met by chance. When the podcast was one of the first items the search turned up, I resolved to not mention it unless she did. I did allude to the podcasts once, but we were interrupted. When she didn't ask about it later, I was sure we were in agreement to keep work and personal separate."

"Your website is scrubbed of any photos, and a million Dr. Lees live in the US alone," Perry said. "After a lot of searching, my assistant did turn up a photo of a Lee in a Stanford yearbook from around the time you would have finished your medical degree, but the photo barely resembled you." Her disbelief was turning into anger. Ming hadn't trusted her enough to reveal her online identity? "And I don't recall you ever mentioning your podcast."

"At the adoption event…when I was trying to talk you into keeping the dogs and you said you were too busy with work to care for them. I said maybe you needed them in your life to show you how to find a better balance between work and your personal life."

"Nothing in that remark could possibly lead me to think you were Dr. Lee. I thought you'd been listening to my podcast."

"When would I have had time to listen to your podcast? I've been swamped with still seeing patients while meeting with my lawyer constantly on selling my practice and my old home, searching for a new one, and packing for the move while still trying to help you find the perfect home for the dogs."

"You had plenty of opportunity during the time we spent together...as friends." Perry heard and felt her icy tone. "I would expect a real friend to trust me enough to come clean about a podcast persona trying to undermine my podcast."

❖

Ming stared at Perry, who had turned stone-faced. This was the cold, controlled version of Perry from that first day they met.

Rayna didn't miss the opportunity to throw fuel on the fire in Perry's accusation. "So should we expect the battling podcasts to become a war, now that you both know who you're fighting?"

Ming quickly corrected her. "There is no battle." She needed to defuse this discussion and talk with Perry in private. "We simply have a difference of professional opinion, not anything personal."

"When one of your listeners asked about Dr. Chandler's recommendation to set a schedule to better organize personal time, you said..." Rayna read from her notes even though the quote suddenly appeared on the screen behind them. "'While this might be the solution for trains, planes, or assembly lines, I'll remind you again that humans are not machines. We'll talk about why this is not a healthy approach...'"

"That wasn't personal," Ming said, struggling to uphold her professional demeanor when she really wanted to slap Rayna to make her shut up. "That was strictly a professional observation."

"I did take it personally," Perry said. "You were effectively questioning my qualifications to advise my clients about how they can ease some of the stress in their lives by being more efficient with their time."

"I was not denigrating your qualifications as an efficiency expert."

"How about when you said Dr. Chandler was 'a single

female without the responsibilities that come with dependents. So, she seems to be struggling with the discussion that keeps circling back to managing shared personal time'?"

"That's taken out of context," Ming said.

Perry's lips had become a fine line. "I suppose Dr. Lee has to suffer the same diseases as her patients to effectively treat them?"

Ming opened her mouth to tear into that ridiculous statement, but Rayna jumped in first. "But haven't you landed a few punches, too, Dr. Chandler?" A new quote flashed on the screen. "It sounds rather personal when you said, 'This Dr. Lee sounds depressing. I wonder how many calls the suicide help line received after that podcast—'"

Ming narrowed her eyes at Perry. "You actually accused me of driving people to suicide?"

To Perry's credit, she stared down at her hands, her ears reddening, and didn't deny the statement. Then she looked up and threw Ming's words back at her. "That's taken out of context."

"Looks like we're all out of time today, folks. Stay tuned, because *Podcast Prattle* will be keeping an eye on the war between efficiency and balance in the coming weeks."

"And we're out," the video chief-slash-director called out.

Perry tore out her earbud and threw it onto the coffee table that was part of the set. "That remark was taken out of context. I immediately retracted that statement and apologized to my audience for being flippant about a serious issue of suicide. Stay away from my podcast and me." She spat the words at Rayna. "I'm calling my lawyer to get a restraining order to prevent you from publicizing any further photos of me, so you might as well call off your paparazzi." She avoided looking at Ming as she wheeled and strode toward the exit door.

"Perry." Ming struggled to leash her anger and catch Perry, who ignored her and continued toward the exit. They needed to talk about this like two adults. But Perry was almost at the door. "Stop, goddamn it."

Perry stopped and turned to her. Her blue eyes were as cold

as her expression. "I'm a daughter only when it's convenient for my parents. I will not be conveniently used by anyone else who is supposed to care about me. Like this vlog, we're out. Over and done. Call Julie when you've found homes for the dogs." Then she was through the door and gone.

Ming was stunned. Then she was furious. How could she have known Perry hadn't figured out that she was Dr. Lee? And the podcast jabs were simply related to work. Well, the suicide comment was over the top and incredibly insensitive. But the back-and-forth had rocketed numbers for both of them. And Perry hadn't even given her a chance to explain.

She was so lost in her tumultuous thoughts, she flinched when Rayna spoke from right behind her.

"Thanks for being on the vlog. That was awesome."

"It was a disaster. I had no idea she didn't know I was Dr. Lee." Ming stalked back to her dressing room to collect her purse, but Rayna followed. "Now she thinks I deliberately misled her as part of a marketing stunt to benefit me."

"Come on. This is only about work. She just needs time to cool off. I bet you'll both see your follower numbers double again. It's a win-win, right?"

"Today has been a lose-lose." Ming grabbed her purse and faced Rayna. Was this woman that clueless? "We were more than friends." She hesitated, then admitted the fear that was gnawing at her gut. "If I can't fix this, I will have lost something much more valuable to me than stupid podcast numbers."

CHAPTER FOURTEEN

Ming ended the call as soon as Perry's voice mail kicked in. She'd left six messages over the past six days asking to talk, but Perry had not responded. She also didn't respond to texts. At first, Ming had been angry that Perry was refusing her calls and texts. She'd even driven to her house and banged on her door. The dogs barked, and Ming had talked to them through the door, hoping Perry was inside and listening. She told them how much she needed to talk to Perry, but Perry still didn't open up. She wasn't sure what to do next. Go back to Perry's condo and ring the doorbell until she opened it?

Ming jumped when the phone rang in her hand and answered without checking the caller identification.

"Hello?"

"Hi, Ming. This is Julie."

Ming's heart nearly stopped. "Julie, I'm so glad you called. I would have phoned you days ago, but I didn't have your number, and Perry isn't answering my calls or texts."

"Yeah. I know." Julie's tone was indecipherable—a mixture of resignation and irritation. "She wants you to stop trying to get in touch with her."

"She needs to talk to me. I thought we meant more to each other than to let one disagreement end everything."

Julie didn't respond for a few long seconds, then ignored

Ming's remark. "She wants me to give you the phone number of a woman she met at the adoption event. She said if the woman hasn't already adopted some other dog, she'd be a good fit for Tucker. Also, I got emails from at least two dozen people interested in JT after I posted his photo on her social media. Perry asked that you find another foster for Molly."

Her message was clear. Julie had called because Perry wanted to divest herself of the last connection between them. She'd not only given up on their relationship, but she'd given up on finding the dogs a forever home together.

"JT will be easy to place." She closed her eyes and willed back the tears that threatened. "I…I have a foster for Molly, too." She cleared her throat. "I'm not in Fresno any longer. The movers cleared out my apartment two days ago. When can I pick them up?"

"Any time. Perry left on an unnecessary business trip, and I'm staying at her place to take care of the dogs. She asked me to make sure the pups were gone when she returned. She got a letter saying she's banned from the dog park, and they're not getting much exercise in her tiny yard."

"I'll come pick them up now."

❖

Located in the most Americanized city in Mexico, the American chain restaurants at the Monterrey airport and on the way to her hotel seemed out of place to Perry. In fact, nothing seemed to fit right since she'd walked out on Ming.

She had put her podcast on hiatus so she could spend the time researching for her next book. But she'd lost interest in the book, because it only reminded her it had been Ming she'd debated the subject with online. She'd mostly snuggled on her couch with the dogs to binge-watch movies and television series until Julie intervened and forced her outdoors for a long run. The fresh air rejuvenated her some, so she began running every day, then twice a day.

When she noticed Julie was calling less often and had quit bringing over food in an attempt to get her to eat, she invited her over under the pretense of completing some work and was shaken by the dark circles under Julie's eyes and the tired lines on her face.

"Who did you think was going to pick up your slack while you wallowed in this depression of your own making?" Julie asked. "Either talk to Ming or get off your ass and get back to work. I'm running out of ideas to keep some of your followers engaged in the podcast. There's a limit to how many 'best of' on whatever subject I can edit together from your archived episodes."

So, she got back to work.

She gave up scheduling her day because she rarely followed her plans any longer. Finding it hard to focus, she bounced from one task to another without completing any.

It was easier to let the dogs dictate her schedule, and Molly had a firm one—morning pee, breakfast, mid-morning nap, backyard break, treats, afternoon nap, dinner, playtime, snuggle time, bedtime. And she was increasingly insistent, barking at Perry until she complied. It was as though Molly had become an extension of Julie, yelling for her to find her groove again. The dogs, like almost everything else, brought up too many memories of the time she'd spent with Ming, and she still couldn't bear to think about their implosion. It was like a knife that gutted her every time she opened that door.

Then she decided a change of scenery would dull the pain and began meddling in the projects her teams were working on. That was why she was in Monterrey.

A huge company had established a battery plant here, and she was personally reviewing the workflow of their production lines to make recommendations her team would stay to implement.

She'd missed fieldwork. It hadn't diminished the physical pain and lethargy that had consumed her since Ming's betrayal, but it grounded her enough that she could finally think about what had happened.

Had it simply been a marketing ploy? She'd thought they met by chance, but did they? Ming knew the dogs' previous owner, so maybe Ming had suggested that her mother dump the dogs on Perry. Okay. That sounded like a weird conspiracy theory, but it was possible. Why else would Ming have kept her identity secret from her?

"Given my recent problem with stalkers, I try to keep my work separate from my personal life."

That was a thin excuse at best. Besides, the remarks Ming made on her podcast about Perry were really low, considering she knew exactly who she was talking about.

"You actually accused me of driving people to suicide?"

Her ears burned at the memory of her own heartless comment. She couldn't explain why she'd used the subject of suicide in such a cavalier way. She knew the pain that could lead to taking your own life.

She'd tried once, after both of her parents failed to show up at her high school graduation even though she was making the valedictorian speech. She hadn't seen her dad for months after her mother kicked him out of the house for cheating on her, and her mother had left the week before graduation on another long research trip. Perry had washed three Oxycontin—all she could find in the house—down with a fifth of vodka. Fortunately, she woke up the next day, facedown on her bed and lying in a pool of her own vomit. She'd showered, cleaned up the mess, and packed her bags for Columbia University, where she'd been offered a full scholarship, and arranged to begin with the summer semester rather than wait until fall.

It was a secret she still bore alone. Nobody knew. Not even Julie. She had no physical scars for anyone to notice. She did see a therapist while at Columbia, but she still sometimes wondered that if she had died, how long it would have taken for anyone to miss her, if they ever did. Those old feelings of inadequacy and anger had pushed her to walk out on Ming.

She hadn't gone directly home that day because she realized Ming might follow her there, demanding they talk. But Perry was too raw. Instead, she'd turned off her phone and drove aimlessly for an hour before stopping at a coffee shop, where she sat at an outdoor table for another hour, nursing consecutive cups of espresso until she was too jittery to sit any longer. She got back into her car, turned her phone on, and called Julie after at least ten phone and twenty text messages downloaded.

"What the hell happened, Perry? Why aren't you answering my texts or my calls? The podcast world is blowing up over that vlog, which has already gone viral. I thought I was watching a Jerry Springer show and you guys were going to stand up and start throwing your chairs at each other."

"I don't want to talk about it. I need you to go by my house and make sure Ming isn't waiting for me. I don't want to see or talk to her."

"I'd save anything you have to say to her for your next podcast. We've got the weekend to nail down a script before Monday."

"I'm putting Timed for Success *on hiatus."*

"Wrong answer. We've got to strike while the iron is hot. I'm sure Ming will."

"I don't care what she does. I'm not going to be a pawn in her marketing scheme."

"If it is a marketing scheme, she's brilliant, and you should take advantage of that opportunity."

"No. I mean that, too. No response to the vlog today and no further comments on Dr. Lee's podcast. If my listeners bring it up, I'll just ignore those questions."

"Perry—"

"No, Julie. And that's final."

"I think you're wrong about Ming. I've seen the way she looks at you. I have a hard time believing she would deliberately do anything to hurt you."

Was Julie right? Had her accusations been too hasty? She played that day over and over in her mind, searching for anything that would reassure her she'd been right to walk away. Or maybe something that explicitly showed she'd been wrong.

Time and distance had not lessened that ache in her chest and the hollow feeling in her stomach.

❖

The dogs barked joyfully and crowded around Ming when Julie let her into Perry's condo. She stooped to greet each one, but Tucker danced away when she reached for him, then ran up the stairs and into Perry's home office.

Julie sighed. "He's been a nervous wreck since Perry left. He won't come out of the office except to go out to pee. He won't even eat unless I take his food up there. It might be because I've been editing clips of her past podcasts to keep something posted. She hasn't done a new one in weeks. He doesn't understand why he can hear her voice but she isn't there."

Ming stood and shook her head. "He's bonded with her, poor little guy. He was bonded to his original owner, who adopted him as a puppy, and she disappeared on him. Now, he's bonded with Perry, and she's ditching him. The older he gets, the harder it is for him to attach to a new person. I really thought she'd give in and keep at least him if we had to break up the pack."

"I thought she'd keep all three after that fiasco of a vlog. She cuddled on the couch with them for two weeks, binge-watching everything she could find on Netflix."

"I've tried everything I know to get her to talk to me after I cooled down from her rejection." Ming looked away, unable to meet Julie's eyes. "I thought I meant something to her, but she threw that away as soon as things got hard." She looked up again when Julie didn't respond to find Julie studying her.

"I'm not going to get in the middle of the drama between you two, but I will tell you a little about my friend that may help you understand her better." Julie motioned for Ming to take a seat on the couch while she sat in the chair across from her.

Tucker stood hesitantly at the top of the stairs when Molly and JT sat next to Ming on the couch, then came down to join them. Ming wanted to scoop him up and hug him, but that probably would send him running again.

"I'll listen to anything you're willing to tell me. I'm still reeling from her over-the-top reaction to finding out I'm her podcast rival. I really thought she knew, just like I knew about her." She avoided looking directly at Tucker but snuck a hand over to scratch his favorite spot on his chest. He finally relaxed and lay down on the other side of Molly, in the safety of his pack.

"I tried to tell her, but she insisted your last name was Davis. I suppose Lee is a nom de plume?"

"It actually was my last name, but I legally changed it to Davis, my father's first name, so Lee wouldn't be on the contract, deed, and tax records of my new home. I had to do what I could to make sure my fanatic fans didn't follow me from Fresno. She never asked about my last name, but I'm guessing she heard my new neighbor address me as Dr. Davis."

Julie nodded. "I did track you down in the Columbia University yearbook by guessing when you might have been a student there. I still couldn't convince Perry that was you. I think she was in denial because she didn't want it to be."

Ming snorted. "I can see how she didn't recognize me. I was

fifty pounds heavier and still the same shy nerd I was in high school. Fortunately, I came to terms with my sexual orientation my sophomore year and discovered Columbia's rowing club. Even I was surprised at the person I found after shedding the extra weight and making friends who built up my confidence."

"You certainly don't resemble that picture any longer." Julie nervously twisted her fingers, then sat back in her chair and held Ming's gaze. "She does care about you, Ming. I don't think I've ever seen her so enamored with another woman. But underneath that confident business professional and public speaker is a kid who had to raise herself. Her parents put their research first in every situation. They didn't have the money for a nanny but hired college students to pick her up from school and take her to any after-school activities. Her drive to excel comes from always feeling she wasn't meeting their expectations. Basically, everything that makes up the adult Perry is rooted in that childhood belief that she wasn't good enough to earn their love."

"She's never talked much about her parents, but I did get the feeling they weren't close."

"They still see her a couple of times a year, but only when it's convenient for them. And Perry always has to go to them or meet them somewhere. When Janice dumped these pups off, it was the first time she'd been to Perry's home. And she didn't even come inside. She said she had a plane to catch and put their stuff on the porch, then left."

"That's rough. What about her father?"

"He lives in England with a woman about Perry's age. She meets up with him every couple of years when he messages that he's in the States for a conference or research consult. Pretty often, he wants to see her because he's trying to impress someone he needs to fund one of his research projects. He uses her status as a best-selling author and international consultant like it's part of his own résumé."

"I guess, given that background, I can sort of understand why she jumped to the conclusion that I was also using her. On the other hand, she's no longer that child, and I'm not her parents. With everything I had going on in my life, taking on a relationship was the last thing I needed." Ming paused as her throat tightened, and tears threatened. "I made time for her. I opened up to her. We shared more than physical intimacy."

Julie rose, and the dogs made room for her on the couch. She took Ming's hand and squeezed. "She's miserable. Pretty much a zombie. I think you scare her because she feels so deeply about you. She's sort of like Tucker. She'll run if you chase her. It's better if you let her work up the courage to come to you."

Ming teetered among her own insecurities. Should she wait for Perry to come around? What if Julie was saying this to get rid of her so she'd have Perry's full attention again? Then again, what did she have to lose? Her current pursuit of Perry wasn't working.

"I hate that she's giving up the dogs and that I'm going to have to split them up."

"I hate that, too. I wish I could take the little darlings." Julie frowned at her. "Why can't you take them? Perry said you bought a huge farm property. Seems that would be ideal for dogs."

"I've got so much going on there over the next few months—renovating the house and building greenhouses. Too many trucks and machinery are constantly coming and going while I'm traveling to find the best seeds and visiting other herb farms to study their processes." Ming managed a weak smile. "Besides, the first thing you have to learn as a foster is that you can't keep every needy animal. My job is to match them with the right forever family. I promise to find them good homes." And, truthfully, they'd be a constant reminder of her monumental mistake that lost the one woman with whom she'd fallen deeply in love.

CHAPTER FIFTEEN

Perry opened the door and rolled her suitcase inside the eerily empty condo.

Julie had texted that she was going back to her own home after Ming picked up the dogs, but their absence didn't really sink in until no happy barks greeted her. No Tucker was zooming around with a bone in his mouth that he would give her after she greeted the other two dogs. She searched for a question or command to give SHA, just to have another voice break the bleak silence.

"SHA, call Julie."

"Welcome home, Perry. Calling Julie now."

Julie's voice came over SHA's speakers. "Well, well. The prodigal boss finally returns."

"Yeah. Want to come over? We can order takeout and catch up on everything." She'd left to spend a week in Mexico but had been gone three because she flew from Mexico to Taiwan to check on another team's progress, and then to see her publisher in New York to renegotiate the deadline on the new book she'd contracted.

"I would, but I have a date tonight with a hot chick."

"Where'd you meet this one?"

"On our jogging trail. I'd seen her a couple of times, but she was running with a couple of other people. When I spotted her at the trailhead, getting ready to run alone last week, I introduced myself and suggested we hit the trail together for safety reasons. Afterward, she asked me out. This is our first date."

"Don't be late."

"I won't be if I hang up now. Sorry about tonight. I didn't expect you until tomorrow afternoon."

"No problem. I'll order in and probably go to bed early. It's been a long day of travel."

"Good idea. Tell you what. I'll pick up lunch tomorrow from Panera and come over so you can tell me about Mexico. I know you don't want to, but we also need to talk about the podcast."

Perry sighed. "Okay. I guess I can't put that off any longer."

She ended the call and walked through her condo to sit in the glider on her patio. Julie had hired a landscaper to replace the artificial turf since it had been smelling like dog urine. The crew had also filled the many holes the terrors had dug in her flowerbeds and put down fresh mulch. The cleaning service had been by yesterday, so every trace of the dogs had disappeared. Melancholy was settling around her, so she decided to take a walk to shake it off.

She waved at Mrs. Mayberry, who was adjusting the drip hoses in her flowerbeds. Then she broke into a jog so her neighbor wouldn't try to engage her in conversation.

After two blocks, she slowed back to a walk. The afternoon was pleasant enough, but she wasn't dressed for jogging. Besides, she felt more like strolling to put off returning to the depressing emptiness of her condo. When she passed the dog park, she wanted to flip a rude gesture at the place. She couldn't believe Molly had been banned because she chased a cat. She was doing what was natural to a dog. Besides, it was supposed to be a dog park, not a cat park.

When she returned her attention to the sidewalk, she was surprised to see a slightly familiar woman walking a dog that looked just like…Tucker! He appeared to spot her at the same time and stopped.

The woman seemed puzzled by his refusal to continue

forward. "What's wrong, Tuck? It's okay. I won't let the other dogs bother you. We can just walk on past, if you want." Her tone was coaxing and kind.

Perry called to her as she approached, in order not to startle the woman. "Hey, so you did get my boy."

Tucker yipped and danced forward, the leash limiting his usual zooming back and forth to greet Perry. The woman looked up and smiled. "Yes. Looks like he hasn't forgotten you."

Perry extended her hand. "Perry Chandler. I remember you from the adoption event. Gigi, right?"

"Yes. Thank you for remembering me when he went up for adoption. I'm sorry, though, that you had to split up their little pack."

Perry knelt in the grass next to the sidewalk, and Tucker wagged his way to her, licking her hands, then standing on his hind legs to bathe her face. He barked and barked happily until Perry quieted him with an ear scratch. "I'm glad you were still available to take him. I had to be out of town on business, but I asked them to call you before they considered any other adopters. He's sort of a special case, and you seemed to understand him. How's he doing?"

"Honestly, this is the happiest I've seen him. He wouldn't eat at first. I tried everything."

"What about peanut butter? He really likes it. And sweet potato, but only when it's raw. He likes turkey and green beans, too."

Gigi laughed. "Yes. I called Ming, and she forwarded a list of treats that your assistant sent her."

Perry's heart stuttered at the mention of Ming, but she shoved the feeling down and decided to head home. "Were you going to the dog park?"

"Yes, we were. Tucker just sits at my feet, but I'm hoping he'll eventually make a friend there he can play with."

"I was out for a stroll but probably should be getting back home, so I'll walk with you back to the park."

The park was less than a block away, so when they arrived, Perry petted Tucker once more and turned toward home. Tucker made his little sounds of worry, then erupted into a frenzy of yelps and barks when it became clear Perry was leaving. She remembered the child who watched her mother leave so many times no matter how much she begged, and something inside her tore open like a never-healing wound. She broke into a jog and then an all-out run the rest of the way to her door, tears mingling with the sweat.

❖

It seemed like everybody in Cutterville had swarmed the farm as soon as the papers were signed. The renovations to the house were nearly done, and four medium-sized greenhouses were finished and nearly filled with seedlings in record time.

Ming rose in the predawn to perform her tai chi on the ridge overlooking the house and barn. Fresh air filled her lungs as the sun peeked over the horizon, and she concentrated on the movements. She would spend her day in the greenhouses, planting more seeds in porous trays filled with rich, black soil, then eat her dinner on the terrace as the sun dipped again below the mountains.

It was everything and more than she had dreamed. And she was miserable.

Her dinner sat untouched while she cuddled Molly against her. She'd placed Tucker with the woman Perry had recommended, and JT went to the couple, Tom and Bob, that Perry had discouraged at the adoption event. They were thrilled to get her call before they headed out to visit several national parks with a caravan of their RV friends. She also had a foster who took Molly, but the man already had five other senior dogs. So, when the flurry of construction wound down at the farm, Ming filled out the papers to permanently adopt her.

Truthfully, she needed Molly's companionship. She'd tried to bury herself in the physical labor of the farm, and she'd even seen a few patients at a small clinic the only local doctor was happy to share. He was a Cutter, of course, and had worked for eight years in a San Diego emergency room before returning home to open a small general-medicine office. He triaged, vaccinated, prescribed antibiotics, set simple fractures, and sutured wounds from everyday accidents—basically handling anything that didn't need to be sent to a hospital in Fresno.

None of this lifted her depression.

The rhythm of the farm she'd felt so easily before eluded her now. Her seedlings sprouted but were not flourishing as expected. Even Collin was scratching his head over their slow growth.

She would lie in bed at night, unable to sleep. She'd put up a notice on her website that she was on vacation and her podcast would return, but she wasn't sure that was true. Her failure to find her own natural balance had drained her enthusiasm for helping others find theirs.

With each day that passed, her hope that Perry would come back to her lessened. Never again would she give her heart to anyone, because when they left without giving it back, only a hollow shell of herself remained.

Perry sipped her coffee and stared out the window in her home office while she half listened to one of her team leaders rattle off their findings at a new factory site. Diego was one of her best, but he liked to conference-call too often to give results she could read in his weekly report. She was rescued from hearing more when her doorbell rang and SHA informed her, "Someone is at your front door."

"That all sounds good, Diego, but my doorbell is ringing. I'll read the rest when you turn in your weekly report. As always, though, call immediately if you come across a problem that requires my help."

She closed the video-call window without waiting for his good-bye and sprinted down the stairs. Who could it be? Julie had a key and normally let herself in without knocking or ringing the doorbell. Could it be…? No. Too much time had passed, and the texts from Ming had stopped several months ago.

Perry's anger, after a few sessions with her new therapist, had burned out, and she realized now that she should have given Ming a chance to explain. She didn't really believe Ming had intentionally used her. Their relationship had been brief but deep. What was more, Ming's podcast was also silent. Neither had taken advantage of the subscriber boost from the vlog. She should go to Ming and talk things out, if she would still speak to her. It was just…well, she was too ashamed and didn't know what she should say. Still, a small flame of hope flickered in her chest as she opened the door.

"Mrs. Mayberry, hi."

"Hello, dear. I think one of your pups got out, and he's been sitting here whining to be let in."

"I don't still—" Perry stopped mid-sentence when she looked down to see what was bumping against her leg. "Tucker!"

"He's such a fine little dog, and I was afraid he might run into the street and get hit by a car."

Mrs. Mayberry prattled on as Perry scooped him into her arms and he licked her face. She'd missed him so much her eyes filled with tears as she returned his licks with kisses to his head.

"Oh, dear. I didn't mean to upset you by mentioning the street," Mrs. Mayberry said, apparently flustered by Perry's tears. "He appears to be fine. I don't think any harm came to him."

Perry wiped at her face, even though Tucker had already licked her tears away. "I'm sorry. Actually, I was just fostering the dogs. Tucker has a great new home with a wonderful owner who lives about ten blocks from here. He must have gotten out, became confused, and came here instead of going to his new home. I'm so glad he didn't get hit on the way here. I'll give his owner a call to come get him."

Mrs. Mayberry gave her an odd look. "I'm sure she's very nice, but it looks to me like you two belong together." She fluttered her hand in the air, dismissing the thought. "Don't pay any mind to me. I'm just prattling on. You have a good day now."

Perry took Tucker inside and put him down on the couch next to her, but he crawled back into her lap, pressing himself against her chest in a doggie hug. She couldn't resist putting her arms around him again and holding him tight while she kissed the top of his head. He relaxed against her. He was wearing a new collar with his name stitched into it, and a blue tag that dangled next to his rabies license was engraved with Gigi's phone number.

She sniffed and cleared her throat. Gigi must be frantic looking for him. "SHA, call—" She recited the phone number.

"Calling."

It rang only twice before Gigi answered. "Hello?"

"Hi, Gigi. This is Perry Chandler. Tucker just showed up at my house."

"Great. I'm glad you were home. I'll be right over."

"Wait. I didn't give you the address."

"Do you live at 3232 Brightleaf?"

"Uh, yeah. Yes, I do. How did you know?"

"I'll explain when I get there. See you in a few minutes."

Tucker pressed harder into Perry's chest at the sound of Gigi's voice.

"It's okay, Tuck. She'll be here shortly."

But Gigi arrived carrying more than his leash. When Perry answered the doorbell, Tucker still in her arms, she found his food, bed, and a box of dog toys on the stoop, and Gigi was wrestling his wire crate out of her trunk.

"What's all this?" she asked when Gigi set the crate next to Tucker's other things.

Gigi reached out to scratch Tucker's chest, and he licked her hand. "This smart little fellow obviously has chosen you, so I'm returning him. I don't want the adoption fee back or anything."

"I don't understand. I was sure you were a good match for him."

Gigi sighed but smiled. "I am, and we've become good friends, but he'd already chosen you."

"But—"

"He's really smart. I think that when we saw you near the dog park, he remembered the way from the park to here. This is the third time I've retrieved him from this porch, so I figured this had to be your address."

"I didn't know."

Gigi laid her hand on Perry's arm. "You'll break his little heart if you don't keep him. But if you can't, Ming needs to find him a home with somebody who doesn't live in this neighborhood. No matter how much he likes me, he's going to keep running away to come back to you because we live so near each other. I'm sorry. He's a really fine little guy. It's going to be hard to replace him, but I've got a few leads on puppies from a group that rescues Jack Russell terriers."

Perry stood flummoxed as she watched Gigi get into her car and leave. She looked over at Mrs. Mayberry, who was conveniently weeding her flowerbed.

"You'll break his little heart if you don't keep him," she said without looking up.

CHAPTER SIXTEEN

Ming stood next to the chair where Mee-maw sat and watched while the Shoshoni shaman chanted and waved a smoking bundle of sage in and around the greenhouses.

Her seedlings still were not flourishing despite consulting with Collin and precisely monitoring water, sunshine, and fertilizer for each group of plants. So, when the ninety-six-year-old Cutter matriarch showed up personally with a Shoshoni shaman to purify the new greenhouses, she consented. What could it hurt?

She was caught off guard again when her uncle drove up with her own grandmother in his passenger seat.

"Hey. What a nice surprise. You should have told me you were coming." Ming helped her grandmother from the car. "I would have prepared something special for lunch."

"We brought lunch with us, sweetie, and we've got plenty for everyone. I wanted to see this farm that's kept you so busy you keep missing our usual restaurant date."

Ming led them over to where Mee-maw sat. "Mrs. Cutter, this is my grandmother, Song Lee, and my uncle, Frank Lee."

Mee-maw rose gingerly from her chair, tugged her mask down briefly so they could see her face, and nodded, rather than accepting Uncle Frank's offered handshake. "Song. What a beautiful name. Pleased to meet you. Sorry for not taking your hand, but at my age, I have to be careful about germs. I'm Leone Cutter, but I'm just Mee-maw to everyone around here. Or you can call me Leone."

"We're pleased to meet you, too," Song said, pulling up the colorful scarf around her neck to cover her lower face. "Frank, will you get my chair out of the trunk, please."

"I've got several more just inside the barn, Grandmother." Ming pointed to the old barn, freshly painted and equipped with a new set of solar panels. "Can you get them, Uncle Frank?"

"Sure thing." He pulled a mask from his pocket, then headed for the barn.

He returned quickly with the chairs, and everybody, including Ming, sat to watch.

The shaman wore jeans, a plaid flannel shirt, and work boots, but a white feather was braided into his shoulder-length, glossy black hair, and several strings of various beads hung around his neck. He chanted in a language Ming didn't recognize as he fanned the sage around the doors of the greenhouses.

"Can you explain to me what's happening here?" Song directed the question to Ming, but Mee-maw answered.

"Ming's plants aren't thriving like they should, even though she's doing everything right. Joseph is a Shoshoni shaman. He's making sure there aren't any spirits that are uncertain about your granddaughter being here."

Song nodded. "Ming, I need a small rug from your house."

"Grandmother, you don't need—"

Song shot her a hard look that instantly silenced her.

"Okay. I'll be right back."

When Ming returned, her grandmother took the rug and approached Joseph. She couldn't hear what they were saying, but after a brief conversation, Song spread the rug on the ground in front of the greenhouses and carefully lowered herself into a lotus position. She closed her eyes and became very still.

"Your grandmother is a shaman among your people?" Mee-maw asked.

Ming choked back a laugh. "She was born here in California and, as far as I know, has never traveled outside the United States. She goes to a Unitarian church because she likes the social activities they offer, but I've never known her to be very religious."

"Maybe you don't know her as well as you think. She has a strong spirit. I could feel it the minute they drove onto this property." She smiled at Frank and shrugged. "Your uncle, not so much. Men seldom have the strength of spirit that blesses many women. It's not their fault. They are warriors and protectors, which requires strong focus and closes their minds to other things."

After a few minutes, Joseph extinguished his sage and lowered himself to the ground near Song's left elbow, mimicking Song's position. Song rested her hands on her knees with palms turned skyward, whereas Joseph turned his down over his knees.

"I hope this doesn't take much longer. I'm starving," Frank grumbled. "Are you sure she hasn't fallen asleep?"

"Hush, Uncle Frank. It's not going to hurt you to have lunch thirty minutes later than usual." Ming loved the grumpy old curmudgeon, because under his crusty exterior was a soft sweetheart she had always been able to charm to do her bidding.

"I might pass out from hunger. I have low blood sugar, you know."

She ignored his typical complaint because Joseph was standing again and offering a hand to help her grandmother up.

"Well?" Ming asked when they approached.

"Let's go unpack lunch. We brought plenty, if Joseph and Leone would like to stay."

"We would be delighted, if Joseph doesn't have to be somewhere."

"I never turn down a free meal," he said.

Molly clearly agreed, following them to the terrace because Song would slip her a few morsels when Ming wasn't watching.

They feasted on cups of broccoli-and-cheddar soup, shrimp

salad, and chicken pot stickers, in case anyone was allergic to shellfish, but Ming lost her patience before dessert.

"Do you two have any insights about why my plants aren't growing very well?"

Joseph looked contemplative as he sipped from his glass of water. "The spirits are happy you are here. The sky and earth welcome you and are not blocking your plants from growing."

"So, what's the problem?"

Joseph didn't answer but looked to Song, who reached for Ming's hand and clasped it.

"*You* are, sweetie."

"I am?"

"I could feel it the moment I got out of the car. I've known you all your life, and I've never seen you so sad and out of balance. Maybe this move seemed like a good idea but wasn't the fix you were hoping it'd be. I feel like you've made a wrong turn off your life path. Have you been taking time to meditate?"

"Yes, every morning." Ming stared at her lap, willing herself not to cry. "You're wrong. I am on the right path."

"Then something else is wrong, and until you are able to center yourself, those little plants will wilt from your distress. What is it, baby girl? You've always talked to me about everything. Don't be bashful. We all can feel your hurt. Well, maybe not Frank, but the rest of us can."

"I can too," Frank said, his deep, gravelly voice gentle. "I hate seeing you so sad. It's not a good look on you."

Tears dropped onto her lap, their concern overwhelming her. Molly pawed at her leg, and she reached down to lift the dog into her lap. She was surprised to find Molly lighter than she'd expected. Had she lost weight? Was she also wilting under Ming's sadness? She clutched her to her chest, and Molly licked her arm. "I screwed up, and Perry doesn't want to see me anymore."

"The woman Ben said was out here with you the night before we signed the papers to sell you this place?" Mee-maw asked.

Ming nodded.

"Who? Why haven't I met her?" Song's words were disapproving, but her eyes held pain.

"Did this girl break your heart?" Frank asked. "I'll take care of her. I know people who can do it."

Song slapped his arm. "You do not."

Joseph was nodding. "This makes sense now. I understand why I see a half-person when I look at you." He made a series of signs that had Mee-maw nodding in agreement. Then he went to his battered hatchback and began to rummage among some boxes in the back of it.

Song moved closer and stroked Ming's hair. The gesture had comforted her through many childhood hurts. Molly gave her arm a few more licks.

"Your feelings for this Perry must be very deep for you to hold them so close that you hadn't even told me about her."

Ming nodded, drying her tears with her napkin. "I think...I think I fell in love with her." She finally looked up into her grandmother's eyes. "I did. I do...love her. But I did something... not intentionally...and she feels I betrayed her. I didn't understand then, but what I did dredged up a very deep sorrow from her childhood. Now, she won't even talk to me so I can explain."

"Sounds to me like she doesn't deserve you," Frank said.

"She's very hurt, and I can't fix it."

Molly snorted and shook her head so hard her ears flapped. Apparently, she didn't agree.

Joseph returned and placed a pill bottle filled with leaves on the table in front of her. "You've been moving very fast recently to remove many toxic things in your life. Maybe too fast and were not careful in sorting the bad from the good. You should act soon before the river of life carries this love truly out of reach, and you spoil this piece of earth entrusted to you."

"I don't know what to do," Ming said. "Her best friend said I should wait and let Perry come to me, but she hasn't. It's been weeks, and I'm wondering if the friend was jealous of our relationship and intentionally gave me bad advice."

"Use all of these leaves to make a tea and drink it one hour before sundown," Joseph said. "Then go to your ridge and meditate on all the good times with her and review every step that led to your parting. Ask the sun to burn away the righteousness you still carry as justification for your actions. When the sun sets, go to the lake and bare yourself to wash away the ashes. Then you will know what to do. Go to the ridge the next night and take the largest lantern you have—it's too dangerous to make a fire—to illuminate the path between the two of you and call to her. She will come."

Frank harrumphed. "Or you can just go bang on her door until she gives in and listens to what you have to say." Song and Mee-maw pinned him with double-barrel glares, and he threw his hands up. "But what do I know?" He stood and gathered some dishes to take inside, pausing to bend down and kiss Ming's cheek. "Just do something. I hate seeing you so sad."

Ming reached up to squeeze his forearm, acknowledging his affection and effort to help. He went inside with the dishes, and she turned back to Joseph. "I'm a naturopathic doctor." She held up the bottle of leaves. "What's in this?"

He smiled. "Today you are not a doctor. You are my patient. It's a Shoshoni remedy I won't share with you now, but perhaps after we know each other better, we can trade our secrets."

She studied him.

"You must get past your distrust of everything," Song said. "It's always held you back. You are always on guard, expecting people to react badly to you being gay or make assumptions about your beautiful Asian features. Sometimes, their words or actions are unintentional, like you say yours were. You have to give them a chance to understand, just like you want Perry to understand you didn't realize your mistake until it was too late."

This wasn't the first life lesson her grandmother had explained to her, and it wouldn't be the last.

"My apologies, Joseph. I meant no disrespect. Only voicing my curiosity. I'll follow your instructions and look forward to learning anything you can teach me."

❖

Ming drank Joseph's tea even though she was suspicious that it included something akin to smoking peyote or consuming some other mild hallucinogenic. Then, as her body began to relax, she closed her eyes to remember her moments with Perry.

She recalled Perry at the outdoor restaurant, animated and motioning with her hands as she told her about a lizard the dogs had brought inside and chased all over her bedroom. She remembered Tucker listening intently as Perry explained her business problem to him as if he could understand, then playfully scratched and tickled him when voicing the problem helped her realize the solution. She could almost feel Perry's soft skin and hard nipples as they made love. And she cried with the memory of Perry's eyes as they lay together postorgasm, and she'd seen more than lust and affection. She'd seen love.

She replayed in her mind every moment of that wretched vlog. She recalled Perry's face when she walked onto the stage. She easily recalled her shocked expression but now saw more. Hurt. Disbelief. She recognized how cavalier her chat with Rayna appeared as trust drained from Perry's eyes and her expression turned hard as stone.

The sun slowly set, but she stayed seated on the ridge until her tears dried and the full moon rose, lighting her path to the lake. She stripped nude to walk into the warm water, letting it wash away her shame.

Then what she should do next came to her like the stars popping into the midnight sky.

❖

She slept only a few hours before rising refreshed to type the script for the podcast she was about to air. Five minutes until airtime, she closed her eyes and took several deep breaths, praying to any spiritual being that would listen. *Please let Perry hear me.*

Carl: You're live in five, four, three, cueing music.

"Good morning. This is Dr. Lee, and this is *Finding Natural Balance.* I hope you're all back with me after the long break. We were talking about decisions to make changes in our lives after living through the devastating pandemic. The podcast was on hiatus because I've been making some huge changes in my life and, honestly, trying to regain my own balance amid all of it. In making those changes, however, I learned a few lessons I want to talk about today.

"When life stops teaching us lessons, it's not because we've learned everything there is to know. It's because we've stopped listening. I could throw a lot of euphemisms at you like 'united we stand, divided we fall' or 'no man is an island'—that saying goes for women, too—but I want to talk about taking time for true introspection. The imbalance you feel as we've emerged from the pandemic might be more internal—baggage you've been carrying all along—than external, like a job or lifestyle. Bear with me for a few minutes while I share a bit to make my point.

"The pandemic lockdown basically imprisoned most of us in our houses and apartments, turning our homes into office, school, and living space. The virus killed many of our family members, friends, and neighbors. The experience has caused a lot of us to reconsider how our priorities are weighted between career, family, and ourselves. I'm still optimistic this experience will be a good thing for our society.

"However, the pressure of our confinement also acerbated some of our worst shortcomings. I'm not going to blame social media, because it's just a vehicle we've used to air our lowest nature in vitriol, careless criticisms, and deliberate misinformation. And we've become conditioned to ignore the damage it's doing to all of us.

"I know a lot of you have subscribed to follow and add to the back-and-forth between this podcast and *Timed for Success*, hosted by efficiency expert Dr. Perry Chandler. Most of you probably watched Rayna Shine's vlog *Podcast Prattle* episode that featured Dr. Chandler and me. Ms. Shine intended to throw gasoline on our professional disagreement and fire up her subscriber numbers. To do that, she originated and spread—my people later discovered—the false rumor that the debate between the podcasts was a marketing ploy to draw more listeners. We still don't know, and I don't care to know, if she hired trolls to initiate the entire debate.

"I don't care how it started because I'm ultimately to blame for taking the bait and making remarks that denigrated Dr. Chandler and her expertise. I am deeply ashamed for giving in to a side of myself I didn't realize existed. If I could erase that vlog and what led to it, I would, because it has cost me the person I'd come to love more than my career and more than myself. I've been rightly humbled and deserve everything reaped from what I sowed.

"I've shared all that to announce I am ending the *Finding Natural Balance* podcast, because I clearly haven't yet found my own balance. I only hope my failure will spur some of you to take a deep look inside yourselves and ask if what you post online truly reflects the person you want to be."

The chat line went crazy, and her staff was swamped with incoming calls, but Ming tossed her headset onto her desk. The chat line would stay open for a few hours to let them talk among themselves, but she wasn't taking calls…unless the caller was the person for whom her heart still ached, the person she needed if she was to ever find her balance.

CHAPTER SEVENTEEN

Tucker stared at Perry from his blanket on the small sofa in her office while she booted up her computers and prepared to check her business email. She was used to his watchfulness, guessing that he was afraid she'd send him away again. She wouldn't. She couldn't. In her mind, he was the lonely child she'd been, ignored by her parents and passed from babysitter to babysitter before being left pretty much on her own.

"Hey. Who's my handsome boy?"

His tail thumped against the sofa. She'd set up his crate in its old spot in her bedroom, but he slept each night on her bed, his nose touching her shoulder or his back warming her leg. Did he fear she would slip away while he was sleeping? She often saw him lift his head and become very still, as though listening for someone. She worried that he was hoping his pack would also find their way back to them.

She was about to offer him another treat, although he'd already had his daily limit, when an alert pinged from her email. She stared at the search bot that notified her any time her podcast was mentioned online. She hadn't received an alert from that bot for almost two weeks. The website link to this latest mention was *Finding Natural Balance*. Had Ming posted a new podcast? Did she even want to listen? The personal line on her cell phone rang. Julie. She answered the call, but her cursor still hovered over the alert as she warred with herself over whether to click the link.

"Hey. What's up?"

"I know you got the alert. Have you clicked on it yet?"

"No."

"Do it. You need to listen to that podcast."

"Julie, I can't."

"Yes, you can, Perry." Julie's voice softened. "I'm your best friend and love you like a sister. Well, maybe not like a sister because I wouldn't have sex with my sister—"

"Julie, just spit it out." Perry loved her, too, but sometimes Julie had trouble getting to the point.

"You need to get your head out of your childhood and grow up, honey. Ming is not your mother. You're miserable, she's miserable, and it's ludicrous that you two haven't talked this out. I'm laying the blame for that on your doorstep."

"You've talked to her?"

Julie paused. "A few times, but it was Danny, the guy she worked with at the adoption event, who told me she'd taken a leave of absence from volunteering with them. He said having to split up your trio took an emotional toll on her. A couple of days after she turned them over to him, she wanted them back, but they'd already been placed in new homes. All except Molly, so Ming made a big donation to their general fund and filled out the paperwork to adopt her."

"She has Molly?"

"Yes, thank God. She was being fostered at a home with a bunch of other dogs and was refusing to eat."

Perry closed her eyes as relief flooded her. "And JT?"

"Danny said JT went to that couple you told me about…Tom and Bob. Is that a gay couple?"

"No. Bob is short for Roberta, I think."

"Whatever. Now put on your big-girl panties and listen to her podcast."

After they ended the call, Perry clicked on the link. Nothing had changed on the website except for a posting that advised listeners the website was closing in a few weeks, but the podcasts would be available for download until then. Perry clicked on the download button for the episode that had just been posted, then stared at the file. She was afraid to open it. Something bumped against her calf, and she realized Tucker was poking her with his nose. He made his little worry noises, so she lifted him into her lap and clicked her mouse to open the file.

"The podcast was on hiatus because I've been making some huge changes in my life and, honestly, trying to regain my own balance amid all of it. In making those changes, however, I learned a few lessons I want to talk about today."

The tears began to fall the minute Ming's melodic tones came through her speakers, and Tucker plastered himself against her chest.

"I know a lot of you have subscribed to follow and add to the back-and-forth between this podcast and Timed for Success, *hosted by efficiency expert Dr. Perry Chandler. Most of you probably watched Rayna Shine's vlog* Podcast Prattle *episode that featured Dr. Chandler and me. Ms. Shine intended to throw gasoline on our professional disagreement and fire up her subscriber numbers. To do that, she originated and fed—my people later discovered—the false rumor that the debate between the podcasts was a marketing ploy to draw more listeners. We still don't know, and I don't care to know, if she hired trolls to initiate the entire debate."*

"That bitch. If I could get my hands around her neck—"

"I don't care how it started because I'm ultimately to blame for taking the bait and making remarks that denigrated Dr. Chandler and her expertise. I am deeply ashamed for giving in to a side of myself I didn't realize existed. If I could erase that vlog and what led up to it, I would because it has cost me the person

I'd come to love more than my career and more than myself. I've been rightly humbled and deserve everything reaped from what I sowed."

Perry didn't hear the rest because her brain was replaying the words she never thought she'd hear from anyone.

"...because it has cost me the person I'd come to love more than my career and more than myself."

Her tears became sobs, and Tucker licked her face, whining. "Oh, Tuck. I let my fear and pride fuck things up royally." She buried her face in his wiry coat. "At least I still have you. I'm so glad you didn't forget me after I let you go. Don't ever give up on me the way I gave up on Ming." He grunted and licked her on the chin.

Regret settled over her. She hadn't allowed Ming a chance to explain. She'd jumped to the conclusion that Ming was using her in a marketing scheme without even tracking down the source of that rumor.

"Stupid, stupid, stupid." She looked at the clock. "Want to go see Molly tomorrow?" she asked Tucker. He jumped down from her lap and danced around barking. Perry laughed. "Tomorrow. It's too late to go tonight, and I need to pick up some things before we head out."

She hadn't decided yet what to say to Ming but pondered the possibilities as she retrieved Tucker's leash from the hallway coat tree. As she watched the scruffy little terrier twirl in circles after she mentioned their nightly stroll, she was certain that, like Tucker, she would never quit until Ming accepted that she was the one, the only one for her.

CHAPTER EIGHTEEN

Ming blinked in the bright sunlight that was warming her. It had to be midmorning, judging from the sun's position, which meant she'd slept about five hours despite being wrapped in two scratchy wool blankets and lying on the ridge's hard, rocky surface. She was stiff and still exhausted, groaning as she gingerly shifted to sit up and extinguish the now-unnecessary battery-powered lantern.

She had driven the Gator to the ridge just before sundown. Molly had barked and protested, but she'd left her in the house. The lovable old dog had been sleeping more and eating less lately. Her passing could be closer than expected, and a night on the ridge might be too cold for her arthritis. Her eyesight and hearing failing, she also could wander off and fall down the steep side of the ridge that overlooked the farm buildings.

Ming had felt a little ridiculous sitting in the pool of lantern light as dark settled around her. She was no mystic and certainly not Native American. But she had promised her grandmother that she would trust Joseph, so she'd reached inside to clear her mind of everything except Perry and how much she longed for her.

She'd visualized reaching out to connect with her and again relived her memories of their time together. After a time, she began to see visions of a future together—her and Perry—then a scene of them and all three dogs together. That image cut through her like a knife and jerked her from her meditative state. That vision would never come to pass because JT and Tucker were gone. Maybe none of it would happen. Perry would never come, Molly would pass away, and she'd be forever half a soul.

Her face had been wet with tears as she returned to reality and realized the night had mostly passed. The sky was a black void no longer studded with stars or softened by moonlight. It was the dark hour before dawn.

Her legs had been so cramped from holding the same position for hours, she'd stretched out between the blankets and immediately fallen into a deep sleep...until now, when the sun woke her. She squinted at her surroundings. Her eyes felt dry and burned. She didn't want to think about what she'd see when she returned to the house and looked into a mirror. Crap. Molly. She needed to let her out to relieve herself. Unlike the boy dogs, she would hold her urine until she got a bladder infection before she'd pee in the house.

Ming loaded the blankets and lantern into the Gator, but movement at the farm below caught her eye. She frowned. Someone was unloading plants from an unfamiliar truck next to the house, but her eyes were too dry and the sun too bright to make out who it might be. Damn. She wished she'd thought to bring sunglasses.

Remembering her urgency to let Molly out of the house, she jumped into the Gator and raced down the rugged farm road so fast she nearly bounced out of her seat.

❖

Perry grunted as she lifted the last plant down from the truck's tailgate and carried it to the terrace. She was second-guessing her carefully arranged display when Tucker barked an alert. Then she heard the motor of the John Deere Gator approaching from between two newly cultivated fields. Oh, God. It was time to face Ming. She ditched her ball cap, throwing it through the truck's open window, fluffed her short hair, and brushed at the soil clinging to her clothes. Ugh. She was sweaty and filthy after unloading the plants. Not very sexy.

But as the Gator drew closer, she saw that Ming didn't look much better. She was covered with dust, her long, black hair a windswept, tangled mess. And she was the most gorgeous woman Perry had ever seen. Her beauty wasn't just physical. It permeated Perry's whole being.

Tucker danced around the Gator with joyful barks until Ming got out and squatted to hug him and kiss his head.

Perry waited her turn and swallowed against the lump closing her throat as Ming stood again and stepped closer. Her eyes held all the unanswered questions between them, and the speech Perry had practiced suddenly eluded her. She blinked, not caring about the tears rolling down her cheeks.

"Perry?"

"I'm sorry." Once she choked out those first words, more flowed…not from her prepared speech, but from her heart. "I was wrong, and I'm so miserable without you because…because I love you. I'm in love with you, and not seeing you is killing me. Even if you won't allow me another chance today, I'm not giving up. I'll be back tomorrow and the next day and the next until you love me, too."

"Oh, baby." Tears dripped from Ming's eyes, too, as she closed the final distance between them to cup Perry's face in her hands. "I already love you. I made mistakes, too, and was angry for a while, but I never stopped loving you." She drew Perry down for a kiss—no tentative brushing of their lips, but long, deep melding filled with apology and promise. The details of who was wrong about what no longer mattered.

They parted and laughed together when Tucker jumped against their legs and barked.

"You already got a kiss from me," Ming told him, still hugging Perry. She couldn't let go now that she had Perry in her arms again.

"Julie told me that you still have Molly," Perry said. Tucker barked excitedly at the mention of his packmate.

Ming stepped back. "Oh my God. I need to let her out. She's been in the house all night by herself." She hurried across the terrace and flung open the door. "Molly. Sorry, girl. Let's go outside."

No Molly appeared, but Tucker ran into the house, barking as he ran from room to room.

"She's probably asleep in your bedroom," Perry said. "She keeps a tighter schedule than I do, and it's about time for her morning nap."

They went to the bedroom, but her bed and the dog bed in the corner were both empty. Ming knelt to look under the bed, and Perry dug her keys from the pocket of her jeans.

"I have a penlight on my key ring."

Ming laughed but took the offered penlight. "You are such a lesbian," she said.

"Lucky for you," Perry said, returning the tease. "And so are you."

"I'm a doctor. I never know when I might need to check pupil response or look down a throat or into an ear." She had missed their playful banter and was happy to so easily fall back into it.

"Good point."

Ming shone the light under the bed but saw only a collection of dog hair and dust bunnies. She really needed to hire a cleaning service since she spent almost all her time in the greenhouses. She accepted Perry's hand to help her stand again and shook her head. "Maybe she's fallen asleep in one of the other rooms."

Ming tried to ignore her growing uneasiness as a search through the house failed to locate her.

"Hey, did you know your front door was ajar?" Perry asked.

"No. I've got a guy coming out tomorrow to look at it because the lock doesn't engage unless you push hard on it. We've searched everywhere in here. She must have gotten out."

They both had seen Molly use her short legs to paw open a door or retrieve a ball wedged between furniture.

They went outside and called for her but got no response. Ming scanned the fields, newly plowed in preparation for a winter planting. No Molly. Her fear swelled as she turned toward the woods that bordered the fields. So many dangers were there, and Molly had had all night to wander until she was lost. "Maah-lee." Their calls were becoming desperate shouts, and Tucker added his sharp barks as he raced around the yard.

Ming finally turned to Perry. "She's been going downhill lately, sleeping like the dead and eating less and less every day. I don't know exactly how old she is, but I'm afraid—" She couldn't finish the thought, must less voice it.

"No. Don't think it," Perry said, wrapping her arms around Ming. "We'll find her." She let go of Ming and slapped her own forehead. "I should have thought of this before." She called Tucker over. "Tuck, where's Molly? Go find Molly."

He appeared to understand now that all the shouting and calling for Molly wasn't just a fun game. He raced back to the front entry and sniffed at the ground before taking off on a zigzag path toward the barn. They ran to keep up with him.

"I thought you checked the barn," Ming said when they followed him inside. All the musty, decaying hay had been cleaned out, and drying racks for her herbs were being constructed in place of the old animal stalls. Tucker ran behind the bales of fresh straw that would later be spread over the outdoor plant beds to protect them during the winter, then returned to jump against Perry's legs and disappear again behind the bales. They followed and stopped when they spotted Molly unmoving on the blanket they had used the day they picnicked at the lake. She was so still. Ming wrapped her arms around Perry, afraid of what she'd find if she touched her. Tucker looked puzzled at their response. He'd found her, like Perry asked him.

After a long moment, Perry pulled out of Ming's grasp and knelt to quietly thank Tucker for locating her. Then Ming held her breath as Perry crept forward and laid a careful hand on Molly's still frame.

Perry stroked her soft fur and spoke hesitantly. "Molly?"

Ming wanted to both laugh and cry in relief when Molly's head popped up, her beard smushed and ears askew. It took a few seconds for her to struggle to her feet with Perry's help, but then she shook herself all over like a typical dog and licked Perry's hand as if she suddenly realized Perry and Tucker were present. Tucker stood very still, tail wagging as Molly sniffed him from head to toe, then joined in her sharp, happy barks as she waddled back and forth between Ming and Perry.

Ming laughed, her heart soaring. "I know. I can see. Perry and Tucker are here." She smiled at Perry, who grinned back. They were nearly complete.

❖

Ming stopped their small parade when she reached the terrace. Now that the Molly crisis had passed, she wanted an explanation.

"What's all this?" She waved her arm to indicate the plants that nearly covered the wide terrace.

Perry puffed out her chest. "I brought you flowers."

Ming shook her head. "Most people stop at a small bouquet."

"I'm not most people, and neither are you. I was up half the night researching this subject and called a friend and former client who owns a commercial nursery outside Fresno at six o'clock this morning to get him to open early for me."

Ming stepped closer to examine the variety of potted plants. "So, you brought—"

"Honeysuckle, hibiscus, lavender, nasturtium, borage, and chamomile. All edible and with medicinal qualities. He looked at me like I had an alien popping out of my chest when I asked if he had any dandelions."

Ming laughed. "You goof. They're a common weed. I'll

likely have an entire field of them blooming in the meadow by the lake next spring." She hugged Perry close, then looked up to reward her with a gentle, lingering kiss. "Thank you for the flowers. I have to say, I've never received a gift so beautiful but practical."

Perry's expression turned serious. "I was afraid you wouldn't give me another chance." She touched Ming's cheek in a reverent caress.

Ming captured her hand and kissed it while still holding Perry's gaze. "I was afraid you wouldn't let me." She took Perry's hand.

Together they secured the front door, made sure both pups were happily snoozing after Molly's big adventure and Tucker's tracking job, then stripped naked and showered to slide between the cool sheets of Ming's king-size bed, where they made slow, sweet love, napped, snacked, talked, and made love again until the next morning.

Chapter Nineteen

Ming set a large, covered tray of finger foods next to the pitcher of lemonade and chilled wine on the terrace's new farmhouse table and looked for Perry.

They'd lasted only two weeks after their reunion before they rented a U-Haul and hired workers to move Perry from Fresno to the farm. They both knew their need to be with each other constantly would ease as their relationship matured, but, for now, they were enjoying the farm, quiet evenings sharing a bottle of wine on the terrace, and long nights making love.

She spotted Perry talking to Joseph next to where workers were installing a heated saltwater swimming pool after Perry had decided that aqua therapy would help get Molly's weight down and gently exercise her increasingly arthritic legs. Checking her watch, Ming waved for them to come to the terrace. Her surprise would drive up at any minute.

Perry kissed her on the cheek, then stared at the table Ming had set. "That's a lot of food for just three of us. Were you planning to include the guys digging the pool?"

"They can get their own lunch," Ming said. "We're expecting a couple of visitors to join us." She saw a large bus-like RV turn in at the other end of their long drive and slowly approach the house. "I've got Molly. You grab Tucker so he doesn't get too close to those big tires."

Perry shot her a puzzled look but did as asked. They were still working on getting the dogs to sit and stay when vehicles approached because Tucker had appointed himself farm security chief, while Molly continued to be the welcome wagon.

The RV stopped, and after a moment, Tom and Bob stepped out. Molly began to bark and tried to wiggle out of her collar when Tom bent to place the furry friend he was carrying on solid ground.

"Let them go," Ming said, her throat tightening around the words.

Molly hurdled toward the newcomer, and, after a slight hesitation, Tucker was on her heels.

"Oh my God," Perry said, her tone disbelieving. "Is that JT?"

"It certainly is," Bob said as she and Tom joined them. "And he sure is happy to see the other two."

After a bit of sniffing to confirm everyone was okay, JT pounced on Tucker, and they ran around the yard chasing and tussling while Molly waddled after them and barked at their antics.

"There's the happy dog we adopted," Tom said.

"Let's sit down and enjoy some lunch while we catch up," Ming said. She introduced Joseph to Tom and Bob, and after plates were filled and drinks were poured, they all sat down to talk.

"How did you guys find us?" Perry asked, never taking her eyes from the romping trio.

"You tell it, Bob." Tom looked at them. "She always says I take all day to get to the point."

They all laughed, then looked to Bob to begin their story.

"Well, we were delighted when Ming called to say JT was available for adoption. He's such a sweet boy and so cute I just want to smooch him every time I look at him. But we've found a fun RV group and have lots of lengthy trips planned as long as we're still physically able to travel. We expect that will be a while, since we're both in pretty good health."

She paused, and they all watched as the dogs, tongues lolling, came to the terrace to drink from the big water bowl reserved for them. Then JT greeted Perry with happy licks before springing into Ming's lap and pressing a doggie hug against her chest. She was so glad to see him, she had to be careful not to squeeze too tight as she hugged him back and kissed his cute little head.

"But this little guy gets sick every time he has to ride in the RV." Tom picked up Bob's story. "We got some medicine from the vet, but we have to keep him drugged up while we're on the road, so he won't puke all over everything."

"Bless his sweet little heart." Bob cut in. "We love him, but he's just miserable. Even when we're home, he seems so sad without his friends. I'm afraid that as much as we care for him, we're going to have to return him."

"Do you think you could find another good home for him?" Tom's grin indicated he knew exactly where JT would find his forever home.

Perry scratched her head. "I don't know. He might make a decent farm dog, if he doesn't chase chickens."

Ming rolled her eyes. "You already know he will."

Perry grinned at Tom and Bob. "Well, then it's a good thing we don't have any."

It was a done deal, Ming knew, because she had already lined up a newly homeless Boston terrier that loved to ride for the nomadic couple.

Ming put JT down, and he sprawled on the cool tiles of the terrace next to Molly, taking his place again as her wingman. She filled wineglasses and pressed everyone to eat more of the food she'd prepared, then settled back in her chair. "So, Joseph, what has Perry talked you into?"

The shaman chuckled. "She wants to build a sweat lodge next to the pool. I told her it's not the structure, but the ritual, that makes a sweat lodge and promised I'd carve some Shoshoni totems into the wood and guide her through the ritual if she'll install a fancy sauna instead and invite me over often."

"It would be more efficient," Perry said, and Ming laughed before leaning near to kiss her cheek. "I'll get in a new sauna with you, but not in some dirt sweat lodge." She put her mouth to Perry's ear and lowered her voice to a whisper. "You, me, naked and sweaty."

Perry flushed, but she grinned at their company. "Decision made. A new, high-tech sauna."

Everyone laughed before Joseph redirected the conversation.

"I've been thinking about getting one of those little pull-along trailers and traveling around a bit," he said. "I like to fly-fish and would love to try out some Montana, Wyoming, and Colorado spots. I could take my grandson along maybe next summer."

Tom's face lit up. "I'll tell you about some great places where we've cast our flies. Bob, here, is one of the best fishermen... fisherpeople this side of the Rockies."

For the next hour, they listened to tales of the couple's camping adventures, and before they waved good-bye, Ming gave them the phone number of the Boston terrier's foster so they could arrange to meet up.

Tom and Bob hugged JT good-bye, and he licked their faces but made no move to follow when they boarded their RV.

Ming and Perry stood in the yard to watch the big bus rumble down the drive behind Joseph's truck.

Two women and their trio of mutts. The pack was complete again, and Ming finally felt the natural rhythm of the farm ebb and flow beneath her feet and in the air.

Balance had been restored.

EPILOGUE

Hi, I'm Rayna Shine, and this is *Podcast Prattle*. Now, I know that the attention span online lasts about as long as a teenage boy's first sexual experience, but some of you might remember last year's vlog where *Prattle* got the hosts of two dueling high-profile podcasts together on stage. If you asked me that day if they would appear again on *Podcast Prattle*, I'd have said 'only when pigs fly past as hell freezes over.'

"Guess what? I would have been wrong. Even though both podcasts, *Timed for Success* and *Finding Natural Balance*, shut down shortly after that vlog, we are fortunate to have with us today those same two hosts, Dr. Perry Chandler and Dr. Ming Lee."

This time the rented auditorium was nearly filled, and all applauded and whistled as Perry and Ming walked onto the stage holding hands. They had contacted Rayna about appearing again but had laid down strict rules for the vlog in a contract Rayna was required to sign. They would answer only the questions they approved prior to the vlog, and their chairs would be placed together rather than on either side of Rayna. They would reveal Ming's first name, but not her new last name, to protect her privacy. They were legally married now, but property records indicated the farm was still owned by M.L. Davis.

"Thank you for hosting us," Perry said before Rayna could dive in. "A lot has changed in the past year, and we asked to come here today to share a few of those changes."

"I understand you both are working on new ventures."

"Both separately and together," Perry said. "I'm writing a new book that addresses the need for diversity and employee satisfaction, the last and long-neglected factor required to achieve optimum production. And I've been assisting Ming in her new venture."

"She's been a huge help," Ming said. "I used to hate spreadsheets, but Perry has taught me their value in any business that involves production and distribution."

Rayna's eyebrows shot up. "I thought you were a physician. What are you manufacturing?"

"I am, and I still work in a community clinic several days each week. But, as you know, I'm also a licensed naturopath. I'm farming and distributing a variety of medicinal plants, things that were long used for remedies before the onset of big pharmaceutical companies. As a physician, I do appreciate advances in medicine and medications, but I think pharmaceutical drugs are overused when nature already supplies a natural remedy."

Ming's seedlings were finally flourishing. She'd found Collin Cutter, who'd previously farmed her land, to be an astute advisor, and they'd formed a business partnership after locating a strong market for the herbs and other plants she was growing.

"She also occasionally collaborates with our local veterinarian when he needs a special poultice or has a patient that could benefit from acupuncture," Perry said.

"Are you guys planning to revive your podcasts?"

"No," Ming said. "As you well know, my people found that your marketing people had manufactured the conflict between our podcasts. Thank you, by the way, for the generous settlement check. The Fresno animal-rescue consortium was able to put the money to very good use."

Rayna, who looked chagrined, faced one of the cameras. "Viewers can read my personal apology on the website of *Podcast Prattle*."

Perry picked up the thread. "We shut down our original podcasts because we were astonished and horrified over how easily people—including ourselves—are manipulated with online goading, misinformation, and partial information meant to divide and incite."

Ming tugged their clasped hands into her lap. "Perry was advising people how to better organize their time, and I was talking about setting priorities for their newfound extra time. If you stopped and thought about it, the approaches actually complemented each other."

Perry smiled at Ming, then turned to Rayna. "That's why the new vlog we're launching together will be called *Think About This.*"

"That's sort of a vague title, isn't it?"

"Intentionally vague," Perry said.

Ming elaborated. "We want to be able to talk about a variety of issues. The vlog will rotate among three themes. First, we want to highlight people who are changing our world in a good way. Secondly, we want to explore a variety of topics that our audience might be curious about. For example, I'll do a segment or two on natural medicine and how it can work with, not against, traditional Western medicine. Or we'll talk to top economists about what actually drives American companies to establish factories overseas. For the third theme, we'll attempt to answer questions that subscribers email in. Those questions might range from 'what is sea glass and where does it come from?' to 'why do we need political parties?'"

"We'll invite fact-checking and make sure to acknowledge any proved mistakes or omissions," Perry said.

"That sounds like a lot of work. You'll need a full staff to support it."

"We plan to have a running blog on the website to keep people up to date on what experts we're consulting, who we're interviewing, and fun snippets of things that crop up in our daily lives."

"Speaking of daily lives, yours have become much more interesting, wouldn't you say?"

Perry smirked at the audience. "Lots more fun." When she wiggled her eyebrows suggestively, the people in the crowd laughed and applauded.

"Okay. Let's start with the rings on your left hands." Rayna pointed to the diamond glittering on Ming's finger.

Instead of showing it off, Ming lifted Perry's left hand so the audience could see the sapphire embedded in an intricately carved platinum band. "I asked Perry to marry me, and she said yes."

The crowd cheered.

"So, of course, I had to buy her the biggest diamond I could find to make sure she didn't change her mind," Perry said.

They cheered again.

"So many changes in the past year. What advice would you give our audience and subscribers?"

"Keep an open mind," Perry said.

"And don't discount where your next lesson may come from," Ming added.

Perry laughed. "Our most important lesson came from three additions to our little family."

Rayna's smile was brilliant. "I understand you brought your advisors with you today."

"Yes. I'm surprised they're being so quiet backstage," Ming said.

"Let's bring them out now." Rayna signaled one of her assistants standing in the wings. "Please, hold down your applause so we don't scare them."

Happy barks preceded the new, much-slimmer Molly that strolled across the stage with JT at her shoulder, as always. After a little coaxing from Perry, Tucker darted out and hopped into her lap.

No clapping, but the audience uttered a lot of oohs and awws and soft exclamations over the trio.

Molly bussed Ming's outstretched hand and, always the greeter, went straight to Rayna, where she licked her hand, then sat on Rayna's foot to stare at the audience. Tucker stayed in his safe spot, Perry's lap, and hid his face like he was at the vet to get a shot. JT went to the edge of the stage and wagged his tail at the audience on the other side of the stage footlights.

Perry introduced them. "We think of them as our children, but they see us as packmates. That's Molly sitting on Rayna's foot, JT's the one upstaging everybody with his cuteness, and this shy one in my lap is Tucker."

"They're all rescues," Ming said, looking to Perry, who nodded. "But truthfully, they rescued us."

"What lessons have you learned from them?" Rayna asked.

Perry shook her head. "So many. JT taught me you have to take a big leap sometimes to get what you're after, even if you could end up with only a mouthful of tail feathers."

JT abandoned his gazing at the audience and trotted over to jump onto Ming's lap to press himself against her chest and lick her chin. She hugged him back. "And that hugs always make things better," Ming added.

The audience chuckled.

"Molly is a girl after my own heart. She believes in keeping a schedule. You could set your watch by her morning nap, and she's not bashful about letting you know it's time for you to fix her dinner," Perry said. "She also taught me that schedules are made to be broken when your packmates need help digging up and dispatching a destructive mole or you come across a spot of warm sunlight that you need to take a moment to soak up."

Ming smiled at the audience. "Also, be welcoming to everyone, and a good howl-along with your packmates will start your day on a high note."

JT stood up on Ming's lap when a few quiet, mock howls drifted up from the audience, then jumped down and began barking at Molly.

"Oh, no. Here we go," Perry said when Tucker finally quit hiding and jumped down to join in as their barks turned to howls. Tucker's was passable, and JT's was awful, but Molly pointed her nose to the ceiling, opened her throat, and let out a long, melodic note, occasionally throwing in a bit of vibrato for good measure.

Laughing, Perry joined in like she often did at home, and then Rayna and Ming added their voices as the audience provided backup. After a minute, Perry slashed her hand through the air, and quiet reigned again.

"Don't you feel better now?" Ming asked.

Rayna looked surprised. "I think I do. That's better than a five-minute Superwoman pose." She looked to the audience. "Right?"

Nods and applause confirmed that almost everyone had enjoyed the raucous interlude.

"And what about the third of your trio of furry advisors... your little shy guy?"

Their howling done, JT had escorted Molly back across the stage to settle at Ming's feet. Tucker looked like he wanted to bolt, then leapt back into Perry's lap when she patted her leg in silent invitation.

"Tucker? He taught me the most important lesson." Perry hugged her little guy closer with one arm, then extended her free hand to the woman she vowed to never let go. She held Ming's gaze, her heart swelling with the affection she saw in her eyes.

"Tucker taught me that love can be stronger than your fears, so you should fight for the one who captures your heart and never, ever give up on forever."

About the Author

D. Jackson Leigh grew up barefoot and happy, swimming in farm ponds and riding rude ponies in rural Georgia. She has retired from her career as a journalist but continues her real passion—writing sultry lesbian romances laced with her trademark Southern humor and affection for dogs and horses.

She has published fifteen novels and one collection of short stories with Bold Strokes Books, winning five Golden Crown Literary Society awards in paranormal, romance, and fantasy categories. She was also a finalist in the romance category of the 2014 Lambda Literary Awards.

You can friend her at facebook.com/d.jackson.leigh.

Books Available From Bold Strokes Books

A Fox in Shadow by Jane Fletcher. Cassie's mission is to add new territory to the Kavillian empire—murder, betrayal, war, and the clash of cultures ensue. (978-1-63679-142-5)

Embracing the Moon by Jeannie Levig. Just as Gwen and Taylor are exploring the new love they've found, the present and past collide, threatening the future they long to share. (978-1-63555-462-5)

Forever Comes in Threes by D. Jackson Leigh. Efficiency expert Perry Chandler's ordered life is upended when she inherits three busy terriers, and the woman she's referred to for help turns out to be her bitter podcast rival, the very sexy Dr. Ming Lee. (978-1-63679-169-2)

Heckin' Lewd: Trans and Nonbinary Erotica, edited by Mx. Nillin Lore. If you want smutty, fearless, gender diverse erotica written by affirming own-voices folks who get it, then this is the book you've been looking for! (978-1-63679-240-8)

Missed Conception by Joy Argento. Maggie Walsh wants a relationship with Cassidy, the daughter she's only just discovered she has due to an in vitro mix-up. Heat kindles between Maggie and Cassidy's mother in a way neither expects. (978-1-63679-146-3)

Private Equity by Elle Spencer. Cassidy Bennett spends an unexpected evening at a lesbian nightclub with her notoriously reserved and demanding boss, Julia. After seeing a different side of Julia, Cassidy can't seem to shake her desire to know more. (978-1-63679-180-7)

Racing the Dawn by Sandra Barrett. After narrowly escaping a house fire, vampire Jade Murphy is unexpectedly intrigued by gorgeous firefighter Beth Jenssen, and her undead existence might just be perking up a bit. (978-1-63679-271-2)

Reclaiming Love by Amanda Radley. Sarah's tiny white lie means somehow convincing Pippa to pretend to be her girlfriend. Only the more time they spend faking it, the more real it feels. (978-1-63679-144-9)

Sol Cycle by Kimberly Cooper Griffin. An encounter in a park brings Ang and Krista together, but when Ang's attempts to help Krista go spectacularly wrong, their passion for each other might not be enough. (978-1-63679-137-1)

Trial and Error by Carsen Taite. Attorney Franco Rossi and Judge Nina Aguilar's reunion is fraught with courtroom conflict, undeniable chemistry, and danger. (978-1-63555-863-0)

A Long Way to Fall by Elle Spencer. A ski lodge, two strong-willed women, and a family feud that brings them together, but will it also tear them apart? (978-1-63679-005-3)

Forever by Kris Bryant. When Savannah Edwards is invited to be the next bachelorette on the dating show *When Sparks Fly*, she'll show the world that finding true love on television can happen. (978-1-63679-029-9)

Ice on Wheels by Aurora Rey. All's fair in love and roller derby. That's Riley Fauchet's motto, until a new job lands her at the same company—and on the same team—as her rival Brooke Landry, the frosty jammer for the Big Easy Bruisers. (978-1-63679-179-1)

Perfect Rivalry by Radclyffe. Two women set out to win the same career-making goal, but it's love that may turn out to be the final prize. (978-1-63679-216-3)

Something to Talk About by Ronica Black. Can quiet ranch owner Corey Durand give up her peaceful life and allow her feisty new neighbor into her heart? Or will past loss, present suitors, and town gossip ruin a long-awaited chance at love? (978-1-63679-114-2)

With a Minor in Murder by Karis Walsh. In the world of academia, police officer Clare Sawyer and professor Libby Hart team up to solve a murder. (978-1-63679-186-9)

Writer's Block by Ali Vali. Wyatt and Hayley might be made for each other if only they can get through nosy neighbors, the historic society, at-odds future plans, and all the secrets hidden in Wyatt's walls. (978-1-63679-021-3)

The Business of Pleasure by Ronica Black. Editor in chief Valerie Raffield is quickly becoming smitten by Lennox, the graphic artist she's hired to work remotely. But when Lennox doesn't show for their first face-to-face meeting, Valerie's heart and her business may be in jeopardy. (978-1-63679-134-0)

Cold Blood by Genevieve McCluer. Maybe together, Kalila and Dorenia have a chance of taking down the vampires who have eluded them all these years. And maybe, in each other, they can find a love worth living for. (978-1-63679-195-1)

Greener Pastures by Aurora Rey. When city girl and CPA Audrey Adams finds herself tending her aunt's farm, will Rowan Marshall—the charming cider maker next door—turn out to be her saving grace or the bane of her existence? (978-1-63679-116-6)

Grounded by Amanda Radley. For a second chance, Olivia and Emily will need to accept their mistakes, learn to communicate properly, and with a little help from five-year-old Henry, fall madly in love all over again. Sequel to Flight SQA016. (978-1-63679-241-5)

The Hummingbird Sanctuary by Erin Zak. The Hummingbird Sanctuary, Colorado's hottest resort destination: Come for the mountains, stay for the charm, and enjoy the drama as Olive, Eleanor, and Harriet figure out the meaning of true friendship. (978-1-63679-163-0)

Journey's End by Amanda Radley. In this heartwarming conclusion to the Flight series, Olivia and Emily must finally decide what they want, what they need, and how to follow the dreams of their hearts. (978-1-63679-233-0)

Secret Agent by Michelle Larkin. CIA agent Peyton North embarks on a global chase to apprehend rogue agent Zoey Blackwood, but her commitment to the mission is tested as the sparks between them ignite and their sizzling attraction approaches a point of no return. (978-1-63555-753-4)

Something Between Us by Krystina Rivers. A decade after her heart was broken under Don't Ask, Don't Tell, Kirby runs into her first love and has to decide if what's still between them is enough to heal her broken heart. (978-1-63679-135-7)

Sugar Girl by Emma L McGeown. Having traded in traditional romance for the perks of Sugar Dating, Ciara Reilly not only enjoys the no-strings-attached arrangement, she's also a hit with her clients. That is, until she meets the beautiful entrepreneur Charlie Keller, who makes her want to go sugar-free. (978-1-63679-156-2)

With a Twist by Georgia Beers. Starting over isn't easy for Amelia Martini. When the irritatingly cheerful Kirby Dupress comes into her life, will Amelia be brave enough to go after the love she really wants? (978-1-63555-987-3)

The Witch Queen's Mate by Jennifer Karter. Barra and Silvi must overcome their ingrained hatred and prejudice to use Barra's magic and save both their peoples from not just slavery, but destruction. (978-1-63679-202-6)

Business of the Heart by Claire Forsythe. When a hopeless romantic meets a tough-as-nails cynic, they'll need to overcome the wounds of the past to discover that their hearts are the most important business of all. (978-1-63679-167-8)

Dying for You by Jenny Frame. Can Victorija Dred keep an age-old vow and fight the need to take blood from Daisy Macdougall? (978-1-63679-073-2)

Exclusive by Melissa Brayden. Skylar Ruiz lands the TV reporting job of a lifetime, but is she willing to sacrifice it all for the love of her longtime crush, anchorwoman Carolyn McNamara? (978-1-63679-112-8)

The Game by Jan Gayle. Ryan Gibbs is a talented golfer, but her guilt means she may never leave her small town, even if Katherine Reese tempts her with competition and passion. (978-1-63679-126-5)

Her Duchess to Desire by Jane Walsh. An up-and-coming interior designer seeks to create a happily ever after with an intriguing duchess, proving that love never goes out of fashion. (978-1-63679-065-7)

Whereabouts Unknown by Meredith Doench. While homicide detective Theodora Madsen recovers from a potentially career-ending injury, she scrambles to solve the cases of two missing sixteen-year-old girls from Ohio. (978-1-63555-647-6)